buried
beneath

buried beneath

kelly ann hopkins

ZENITH PUBLISHING

ISBN (eBook): 978-1-952919-47-3
ISBN (paperback): 978-1-952919-48-0

For David and Kelsey

ONE

WHEN YOU'RE LITTLE, you don't realize your family operates differently than others. I'm talking when you're in kindergarten, maybe even first grade. You think everyone eats SpaghettiOs straight from the can with a plastic spoon and a ten-inch-deep carpet of dirty laundry coats all your classmates' hallways.

But it's when you get to be a fourth-grader, on the cusp of the middle school experience, that your perception shifts—ever so slightly. You get smarter, more aware of the subtle variations in the way the world operates based on your personal geography. You begin to figure out the other kids in your class have parents who come to end-of-the-year events and never miss teacher conferences. You wonder why they talk about kids sleeping over on the weekends and why you've never been asked. You get something's seriously not right in your version of reality, but you're too young and naïve to figure it out without someone holding up the wreck of your life in front of your face like a busted mirror.

Then the lightbulb blares on in the refrigerator.

And suddenly, you see what they see, and you want to close the blinds, turn off the lights, and pretend your life isn't a landfill of crazy that one day might swallow you whole.

Thirteen-year-old self asks: How did this happen to me?

Almost-seventeen-year-old self asks the harder question: Why did this happen to me?

Neither query has an easy answer, especially if you've ever heard the BS story about the lobster not understanding it was boiling to death. Maybe the stupid crustacean figures it out right between "it's getting warm in here" and "oh no, I'm dead." Living with a mother who suffers from hoarding disorder is kind of like that when you're a kid. For a long time, I didn't comprehend the growing piles of debris around me for what they were— my mother's inability to cope with my father leaving and her raising me on her own.

No. It wasn't like that for me. We had a lot of *things*. Overzealous clutter. So what? We weren't different from the rest of the world, right?

Uh, wrong.

I imagine a lot of kids growing up in houses overrun with piles of junk figure it out sooner or later. It's like, one day, your eyes are opened, and you sneak around at night completely mortified, trying to collect the food wrappers, the moldy containers of strawberries, the sour-stiff milk, the dirty clothes, the papers, out-of-date magazines, paper plates, glass plates, forks, knives, and spoons into something resembling the kitchen of your childhood only to have your mother fly screaming into the room and clutch the rotten fruit to her chest like a golden prize.

"Someone can use that!"

You stop and stare at the heaving, red-faced person you don't pretend to know and ask, "Who, Mom? Who?"

For a long time, I lived the blame game, believing that maybe I could have done something to make her change. Maybe if I got good grades and made the swim team, she'd decide I was worth the effort. Total teenaged delusion. Kidding myself, believing change might be possible as the piles of debris grew deeper. And deeper. But she wouldn't change. Not for Dad, not for me.

And there's the rub-me-the-wrong-way truth.

My life could've been so different. I knew. I'd seen what could have been. The first outside birthday party I went to was at Molly Shore's house, a couple of blocks away in our neighborhood of smart middle-class houses with sparkling front yards. I remember walking into a clean and uncluttered home—one that smelled good, like cinnamon and lemons. Kids sat *on* the sofa and watched television, and Molly's mom yelled when the potato chip bowl got dumped on the floor.

I remember staring at the vacuum marks on the carpeting after her mom sucked up the crumbs. My fingers had played over the patterns in the spotless beige carpet's nap.

A vacuum? What magic was that?

And suddenly, at ten years old, sitting on my friend's floor, the broken mirror started to knit itself back together, just enough so I could start to understand the big, ugly picture of how I lived.

Once I turned seventeen, my blinders were pulled off like a full-body waxing.

A stranger who happened by would see something seriously wrong with the way we lived behind the cheery yellow walls of our house. But no one could find out—the secret must be kept at all costs—for my mother's sake. I lived in a world that didn't know who I really was. That was my superpower. Or my curse. The world outside could never know what she'd done to our home or they'd take me away from her.

So, instead of telling someone the truth, I lived with it. The shame. The guilt. The rage. Bottled up in a super-carbonated liter of pure hatred for my mother's disaster. I couldn't control what she did. I could only control what I became as a result.

That day I tried to clean the kitchen, my mother banished me to my room, the single twelve-by-fourteen-foot square of real estate in our three-bedroom home to not disappear under the weight of her desiccated brand of crazy. Too bad I didn't learn my lesson.

Not long after the strawberry incident, I committed the mortal sin of inviting a friend over. We sneaked in the back door past the piles of wreckage to the sanctuary of my room. I silenced her with the fear of waking my sick mother. Big mistake. I saw it on Pam's face. The disgust. The shock. The way her nose wrinkled up at the aroma I grew nose blind to. Then came the horror when my mother found us huddled in my room, listening to music on Pam's iPhone, and Pam grasped Mom wasn't sick the way she thought.

No, Pam. She was worse.

And my former friend made sure everyone at school knew it, ending any shot I had at having a life. I lived in fear of opening my locker after the first cafeteria trash can had been emptied over my books.

But my mom wasn't always this way. There was a time when normal was just . . . normal.

Sketchy, happy, sweet-smelling memories remained from my early childhood of my dad cooking hot dogs on the grill, and me splashing in the tiny, blue plastic swimming pool in the backyard (still in the shed, go figure). The day Dad built my swing set, Mom took pictures while I waved from the top of the slide in our pristine backyard.

Those moments were illusions, dreams, fantasies.

But those happy times *had* been real. I was sure of it. Especially the ones with my dad in them before they fought and the weight of my mother's hoarding became too much for him to bear. The memory of him that remained the clearest was the day he left for a normal business trip when I was eleven, except he never came home.

I sighed and breathed in the scent of the air fresheners I plugged into both outlets in my room. I kept my window open no matter the weather or season––winter, spring, summer, fall, 365 days, 24/7. It was the only way I could survive. Outside my room—in the hallway, the kitchen, the dining room, the main bathroom, the living room, everywhere—were my mother's "collections." Newspapers going back a full decade, out-of-print magazines. Tangled knots of clothes that fit me in eighth grade, seventh grade, sixth grade, fifth, fourth, third, infancy. The rotted shells of past

Christmas trees and smashed Halloween pumpkins, Styro-foam coolers, and trash bags she filled but never set out by the curb. Dishes she never washed. Food she never ate.

Garbage.

Trash.

Debris.

Wreckage.

Home.

With my door closed and four air fresheners blasting the scent of clean laundry, I could pretend it wasn't there. But it was. Recently, I smelled it on every inhale and tasted it on every exhale, heaving my stomach and clenching my throat. And somewhere in the metric tons of debris was my dog, Randy. He used to dig around looking for bits to eat under the snarl of old toys and empty cereal boxes. One day he went missing in the piles of stuff. I was thirteen then, maybe fourteen. I heard him whimpering. He was somewhere in the dining room, but no matter how hard I dug or cried, I couldn't find him. Mom tried to help me until the stress was too much for her, and she hid in her room.

A couple of days later, Randy stopped crying. Then the smell of his death wafted through the house. I failed him. Like my mother failed me. I shook my head, clearing the bad memories, and picked up my brimming laundry basket. The laundry room was the only other place in the house still functional because I had to have clean clothes to go to work so no one would find out about how I lived. What my mother did and wore was her business. In the years I lived this way, I'd grown a thick shell around my heart—thick and heavy enough to protect me from feeling anything where she was concerned.

Taking one last fresh-scented breath, I opened my door and set the laundry basket down on the clear patch of murky carpet outside. My room was my island in a sea of insanity. The rock I clung to when the house tried to drag me under. I drew my door shut and snapped the padlock on the hinge installed to protect my space from my mother's hoarding. I had to keep my sanctuary safe at all costs.

"Shelly Marie, is that you?" Mom called from some-where in the front of the house, her voice muffled as if she were stuck in a collapsing tunnel. Hundreds of books my mother never read lined the hallway floor to ceiling, some three-deep against the walls. I wiggled my way through the space, tilting the laundry basket against my hip so I could pass. The flimsy columns swayed, ready to come crashing down.

"Doing my laundry," I yelled back. I couldn't see her at the end of the book tunnel. I didn't want to see her. Most days, I couldn't bear to look at her.

"That's a good girl," she said. "I'm ordering pizza tonight. Can you wait on the porch for the delivery? Should be about fifteen dollars."

I gritted my teeth. This was the third day in a row she ordered pizza and expected me to pay for it out of my minimum wage salary. The child support money kept the lights on, but it didn't cover her pizza habit. The boxes were stacked ten high in the living room and filled with the old slices. She nearly ripped my head off when I tried to throw them away.

The noxious reek of week-old, moldy pizza slammed into my throat, kicking up bile from my empty, clenching stomach. *I can't eat it again. I can't.*

"Mom, will you order me a salad?"

"Pizza not good enough for you?"

The rancid aroma of sour, milky cheese rushed up my nose, down my throat, and punched a hole in my guts. I braced myself against the laundry room door, my eyes squeezed tight against the tears I refused to shed, the basket pressed against my chest holding in the pain.

"I just need a change."

"Hmph. So did your father."

My vision went nuclear. *Everything* wrong in our lives was my father's fault. As if he appeared to throw more debris in the living room when we weren't looking.

I shoved the door open as far as it would go, slamming into the pile of books and sending them flying. I didn't care about her books, not when I couldn't stop the burning tears. If not for the clothes I needed for work, I'd never come out of my room. I'd let the pizza delivery person bang on the door until hell grew upside-down icicles.

Except, my job was my only escape from the claustrophobia of my house, and I took every shift offered to me. One of us had to do something to create income besides the ransom my father paid for his freedom. With my online school out for the summer, the responsibility fell to me because Mom never left the house.

My father got his change, all right. Took it and ran away. *Thanks, Dad.*

Although resentment burned in my chest, I didn't respond to her jab. I couldn't. Nothing I could say would make this life better or make her acknowledge her responsibility for his flight when I was a kid. I didn't blame him for going anymore. I couldn't. I missed him too much.

Time had given me perspective. The truth? I wish he would've taken me with him.

For spite, I slammed the washer lid and kicked the overflowing trash bin across the room, spewing old dryer sheets and lint over the tile. I collapsed against the filling washing machine, my hands covering my face. My empty stomach churned, and my head thumped. When? When would this ever end? When could I leave this mountain of unwashed reminders of my mother's inability to cope?

One year and one week. Then I'd be eighteen. The law might say I was old enough to strike out on my own, but what would I do with my mother? She couldn't survive on her own, not if she wouldn't leave the house. Maybe when I became an adult, I'd have the guts to turn her in. Maybe then she'd get some help.

Wiping my tears on my sleeve, I leaned down and collected the trash into the bin and carried it to the sanctity of my room. Hidden under my mattress were two dozen empty heavy-duty trash bags. Every week, I filled seven or eight, quietly, carefully, and tossed them out my bedroom door onto the deck. After my mother fell asleep, I would drag them out to the curb and celebrate my small victory against the house.

The trash service discretely picked up the bags at the edge of our property—far enough away I could swear to my mother the mountain of bags belonged to the neighbors. It was the only way to endure. Beating back the hoard box by box, wrapper by wrapper.

I returned the empty trash bin to the laundry room, filling it with debris I picked up along the way. Mom would find a bin with trash in it, not an empty one. No questions. No arguments.

Score one for Shelly Frank.

My five o'clock shift at the Quick-Serve couldn't get here soon enough. I tugged on jeans and a black shirt and then slipped into my favorite pair of Vans. With any luck, I'd be long gone by the time the pizza arrived.

"The delivery will be here soon," she called again from the front of the house, as if we never quarreled. I stopped at my dresser mirror and ran a hand through my unruly auburn hair before grabbing a bottle of water from the case in my room. I stuffed it and a granola bar in my pocket and stomped into the living room, crushing papers under my feet as I went.

"I have to go to work. I'll put the money and a note on the porch. You have to get the pizza when they leave it." I glanced in the direction of the front foyer. A barely discernable path led the way to the door.

Her jaw twitched nervously. "Can they leave it right by the door? So I can reach it?" My mother wore sweatpants and a hooded sweatshirt. An old quilt nestled against her back. She was always cold because I kept the air conditioner cranked high to keep down the stink.

I half shrugged. "Yeah. Sure."

"What time are you home tonight?" she asked.

"Late. Maybe eleven." My shift ended at ten. Afterward, I'd find a quiet parking lot and drink iced tea until I got tired enough to go home.

"Don't forget the note. Right by the door," she said. Her fingers played with the strings of her sweatshirt.

Back in my room, I swore under my breath as I scrawled a note at my desk.

DROP PIZZA BY DOOR

$$$ UNDER LADYBUG

Good enough. I opened my tiny refrigerator and pulled out half of a protein bar. I shoved it in my mouth and chewed like a chipmunk with a full nut load. Enough mash to settle my stomach and hold me until break time.

In the middle of the kitchen, the source of the recent sour milk odor was revealed: a puffy milk carton on the floor outside the refrigerator. Why? Why did she do this to me? I gingerly set the carton on the back deck and stuffed trash in a bag as fast as I could. On my way to the back door, I stepped over an unopened Amazon box. I kicked the logo right in its salty smile.

Heavy box. Had to be more books. Volcanic rage scrunched up my face as I counted to five before hauling my trash bag out to the deck and inhaling the unpolluted air.

Outside, oh beautiful, wonderful outside! My world expanded, filled its lungs with fresh breezes, and I spun in lazy circles gazing up at the vast expanse of the uncluttered sky. Summer in New Jersey had turned balmy and semi-tropical. The air draped against my skin like a light fleecy blanket, and the grass brushed my sneakers as I walked past vibrant flower beds and squat rose bushes loaded with fragrant blooms.

Around the front of the house, summer was in full swing in our neighborhood. Kids ran and rode bikes. Dads cut the sweet-smelling grass, and moms toiled over heavily mulched flower beds or swept grass clippings from white sidewalks.

At least, the normal moms and dads.

My mother never came outside, which was why our yard looked the way it did—untouched by her tendencies. Flower beds hummed with bees where early petunias in pinks and purples promised a riot of color across the front of the porch. Bright red geraniums thrived in clay pots on the edges of the porch and at the bottom of the steps. The last magnolia blossoms dotted the rich green of the matching trees on either side of the front yard. Our mailbox stood straight and clean, no bird bombs in sight. A swell of pride filled my chest as I twisted my hair into a messy knot at the back of my neck. I loved my yard as much as I hated my house. Like my bedroom, it was the only other place I could escape the chaos of the nest behind me.

That's what I decided to call it when I understood what it was. My mother's nest.

I stuffed fifteen dollars under the stone I painted to look like a ladybug, stuck the note to the door, and headed for my car.

TWO

I RECOGNIZED him the second he stepped into the store, but I couldn't recall his name. Grass and mud stains covered his bright blue Titan Lawn Service T-shirt. Tall, dark, and different, he had appeared like a ray of sunshine my junior year in late September. But I left Randolph High right after Thanksgiving for my self-imposed exile to take care of my mother without ever speaking to him.

He wove through the potato chip racks back to the cooler where we kept the energy drinks. The cute guy glanced once in my direction. It wasn't one of those quick, look-my-way glances either. He suspected he knew me, too. Instead of acknowledging him, I pretended to organize a counter display of Fourth of July sparklers. Ugh. I hated when kids from my old school appeared in the store like bad high school dreams on repeat.

I am invisible. Don't recognize me. Don't remember who I am.

He made his selection, straightened, and looked

square at me. Again? Once was a coincidence but checking me over twice, not so much. My body stiffened. Someday, I'd send Pam a Christmas card with a dead Santa on the front, just to show my appreciation for spreading my secrets. I swallowed, hoping he'd buy his drink and disappear without mentioning anything about me or my sideshow life.

At the iced tea cooler, he lifted his gaze. I groaned. Now he knew I knew he knew. *Great. Just great.* Maybe if I acted all friendly, he would pay and flee. What was his first name? He'd expect me to recognize him when he got up to the counter. I cursed myself. *Fool!* I'd made deliberate eye contact.

Was it John? Jimmy? Jamil?

Joshua. Yep. Joshua . . . something. Too late to worry about the last name. I busied myself with the sparklers while he dropped a Red Bull, a peach iced tea, and a bag of pretzel twists on the counter. I scanned his selections without meeting his gaze.

"Hey, didn't you go to Randolph?" he asked.

I barely lifted my head to side-eye him. "Uh . . . yeah."

"I thought so. I saw you in here the other day." He adjusted his sunglasses on the brim of his cap.

"Mmm," I said. When had he been in the store before? Once was coincidence, twice was practically stalking.

"I remember you. You were in Environmental Science. You sat in front of me." He motioned with his hands. "Well, sort of. In front and off to the right." The corner of his mouth turned up, exposing a dimple. "I'm Joshua Evans. Aren't you . . . Michelle?"

"Shelly," I corrected him as I pulled a plastic bag free of the rack. "I'm Shelly."

He nodded. "Yeah. I remember you."

"Six seventy-eight," I said.

"Uh, what?"

I pointed at his purchase. "Six seventy-eight?"

"Oh, yeah." He fished his wallet from his back pocket and handed me a ten. "Did you transfer? You kind of disappeared after Thanksgiving."

The memory tightened my throat. My mother had a particularly bad couple of weeks leading up to the holiday. The principal got tired of her calling the school to find out where I was. "Um, no. I withdrew. I go to online school now." Except I never *went* anywhere, which was a problem.

"Do you like it?"

"What?" I dropped his items into the plastic bag.

"Online school or whatever."

"It's okay." I hesitated before handing it over. Some impulse drove me to ask, "Why?"

"I wondered what happened to you," he said with a one-shouldered shrug. "One day you were there in front of me; the next day you were gone." He stuffed the change and wallet in his front pocket.

I risked a glance at his profile, trying to remember him from class. Dark hair, dark blue eyes. Tall and tanned. Yeah, I remembered him from school. The girls went nuts when he showed up.

He caught me staring at him. My cheeks burned. "I didn't think anyone noticed I left," I said, my voice strangled in my constricted throat.

Joshua's shoulder lifted a fraction, and a dimple reappeared in his cheek. "I noticed."

"Thanks," I told him. Part for the sale, part for realizing I existed.

He lifted the bag. "Good to see you again."

"Um, yeah, you, too." I clumsily grinned until the bell jingled, and Joshua slipped out the door. My breath expelled in a whoosh. What was with the third degree? It was nothing. A nice coincidence. Still, he admitted he'd been in the store more than once. He didn't seem to know about my mother.

Maybe he would come back. A girl could dream.

CLOSING TIME. I rushed around the store, mopping floors and straightening racks. My Joshua Evans distraction cost me time at the end of my shift. I dumped the trash cans into a monster bag and headed outside to empty the trash at the gas pumps. A big, black pickup truck idled in the parking lot with the dome light on. Joshua sat inside looking at his phone, his bass-thumping music drifting over the lot. He lifted his iced tea and drank while I spied on him from behind pump number four. Two lawn mowers sat on a small trailer behind the truck, and a bright blue Titan Lawn Service sign decorated his door.

My brows furrowed. Relaxing after a long day? I guessed I was no different. When I finished at the Quick-Serve, I planned to drive over to McDonald's for an unsweetened iced tea and large fry and sit in the parking lot for half an hour to decompress before going home.

Tonight would be no different—not with crickets singing in the grasses. It was a perfect summer night. I didn't want to waste the weather.

I lifted the lid on the gas-pump trash bin and tugged on the bag. Great. Wedged. I kicked the side of the can to loosen it. Kick. Tug. Kick. Tug. Nope. Not moving. Oh, well. Leave a note for my boss and let him deal with it.

"Need a hand with the trash?"

The lid slipped from my hand and clattered on the pavement. I stared at Joshua. "That would be great."

He grabbed the bag while I held on to the can.

"What the heck is in this bag? A body?" With a grunt, he yanked it free. "Man, this sucker weighs a ton." He looked around for a place to put it. "Where does this go?"

"The dumpster in the back. Thanks." I gathered up the store trash bags, and Joshua half-carried, half-dragged the mammoth bag. We heaved it all into the dumpster.

He wiped his hands on his shorts. "Man, garbage stinks in this heat," he said, waving a hand in front of his nose.

I cringed, imagining the landfill at home. "Thanks," I said again. "You didn't have to help."

Joshua flicked a bit of paper off his fingers. "No problem. I was just hanging out. You closing up?"

"Yeah. We close at ten." I eyed him with suspicion as a thousand reasons for his question collided in my brain.

"You need any more help?"

I brushed off my hands and wished for sanitizer. "No, I just have to wash up and turn off the lights."

"Okay. Oh, I forgot to ask you." He fished in his pocket and pulled out his lawn service business card. "Can you tack this up on the board by the door?"

I took the bright blue card. It read:

TITAN LAWN CARE

JOSHUA EVANS, Owner

My boss didn't like a lot of business cards hanging around, but I'd stick it on the corkboard by the deli and pretend I had no idea how it got there. Rich would never notice. He rarely bothered to stop in.

"Yeah. Sure."

Joshua followed me inside. I tacked the card to the bulletin board beside Mark's Power Washing.

"Thanks. I'm trying to get more customers."

My curiosity was piqued. "You graduated, right?" I scrubbed my hands in the prep sink and offered him a squirt of antibacterial soap.

Joshua nodded as he washed. "Yeah. I'm done."

"Congrats. I've got one more year."

"You planning on going to college?"

I gestured to the store. "I'm planning on getting out of here."

He chuckled. "Yeah. I'm taking the year off before I decide where to go. I'm trying to build up business and stash some money away."

We dried our hands with paper towels. Joshua crumbled his and launched a hook shot into the trash can.

"Lots of people in my neighborhood use lawn services," I said. *What?* What was I saying? Did I want

Joshua to find out where I lived? How I lived? The details of my landfill life had been kept from him—a shot of good fortune. Maybe he hadn't been at the school long enough for someone to fill him in.

"Where's that? I made up a flyer to drop in mailboxes."

Now I backed myself into the corner. "I'm in Logan Park."

"Yeah," he said, nodding. "I've been there." He didn't say anything about his opinion of the area, which gave me hope my secret was safe.

"Thanks for helping with the trash. I'm gonna close up and head home."

"Sure," he said. "Maybe I'll catch you in here again." His statement sounded more like a question.

"Yeah." I lifted my palms in a "sure thing" gesture. "I .. . uh. I'm always here."

"Cool. See you around." He waved and headed for his truck.

I flipped the lock on the door, then hit the light switch. Joshua climbed into his truck while I hid behind the candy rack until he drove out of the parking lot. *What just happened?* More than slightly panicked, I grabbed my purse and keys. For a long time, I sat in the dark car and stared at the spot where his truck disappeared.

THREE

I WOKE to sun streaming through the window above my bed. The rays sparkled on the assortment of crystal suncatchers I hung from the curtain rod. Tiny prisms shot rainbows to the walls. My room was warm but not hot, and the ceiling fan whirled above me, distributing the central air in cooling breezes. I stretched in bed. I didn't have a shift at the Quick-Serve, so the day belonged to me, which meant I'd spend most of it outside hiding from my mother.

My mind drifted back to the end of my shift and Joshua's timely arrival. Was it a fluke he showed up when he did, just as I was about to close? A coincidence had to be the reason. Still, I wondered.

After a quick shower, I sipped on a yogurt drink while I cleaned my already spotless bathroom until the tile gleamed and smelled of bleach. I plugged in a new air freshener and breathed deeply. Clean linen. My favorite. And no malodorous hint of the nest just outside my door.

Jean shorts and a baggy teal tank top sounded like a

plan. I twisted my hair into my trademark scraggly knot at the back of my neck and perched my sunglasses on top of my head. Ten bags of mulch sat in the back of my car. The poor Honda sagged in the rear so much I drove home at twenty miles an hour. But the yard would keep me busy and away from my mother for most of the day. I checked the padlock on the door, grabbed a water bottle, and slipped outside through the French doors, breathing in the morning.

Glorious. Just glorious. At nine fifteen, the world was awake and vibrating with life. Birds hopped beneath the colorful feeders I strung on low branches, and butterflies jockeyed for position on clusters of red bee balm. Down the street, lawn mowers and trimmers hummed with the vibrancy of summer.

I flinched as a hummingbird zipped past my head, but my face broke into a smile. I lived for mornings outside like this, with the sun on my skin and a fresh breeze rustling my hair.

In the shed, I retrieved my gardening gloves, wheelbarrow, rakes, and a trash bin for the weeds. I always started at the mailbox and worked my way back to the deck. I loaded two bags of cedar mulch into the wheelbarrow and swore my ancient Honda, Bennie, sighed in relief as I patted its fender. "I appreciate the effort, buddy."

For the next hour, I mercilessly attacked dandelions and weeds, fluffed mulch, and split up overzealous clumps of ornamental grass, repurposing the new plants around the side of my deck. After wiping my sweaty face on the edge of my shirt, I paused and admired my handiwork. With a fresh bed of mulch and some new miniature rose bushes, the deck garden would be something to behold in the late summer. Rose bushes and maybe Shasta daisies. A nice contrast of red and white in front of the variegated summer grasses. Perfect.

That meant another run to the garden store later to pick up the roses and mature daisies. I calculated the number of plants I needed. I should have just enough cash to cover them.

"Looks great."

My feet all but left the ground as I spun. "What . . . ?"

Joshua Evans stood behind me, holding up a hand in apology, a wry smile on his lips. "Sorry. I should have announced myself."

"You scared the crap out of me." I gathered my spiraling thoughts as I peeled off my dirt-crusted gloves and knocked them together to loosen the earth. My empty stomach plummeted, and the beginnings of a headache thumped behind my eyes. "What are you doing here?"

He chuckled from behind his mirrored aviators. "I'm here to cut your grass. It looks a little shaggy."

I glanced around the immaculate yard. Shaggy my butt. I'd seen golf courses shaggier than this.

"Really?" I countered. "I have a perfectly fine push mower that says otherwise."

"You push this yard?" He whistled through his teeth. "What is this? An acre?"

"And a half," I told him. "We have a double lot."

He pointed over my shoulder. "Yeah? You see over

there by the hedges?" He clucked his tongue. "Sh-sh-sh-shaggy."

I pressed my lips together to keep from laughing. "Uh-huh. And what's this going to cost me?" I was beginning to believe this sudden urge to mow my lawn had nothing to do with money.

He gestured to the bottle of water on the ground. "How about a couple of those?"

Instead of answering his question, I asked one of my own. "Joshua, what are you doing here?"

His shoulders pushed up toward his ears and confirmed my suspicion that he didn't have a real excuse. "I decided to drop flyers in the neighborhood. I noticed your car out front."

We stared at each other for what seemed like a week before I cleared the cobwebs out of my throat.

"So, I better get to work," he said, making no move to leave.

My brain screamed at me to stop him, to say something, so I blurted, "You like cutting grass in this heat?"

"Not really. But it pays my truck payment." He wiped his face on his sleeve and shook his head.

"Good point." I heaved a bag of mulch out of the wheelbarrow and dropped it next to a rhododendron I just finished trimming.

"You do all this yourself? Doesn't your dad like to plant and stuff?"

The question shocked me for a moment until I found my voice. "My parents are divorced."

He covered his eyes with a hand. "Uh, sorry. I'm a jackass."

Shaking my head, I said, "No, you're not. You're just uninformed."

He grinned, and blood rushed to my brain.

"If you say so. I better get mowing." He walked back to his truck in the driveway, his long, tanned legs eating up the distance. Joshua was tall, maybe six feet, his shoulders not too narrow, not too broad. Plus, he had that great smile.

A tap on the window made me swear under my breath. I glanced up. The tightly closed window blind slipped back into place. My mother wanted something.

Fan-freaking-tastic.

The mower roared to life on the side of the house. Inside my bedroom, the air conditioning turned my sweat-dampened shirt to instant ice. I pulled off the padlock and clicked it shut on the other side of the door before heading into the nest to find her.

"Mom?" I called, then covered my nose with my hand. Something smelled worse than usual.

"In the bedroom," came her muffled reply.

Hah. The word "bedroom" gave the impression the room was in some way used for slumber. Not so much in this case. It was more like the unapproved annex of an overflowing landfill.

I kicked shoes out of the way in what used to be the dining room and shimmied between the china cabinet and the back of a broken wooden dining chair. Edging around a pile of laundry baskets stacked six high, I made it to the hallway outside the bedroom without incident.

Inside, my mother stood on an abandoned end table, the only island visible in the sea of knotted belongings and newspaper that used to function as a place to sleep. I ignored the bright pink walls of my youth and tried not to picture my childhood twin bed buried beneath the compost of the past ten years.

"What?" I asked her. I swallowed hard and tried not to gag.

"I heard you talking to someone," she said, frowning. Mom wrung her hands over and over, her anxiety spilling out in her motions.

My sigh rattled the depths of my soul. "There's a guy here to cut the grass." I was not about to tell her the how and why of Joshua showing up at our house. I still hadn't sorted out those questions for myself.

"Oh. I thought you cut the grass." She frowned, her eyes filling with tears.

"I do. The mower's acting up. What's the matter? Are you hurt?"

She glanced around her feet as if confused, her reading glasses perched on top of her head. "I'm looking for my other sneaker. I wanted to come outside and help you with the flower beds." Mom shoved loose strands of dark hair threaded with gray back toward the clip at her nape.

I stared at her for a full minute without speaking, waiting for the punchline. My mother never left the house. In fact, the last time I recalled her stepping outside had been my junior high graduation. Once I got my driver's license, she no longer needed to leave the four walls of her self-imposed prison. I did the shopping. I went to the bank or the post office to pick up the stuff she ordered.

"Yeah, right," I said. "It stinks like crap in here."

Mom's eyes sparkled and narrowed. Her next words were laced with insult. "You don't think I can push a wheelbarrow like you?"

"You've been watching me out the window? How pathetic." Had she seen me talking to Joshua?

"Don't you dare speak to me that way. I need my sneaker." She pointed to the piles of debris threatening to swallow her whole. "It's down there."

For a moment, I imagined her as Rose from *Titanic* on the stupid slab of wood, adrift in the frozen Atlantic. Somewhere in the tumult were the memories of my father, lost in a sea of my childhood, castaways with Rose's dead boyfriend.

"I don't know what to tell you. I'm not digging for it." I turned on my heel and left. I certainly wasn't going to burrow through the room looking for a sneaker she hadn't worn in years. Besides, I didn't need her coming outside, especially with Joshua riding around on the mower. All I needed was him asking questions I had no intention of answering.

"Come back here!" Her muffled complaints followed me to my room where I relocked my door. I took two bottles of water from my refrigerator and headed outside.

Joshua's mower clattered around a lilac bush. I held up a water bottle and waved it at him. He shut off the blades and drove toward the deck. Warily, I glanced over my shoulder. No mother in sight. She'd never come out without her shoe, which meant I had nothing to worry about.

"That for me?" He killed the motor and hopped off as

I underhanded him the bottle. He caught it and twisted the cap free. "Thanks. I needed this." He gulped half the bottle in seconds.

We sank into the plastic chairs I bought for the deck. "First installment of your payment. Thanks for coming over to cut the grass."

He made a face. "What are you talking about? It's my job."

"Yeah, right. I didn't call you, the grass didn't need cutting, and it's Saturday. Titan doesn't cut on Saturdays."

His lips twisted, and it was his turn to look shocked. "And how would you know?"

"Because it said so on your card."

Joshua shrugged with a wry grin threatening the corner of his mouth. "Busted."

"So why did you decide to cut my grass that didn't need to be cut?"

"Would you believe I was bored?'

I laughed at the sincerity in his voice. "Not a chance."

"Guess there's no point in making crap up. I wanted to talk to you again."

My heart tripped, sputtered, and tanked somewhere near my knees. I was oh-so-unprepared to form an answer. Nope. Not a chance of a snappy comeback. Instead, I dropped the best line I could drum up, which left a lot to be desired.

"Why?"

He smirked and shook his head. "Well, let's see. Pretty girl with a cool private deck, a sunny day, and I have nowhere to be. Sounds like a great use of my time."

I couldn't breathe. "I'm pretty?'

Joshua leaned in toward me, his elbows on his knees. "I don't see anyone else here but you."

Yikes! Now, who was busted? My mouth opened and shut.

"I didn't mean to embarrass you," he said.

Sucking on the inside of my cheek, I somehow managed eye contact while my face went up in flames. "It's okay."

"Good. But your grass isn't the only reason I'm here." His gaze traveled around my yard, and he guzzled the rest of his water before continuing. "I have a business proposition."

"Business?" I frowned.

"You do incredible work, and I can't tell a tomato plant from a sunflower. I have a huge landscaping job next week." He pointed at his chest. "Grass cutting, trimming, mulching with a big shovel. Those are my specialties. This planting stuff I'm not built for."

"You mean you want me to do the plants?"

"Yeah. They want grasses and flowers that come back every year around this bank. It's a big contract. If I do a good job, they'll give me more buildings." He pursed his lips. "I was gonna go to the nursery and play dumb. But you know this stuff. I'll pay you, too. What do you think?"

A rustling in the kitchen drew my eyes in the direction of the back door, just before it opened.

"Shelly? Who are you talking to?" My mother stepped onto the porch like a bear emerging from its winter cave. Instead of sneakers, she wore one yellow slipper embroidered with pink flowers and one red quilted one. I froze in terror, unable to breathe. At least she wore clean jeans.

"Who's this?" she asked.

My voice broke through the shock of seeing her outside. "Mom, this is Joshua. He's here to cut our grass."

"Nice to meet you," he said as he stood. *Wow.* He was sweet, good-looking, and polite.

My mother ran a hand over the frizz on her forehead. I'd inherited the texture of her crazy, curly hair, but I spent time on mine, straightening and smoothing so I didn't look like a red-headed Chia Pet.

"You work for Titan?" She glanced between Joshua and me as my blood pressure skyrocketed. He brushed the grass clippings from his Titan shirt.

"Yeah, it was my Uncle Rob's business. I took it over this year."

She nodded. "They do a great job on the pizza."

I leaped out of my chair to shoo her back toward the house. "Mom, Titan cuts the grass. Paulie's delivers your pizza. They're two separate things. I'm going to help Joshua pick up his tools. I'll be inside in a little bit."

"Okay. Nice to meet you, Josiah." Mom waved a hand and smiled as she retreated into the nest.

When the door closed, a different kind of shame burned in my chest. "I'm sorry. She gets confused."

"It's okay. Is she sick?"

I bit my bottom lip, swallowed the endless well of emotions, and nodded, knowing he could never understand what her illness meant. How do you explain a woman who won't throw anything away? Who believes every possession she's ever purchased retains its value regardless of the layer of crusty white mold?

"Yeah. Sorry."

He shifted in his seat. "That's tough. It's all on you?"

I sighed. "Me, myself, and I."

"If you need to go help her—"

"It's good," I cut him off mid-sentence. I didn't want his pity. I carried enough self-loathing for both of us. "I've got to finish out here."

He backed up a step, and I instantly regretted the way I responded. But the less he learned about my mother, the better. I couldn't let another person into my hell. The last thing I needed was another Pam debacle.

"Okay, then," he said, stuffing the empty water bottle into his shorts pocket.

Joshua rolled the tractor up the ramps and onto the small trailer behind his truck. No doubt about it, I blew my chance with this guy, the only guy to glance my way since fourth grade.

If only my mother stayed in the house. I stabbed my trowel into the ground up to the handle. Why? Why did she pick today to venture out into the world and spoil the one good thing that happened to me in forever?

He tugged on the straps holding the mower in place. It was now or never. He was leaving.

"Hey," I called and walked toward him, my legs mushy and heart thundering like a herd of gazelles. "When are you doing the landscaping job?"

His careful expression didn't change, a bad sign. "Tuesday. I need to go pick out plants tomorrow. I have lawns lined up on Monday."

I smiled brightly. "Okay. I'm off tomorrow, and I don't go in on Tuesday until five." I clasped my hands. "It's the least I can do. You cut my grass for a bottle of water."

"Okay," Joshua said with a cautious grin. He leaned against the side of his truck. "I can pick you up tomorrow. Maybe ten? If you don't mind giving me a hand picking out stuff that isn't gonna die twenty minutes after I plant it."

"I'd like to. Can you show me where the plants are going first?"

"Yeah. Sure. Absolutely."

I breathed in. "Okay. I'll see you tomorrow."

"It's going to be fun working with you." He climbed into his truck, waved out the window, and drove away.

Fun? Like walking on eggshells fun? Like avoiding questions about my mother fun? I sighed. The house loomed over me like a ravenous creature, waiting to suck me back inside as soon as my new business partner turned the corner.

Maybe, just maybe, away from the house, I could examine how I felt about him showing up on his day off to cut my grass. Maybe, without my mother spying from the windows, I could relax enough to forget I had to go home again and accept that maybe this guy might like me a little.

"It would be fun," I agreed.

FOUR

AFTER JOSHUA LEFT, I finished my mulching and stored my tools and extra mulch in the shed. Because of its distance from the house, the shed escaped my mother's clutches. Inside, I hung yard tools on hooks and created a potting bench from a thick board laid on top of two of my father's sawhorses. I ran my finger over his initials carved into one of the timbers.

WF. William Frank.

This was the only place I could be with him. He'd built the shed when I was little. Though I couldn't remember doing it, my handprints had been set in the concrete just inside the door. He'd set them, leaving his mark and mine on this sanctuary in the storm, right before he abandoned the ship.

My heart burned with missing him, with hating him. I hadn't seen him since he left, and I hadn't spoken to him in almost three years—since my fourteenth birthday. He lived in Florida with his new wife, Mindy. They owned a house somewhere near Orlando, but I wasn't sure where exactly. For all I knew, they lived in Mickey Mouse's backyard. Florida was where he went when he left us all those years ago—where he fled. What I couldn't understand was why he left me behind. Didn't he want me? Was I a bad memory of his time with Mom as she grew sicker and sicker?

My fingernail caught on the edge of the carving, and I picked away a loose splinter, revealing fresh wood beneath. Clean, golden pine. I dug another chunk free until his *W* looked as if it were growing a bright, new branch. The anger surging in my blood urged me to obliterate his name altogether.

I drew in a calming breath. Would he recognize me if I ran into him on the street? I was taller, older, thinner. Would he ask about Mom or pretend she didn't exist? Simmering resentment and hurt welled up from my clenched, gnawing stomach. I grabbed my trowel from its hook and drew the blade across his initials, scarring the wood. Scratching him from my memories, my soul. I slammed the shed door and locked the pain away.

Inside my room, I abandoned my filthy, sweaty clothes in a heap on the floor and ran the shower as hot as I could stand. Leaning against the cool, soothing tile, I wept for my father, my mother, and myself. Tears mingled with the spray, swirled disappointments down the drain. I might never find an answer to why he left. It was time to stop asking the question. I had a year. One year, and I'd be eighteen. Then I'd flee the house, leave Mom, and never look back.

I was, after all, my father's daughter.

After I gathered my dirty clothes into a pile and

mopped up my bathroom floor with a towel, I sat on the bed stalling, delaying facing her again. Reluctantly, I unlocked my padlock and stepped into the hallway.

My mother occupied the front of the house, usually staying in the living room, and I avoided the area like it was under quarantine. The only space I ventured to beyond the laundry room was the hall bathroom. Every week, I cleared out the accumulation of debris, cleaned the tub and toilet, and returned the room to some sort of usefulness. I hated it. Despised the time I spent surrounded by her things. But the alternative was to have her use my bathroom, which was totally out of the question.

She looked up from a crossword puzzle book balanced across another hardcover on her knees. At least ten puzzle books lay at her feet, most finished. My mother was linguistically and mathematically brilliant. Sudoku, crosswords, brain teasers. She solved them all, usually in minutes, even though she rarely remembered what day it was. Except she wouldn't discard the old books when she finished them. They clustered around her until she tired of tripping on them and tossed them into the hoard.

"Finished outside?" she asked.

"Yeah."

"Is the boy gone?"

I bit my cheek, wincing at the cut of the tender flesh. "Yes. He left a while ago."

"Good. I was waiting on you to order dinner."

My gaze shifted to the grease-stained, rank pizza boxes just inside the dining room door. "I'm going to have some soup in my room. Do you want me to make you one? I have chicken noodle." The idea of another pizza arriving at the house turned my stomach inside out. Worse, the reek of week-old cheese permeated the air, hovering above the regular stench and coating my throat with moldy grease.

"I wanted a fresh, hot pizza, but if you're not having some . . ." Mom tipped her head back and forth as if trying to decide. "Soup it is. If you don't mind cooking."

Relief swept through me. No pizza. "Sure. We could eat on the deck."

"There aren't too many bugs out there?"

"I'll light a citronella candle."

She smiled and adjusted her glasses on the tip of her nose. "Okay. I'll be out as soon as I finish this puzzle."

I retreated to my room and dug two cups of microwave soup out of my closet and grabbed a container of oyster crackers from the shelf. Outside on the deck, I set two cold bottles of water and the tub of crackers on the table. Mom opened the kitchen door as I carried the steaming bowls of soup out of my bedroom.

"This is nice," she said as she took a seat opposite mine. "You've made this pretty." She bent to admire the geraniums I planted on the edge of the deck and the cascade of sweet potato vines running over the railing.

Her fingers grazed the leaves, and I flinched as if she were contagious. "Thanks." I offered her a spoon.

She studied the etched floral design on the handle. "These are your grandmother's. Where did you find them?'

I swallowed. I didn't want to tell her I'd taken all my

grandmother's quilts, china, and silverware last year and stored them in my closet. I wanted to protect Nana's memories. I still did. So, I lied—again.

"I found them in the kitchen drawer. They must have gotten mixed in."

Mom laughed. "Oh, Nana. She'll be upset she's missing them."

I stared at her in disbelief. "Mom, Nana's dead. You know that, right? She died when I was seven years old."

Her lips twisted a minute, her eyes clouded. With anger? Grief? Surprise? I wasn't sure. But her forehead smoothed back out, and she nodded. "Of course, I know. Why did I say something so silly?"

"We better eat before it gets cold," I told her. My hand trembled as I handed her the crackers.

Outside, on the deck, it was easier to be with her as I dodged the funky chicken in my cup. The sun played over the natural highlights in her hair, turning the dark auburn strands golden. Her skin didn't show signs of age. She still appeared young, maybe in her thirties, even though her forty-fifth birthday was coming up in December.

After the noodles in my soup were gone, I sipped my water and munched on a handful of crackers. The incessant gnawing in my stomach eased. The humid, evening breeze cooled, and I lit the citronella against the hordes of mosquitos about to descend.

"The yard looks so nice, Shelly." Mom turned and smiled at me, patting my hand.

"Thanks. I'm going to plant some roses out here, next to the deck. Some daisies, too."

"I've never been any good with plants," she said, her expression wistful.

"I learned a lot from Dad," I said, my tone cautious. Mom *never* talked about my father. It sometimes felt like the happiness I experienced with him had happened to someone else. Like I watched my childhood through a two-way mirror.

Surprisingly, she grinned. "He did have a green thumb." Mom pointed to the shed. "Did you know he built the shed?'

Disappointment slammed into my stomach, curdling the soup. For a moment, she seemed lucid.

"Uh . . . yeah. You told me."

"You were only four or five. He put your handprints in the floor." She talked as if I hadn't said anything, and she visited somewhere better in her mind.

"I know." A tiny bird landed on a spike of maiden grass and bobbed in the breeze as I blinked back tears. There were so many questions I wanted answers to—about their relationship and why he left. If I asked them, would she be able to answer? I blew out a breath. What was her sudden interest in being outside? Maybe the disaster in the house was finally getting to her. I figured it would be a good idea to test those waters.

"Mom, I've been thinking. I'd like to paint the kitchen this summer."

"That would be fun. What color?"

Encouraged, I said, "I like the yellow. But it's all faded. Would you mind if I gave it a fresh coat?"

"Only if I can help you," she replied, squeezing my arm. My heart plummeted. Her offer of assistance was

Mom-speak for making sure I didn't throw anything away.

Still, I went along with it. "I'll pick up some paint charts. We could pick one out."

"That sounds like a great idea," she said. Mom stood and brushed her hands over her arms. "It's getting buggy out here. I'm going to head inside." She gestured toward the soup bowls and spoons. "Do you want me to wash those for you?"

I shook my head. The kitchen sink hadn't been seen in some time. "No, I've got it."

"Okay. See you later. Thanks for dinner."

Tears crested my lids as the door closed behind her. It felt so real, this last hour with her. Like a relationship. Like she cared. Even though she slipped away from me every now and then, she *had* been better. She held on to reality longer outside. Maybe getting her out of the house more often would help her lucidity. But how? It would take a miracle to separate her from the nest. Or a disaster.

I pondered the possibility of both options and hoped for the miracle as the candle flickered in the gathering dusk.

FIVE

I PACED the deck until ten minutes to ten, waiting for Joshua. What if he changed his mind? What if I imagined the entire thing and he didn't ask me to help him out today? But the rumble of his truck on my street told me I hadn't been dreaming. My face broke into a smile as I picked up my garden gloves and headed around the house to the driveway.

He pulled in without the trailer in tow. Of course. This was plant shopping day. No need for the mowers.

"Morning!" he called as I swung up into the cab. "I have doughnuts if you're hungry." He teasingly opened the box.

I laughed as my stomach rumbled, and I selected a jelly-filled. "Thanks."

"You bet." He picked up a powdered sugar ring and clamped it with his teeth as he backed out of the driveway. "It's a good day for this," he mumbled around the pastry.

It was true. The sky was the burnished blue of high

summer with a scattered cloud here and there to break up the perfect ocean of sky. The sun promised today would be hot, but now the breeze brushed cool against my arms.

"So, where's the bank?" I asked, my elbow on the door sill, the wind swirling in the cab.

"Not far from the Quick-Serve."

Ah. That explained why he'd been in the area.

Joshua cranked The Weeknd on the radio, and we sang along to "Blinding Lights." Ten minutes later, he pulled into the First National Bank's parking lot. The building was small, tan with red brick trim, but not much more than coffee shop size. The drive-thru dwarfed the rest of the structure.

"This is new," I commented as we hopped out of the truck.

"Yeah," he said. "Opens in a week."

Around the building, planting beds were marked off by bright white curbs. One large bed curved around the front of the building to the side door. The other sat like a small island in the center of the freshly paved parking lot.

"Just these?" I asked him.

He nodded. "Yeah. Plants and mulch. Oh, there's another one out back, maybe half this size."

"Okay." From my bag, I took my old digital camera and snapped a picture.

"Wow! An antique. Don't you use your phone?"

"Uh, my camera on it broke." I bristled and stuffed the digital camera in my pocket. The ancient Android phone I used had been my father's. I didn't have the extra cash to spend on a big flashy smartphone with lots of megapixels.

He cleared his throat and shifted his feet. "You ready to head to the store?"

I smiled even though I wanted to crawl into a pothole and vanish. First, he meets my mother, now I freak out about my elderly photography methods. Way to impress a guy.

"Yep."

My new business partner took me to a different nursery than the one I usually haunted. It was twice the size and crowded with Sunday shoppers. He turned to me when he cut the engine. "What are you planning for plants?"

"Definitely perennial grasses, nothing too tall. Maiden is my favorite, but you're going to have to split it up every couple of years." The white and green would stand out against the brick, and I loved the way it moved in the wind.

"Okay. You lead the way because I can't tell one from the other."

We wandered down rows of swaying grasses until I found a variegated maiden grass I liked. "Here. This is what you need. Three of these on the front of the building and one on the side."

"What about the island?"

I shook my head. "No, it'll get too tall. We need something shorter." In the next row, I spotted what I was after. "There. Fountain grass."

He chuckled as he loaded the containers of grass onto our hand cart. "If you say so."

I added six of the shorter grasses to the cart. "Okay. Now for color."

Joshua followed me toward the perennial section.

"I like the dwarf rose bushes. They don't require lots of attention." I showed him the bright pink blossoms but decided on the scarlet blooms beside them.

"Those will make people look at the building."

"Exactly. They want people to see the bank's open for business. And these . . ." I picked up a pot of yellow daylilies. "You can use these in front of the bank and in the island. They bloom a bit earlier." I set them next to the scarlet red roses. "So," I said, counting in my head. "Twelve for the bank and four for the island."

"You've got an eye for this stuff," he said.

My body warmed, but not from embarrassment this time. "Thanks. Make sure you water these good tonight."

He paid for the plants, and we loaded everything into the truck. "Tuesday, can you meet me there at seven thirty? I've got to pick up a load of mulch on the way over."

"Sure," I replied, wiping sweat away.

"How about a couple of iced teas?" Joshua asked as he closed the tailgate.

I licked my parched lips. "Let's do it."

AFTER JOSHUA DROPPED ME OFF, I walked around the yard, picking up sticks and grass clumps until rain clouds chased me back inside. I entered my room from the deck, counted to ten, and decided my mother hadn't heard me enter.

I flopped on the bed beneath the flying ceiling-fan blades. What had last night and this morning meant? Yes, Joshua was a former classmate. Maybe he would've talked to me at school if I didn't bail. Sooner or later, though, someone would've filled him in on my dirty little secret. He'd seen my mother yesterday, but her odd behavior hadn't put him off. Another confirmation he didn't know the truth.

I sighed. Tuesday would be another day to figure out what Joshua Evans was up to.

My stomach gurgled and burned. Two thirty and no lunch. I popped a couple of antacids in my mouth and opened my refrigerator, chewing as I made my selection. Yogurt and an apple. A trip to the grocery store was in my future. Rain cascaded over the windowpanes. I washed lunch down with a full bottle of water and braced myself to go check on my mother.

She was in the hall bathroom, applying eye shadow with a bent cotton swab. "What are you doing?" I asked her.

"Getting ready," she replied with a smile.

I caught her gaze in the mirror. "For what?"

"I wanted to go for a walk."

"A walk? Outside?"

She smiled. "Of course! Where else?" A clap of thunder made her frown. "I didn't know it was going to rain."

Frustration expanded my chest. "How could you? We couldn't open a window in this place to save our lives."

Her fist clenched the cotton swab. "It's not my fault."

I shook my head. "No? Whose is it? I don't see anyone else in here but me, and my room's clean."

"That's not fair," she replied. The eyeshadow palette dropped to the floor, scattering cracked makeup at her feet.

"Ha! None of this is." I stalked away to my room and slammed the door.

WANT to know the best day of the week?

Trash pick-up day.

I set my alarm for four thirty in the morning. As soon as my phone chirped, I was out of bed, digging contractor-sized trash bags from beneath my mattress. I swiftly emptied my small trash can and the one in my bathroom before unlocking my bedroom door. In the hallway, I listened. My mother slept in the living room since the bedroom was uninhabitable, a fact which totally sucked. It meant I couldn't throw anything in the living room away unless she was in the shower. Those fifteen minutes of privacy were like those contests where people win a shopping spree in Walmart, except I had to make sure my disposal activities would go unnoticed. I bagged magazines from behind the couch, crushed three or four of the oldest pizza boxes, grabbed water bottles and soda cans like a whirlwind, and bearhugged the bags back to my room.

But my Tuesday morning expeditions were much more relaxed. I headed away from her bed on the couch and attacked the kitchen, tossing mail, wasted food, paper plates, and old newspapers. She didn't spend much time in this part of the house, which allowed me more freedom to throw. I was determined to find the top of the kitchen table by the end of next week. The counters would be next. After I filled three, large, black trash bags, I moved some of the counter clutter to the table, evening out the appearance. Satisfied she wouldn't notice my work, I dumped the last two bags outside my room on the deck and filled another bag from the book stacks in the hallway.

The garbage truck came at six o'clock sharp, and I finished hauling my load to the curb as the vehicle's headlights rounded our corner. The men loaded my eight bags of nest into the back of the truck. I wondered if they'd let me press the compactor button if I asked.

Back in my room, I celebrated my success and hid the rest of my trash bags under my mattress. Time to get ready for our landscaping gig at the bank. As I brushed my hair, I allowed myself to dream about Joshua. I waited all night yesterday for him to make an appearance at the store, but he never showed. Talk about disappointment.

Where was he? Did he change his mind? Maybe the better question was why it mattered so much to me. But the answers didn't really matter. I'd see him today.

My mother was still sleeping when I backed out of the driveway in my ancient Honda Civic, surveying the property as if it was some grand estate. Like the yard, the inside of my car was pristine regardless of the faded red paint and sizable dent in the front fender. I washed, deodorized, and vacuumed at least once a week, whether Bennie needed it or not.

The faded gray interior felt spacious and elegant, a far cry from the life I lived inside the nest. I turned on the radio and opened the windows, smiling at the sun while Taylor Swift sang about sweaters under the bed.

Girl, we can relate.

My life had become divided by inside and outside, and the masks I wore depended upon my locale. I was my mother's daughter inside: tolerant when I could be, living amid her hoard, and unable to convince her to throw even a Styrofoam cup away. Outside, away from the house and frenetic school hallways, no one comprehended the chaos of my life, hidden by a carefully constructed smile and an illusion of happiness. Quiet, calm, serene. Sometimes on the outside of the nest, I struggled to remember who I was when every moment of every day I wanted to forget.

But today? Today, I was Joshua's landscaper.

In the bank parking lot, I unloaded my tools. A familiar rumbling engine spiked my pulse, and I tugged on my peach tank top to smooth it. Joshua drove in with a load of steaming mulch on his trailer. He hopped out of the truck, and I immediately burst into fits of laughter.

"What?" he demanded, his eyes narrowing on mine.

Struggling for breath, I asked, "Did you wear your sunglasses all day yesterday?"

"Yeah, why?"

"You're sunburned. You look like a raccoon!" I clamped a hand over my mouth. *Did I say that to him?*

"Aw, no," he said, rubbing his cheeks. "I used sunscreen, too."

Perfect outlines of his aviators ringed his eyes. He checked out his new look in the truck side mirror, laughed with me, and shrugged. "It's a hazard of land-scaping." He set his sunglasses on his nose. "There. All better?"

I gave him a thumbs up.

"Where do you want to start?" he asked me.

"With the big stuff in the back. Let's grab the maiden grass first." We carted the heavy containers near the bank's rear wall. I paced off a couple of steps and set the first one down. "You have a shovel?"

He reached into the truck bed for his tools. "Guess I know what my job is."

Joshua dug while I set and replaced the dirt around the grass plants. I positioned lilies and roses so the yellow would bloom on the backdrop of scarlet.

"Can you dig the holes for these?" I asked.

"Is this where you want them?"

I wiped my grimy hands on the bottom of my tank top. "Yep."

Once the plants were set in the rear and front of the bank, we grabbed water bottles from the cooler in the truck. We found a spot of shade behind the building and sat on a low stone wall while customers in the Dairy Queen drive-thru next door placed orders.

"Do you smell something?" he moaned. "That's a cheeseburger calling my name."

I took a sniff, and my stomach lurched. "Smells good," I lied. The grease reminded me too much of pizza.

"You want one? I'll buy?"

I would never be able to eat a hamburger, especially not in front of him and in public. Not with my guts in knots and no antacids on hand. The water I guzzled threatened to rebound.

"Thanks. Not in this heat."

"Yeah, you're probably right. I don't need to upchuck over all our hard work."

"Exactly," I said, nodding.

"Should we tackle those plants in the parking lot?" He reached out a hand and pulled me off the wall, but his fingers lingered for a moment. My heart joined my stomach in a full stop.

"Thanks," I mumbled.

When we finished the plantings, I stood back, imagining what they'd look like in full bloom next year, excited to be able to drive by and see them.

"I'll start the mulch," he said. "You want to pick up the empties?" He handed me a trash bag from under the seat of his truck.

I walked around the bank and gathered up the empty pots and my gardening tools. Joshua finished the front mulch and was working on the back of the building. I picked up his rake. "You shovel, I'll rake," I said.

"Thanks. It'll be easier than me climbing up and down."

Mulch flew, and I raked like a fiend to keep up with him. Lightheaded, I closed my eyes and leaned on the rake when he moved the truck to the next spot. Ugh. The granola bar I ate this morning had long burned away.

"Not so bad on the time. It's not even two o'clock," he

said as he tossed the tools back into the truck. "You want to grab some lunch?"

My stomach quivered and burned, and the thumping in my temples told me I needed nourishment.

"Sure," I told him.

He leaned against the truck and pointed at the Dairy Queen. "We're both a mess. How about a sundae? Might be easier than a heavy burger."

"Sounds good." Ice cream I could handle. Vanilla never failed to soothe and settle my stomach.

We walked across the parking lot. Inside the restaurant, we ordered and took our food outside to an umbrella-shaded table. I sank down on the seat and drank thirstily from my unsweetened iced tea.

Joshua took off his sunglasses and set them on the table. He wiped his face on a napkin, leaving muddy sweat streaks behind. "Thanks for today. I owe you at least two more lawn cuts."

"It's no big deal," I told him. "It's what I like to do. This was fun."

"So why don't you get a job at the garden center? Instead of the convenience store?"

"There's nothing wrong with the store," I said, my tone sharper than it should have been. If I offended him, he covered well.

He took a bite of his massive burger and chewed for a moment until he could speak. "No, not what I meant. I . . . you like plants. You should do what you like. That's all." He paused to drink his Coke. The ice rattled in the bottom of the cup. "What do you like to do, for fun?"

"Um, you know. Work outside, read." I smirked at my

boring list. "Sounds exciting when I say it out loud." My phone buzzed in my pocket. Mother bear finally awakened.

"There's nothing wrong with doing what you like."

I picked at a fry. "No, it's just . . ."

"What?"

"Complicated," I told him. I couldn't go where he was asking me to. I didn't want to ruin this, whatever it was. Friendship? That's what it felt like. He wanted to be my friend. God, how I needed one.

My phone vibrated like an annoying insect.

"I get it. It's tough to decide what you're gonna do for the rest of your life." Joshua turned wistful, as if he'd been thinking about the topic a lot. "I work two jobs. I help my Aunt Kay in her restaurant when I'm not cutting grass."

"Which one?"

"Paulie's Pizza," he said.

I stared at him and nearly choked on a nibble of French fry. "It's my mother's favorite."

"Yeah, I figured when she mentioned it the other day. Maybe she recognized me. I've delivered to your place a couple of times. Money's always under the ladybug," he said with a smirk as I snagged one of his fries.

"I had no idea," I said. "Maybe I should wait on the porch more often." Now that Joshua might be delivering to my house, I'd be waiting.

He crumbled up his wrapper and attacked the French fries. "I only help on the weekends, and once in a while at night—because of the grass cutting. It keeps me out of trouble."

"Why did you transfer to Randolph in your senior year?" I asked him.

It was Joshua's turn to go quiet. He stared at the remnants of his burger for a time before he spoke.

"My parents got killed last August. I came to live with my aunt."

"Oh, no. I'm sorry. I didn't mean to ask."

The corner of his mouth turned up. "It's not your fault. You didn't know."

"Yeah, but I feel like an idiot."

"It's all right. I mean, I'm not over it or anything. I miss them like crazy. But every day it's easier."

"How did it happen?" My dad wasn't around, but he was still alive. I couldn't imagine the pain he dealt with.

He rubbed his eyes under his sunglasses. "My dad was a pilot. He had his own plane. My mom was flying with him. They went down outside of Las Vegas in a bad storm."

"I'm sorry," I told him. I reached across the table and squeezed his hand. A pang of sorrow settled beside my heart. Joshua's parents were gone. Sometimes I was angry enough to wish mine were.

His gaze dropped to our joined fingers. "Do you have to work tomorrow?" he asked.

"Yep. Two to close."

"Good to know." He squeezed my hand as he rose to dump our trash.

In the parking lot, we stood awkwardly beside our cars, unsure of how to take this parting. "I'll be doing deliveries for Aunt Kay tomorrow night."

Was he giving me a hint to order pizza? I stepped back toward my car.

"Thanks for lunch. The landscaping looks fabulous."

Joshua nodded. "It does. As soon as I get paid, I'll get you your part."

"Sounds good." The handful of fries I devoured rolled in my stomach like logs in a fast-moving river. I should have stuck to ice cream.

"You bet. I'll be by to check on the lawn."

"Okay, well, see you later." I slid behind the wheel, hoping to get out of the lot before I puked up my lunch.

Joshua stood beside his truck as I waved and drove out of the parking lot.

SIX

"WHAT? WHAT IS SO IMPORTANT?" I asked her as soon as she answered the phone.

"I wanted to tell you what's happened."

My churning stomach dropped into the floorboards as I braked for a traffic light. If I wasn't sick before, I probably would be in a moment. I pinched the bridge of my nose. "What did you do?"

"I bought a refrigerator!"

I pulled into a grocery store lot and slammed on the brakes. "You did what?"

"We need one. I ordered it online."

What the hell? She had no money. No way to pay for her own pizza, let alone an expensive appliance.

"How? Where? *How much*?"

"Don't worry. I got a credit card!" She sounded so pleased with herself. I wanted to scream.

"I'm on my way home, Mom. We'll talk about this when I get there." The problems with what she'd done were too numerous to name. One, paying for it. Two, getting the old one out of the house. Three, getting the new one into the packed kitchen.

"It has an ice maker. And the water dispenser in the door. I saw it on Pinterest."

Closing my eyes, I leaned my head against Bennie's steering wheel. "I'll be home in a little while." I ended the call and stormed into the store. At least fury helped settle my stomach.

Bennie and I drove home the long way. I sipped on a peach-infused iced tea, avoiding the moment I had to step into the house and deal with her and her hot buy. Too soon, I parked in the driveway and turned off the car. For several moments I sat there, admiring the pale-yellow exterior, the white shutters, the overflowing flower boxes. Crippling sadness held me to my seat.

Why couldn't this be real? Why couldn't I walk into a house that looked like this inside, too? I imagined tiled floors, off-white walls, a cluster of family photos over the couch, my dad grilling burgers on my sanctuary deck. A home where love oozed from every corner of the room instead of unidentifiable substances.

At the back of the house, I tried my bedroom door and cursed under my breath. I forgot to leave it unlocked. I silently let myself in through the kitchen. It was close to my room, but my steps led through the wreck of our sunny, happy kitchen. There was a time when Mom made cookies, and we sat at the breakfast table drinking lemonade on hot summer days.

The ancient, busted refrigerator sat wedged behind boxes of God knew what. If I cleaned out the kitchen, I could close the dining room and hallway doors, blocking out the rest of the disaster. Maybe the store could deliver it. Except finding the kitchen was no small task.

The corner of the counter's ceramic tile top mocked me, buried under next week's trash load.

I picked through the pile of envelopes, collecting the junk mail and searching for the newest bills that needed to be paid. Last year, I set up most of the house bills to automatically deduct from her checking account the day her disability payment and child support arrived.

Someone had to keep the lights on.

Someone had to be the adult around here.

The padlock from my door clicked free, and I slipped inside as she yelled from the living room cave. "Shelly? How was your day?"

"Fine," I ground out between my teeth and thumped my door shut. Mom believed I'd been at work—at the store.

I smiled at my successful deception and set my purse on my spotless dresser before surveying the room for signs of my mother's presence. She freaked the day I installed a padlock on the inside and outside of my door after I'd come home from work for the second day in a row to find dirty dishes on my bed.

Ever since, we played this uncomfortable game of hide-and-seek.

I hid. She sought but couldn't get past the closed drawbridge unless I let her in, because I held the key.

Outside in the hall, she shuffled toward my door, and I lunged for the interior lock, snapping it closed as the handle rattled. "Open the door, Shelly. Where were you?

You were gone all morning." She tapped on the door. "I want to show you a picture of the refrigerator!"

"I'm getting changed, okay? Can I have some privacy?" I stood in my room fully clothed and stared at the door until her shushing footsteps faded.

With a weary sigh heaved up from somewhere in the vicinity of my toes, I stripped out of my sweaty work clothes and yanked a clean blue T-shirt over my head. *Great.* She wanted to talk again. A deep, stirring conversation would be the only reason she'd make the trek down to this end of the hall. Now what?

If I didn't go to her, she'd be back, pounding on the door until I let her in.

I found her perched on the edge of her chair in the living room. In addition to the crosswords, books and novels piled as high as the recliner's arms, and the ragged tome she held in her lap was bound together with criss-crossing strands of masking tape.

Gone with the Wind. The only book she ever read. Maybe she envisioned herself to be the Scarlett to my father's long-absent Rhett. Except Dad wasn't coming back to sweep her off her feet, and this place sure as hell wasn't Tara.

"There you are," she said brightly, and for a split second the pretty, petite redhead my mother used to be appeared, the mother I briefly encountered the other night at dinner, the one who used to come to functions at my elementary school when I had to dress up like a flower or a squirrel. The one who used to bake red velvet cupcakes with homemade frosting because they were my favorite.

"Tell me what you did," I said.

She shook her head. "Nothing. We needed it. It'll be here on Thursday."

Two days. I had two freaking days.

"What's the matter?" she asked me.

I pinched my lips together and held my temper until it boiled in a pit of caustic rage. "I have to clean out the kitchen," I began slowly. "So we can get the old one out and the new one in."

She waved her hand dismissively. "Let the delivery men do it."

"We can't let anyone in this house." Her brows drew down as if she didn't understand what I meant. I squeezed the back of my neck and closed my eyes. "Never mind. Forget it. We'll just cancel it."

"No! I bet your father has a new refrigerator. Why shouldn't I have one?" Anger colored her cheeks.

I threw up my hands at the inevitable shift to Daddy-blame. "Who cares what he has?"

My mother burst into tears. *Oh, for the love . . .*

"Mom, stop it. Okay? I'll make a path in the kitchen. You stay here."

"I'll help you," she quavered.

I held up a hand imagining the battle we'd have. "No. I've got it."

If I had to stay up all night and all day tomorrow, I'd get it done. Plus, I might be able to use the kitchen for a couple of weeks before she destroyed it again. Leaving her to her fantasy world, I headed for my room. I'd have to run to the store for more bags. Four dozen ought to do it.

"Wait, Shelly. It's your birthday next weekend. I ordered you jeans from the shopping channel. Are you sure you want a size six?" She frowned and looked me up and down. "You're really skinny lately."

"Are you kidding me?" This was not the conversation I wanted or needed to have, not with disaster looming over our heads. Besides, it was hard to gain weight when I walked around trying not to upchuck from the stench of rotten food. Not like she understood why my stomach burned all the time.

"There's plenty to eat," she said, waving her hand toward the old pizza boxes.

I bit the inside of my tattered cheek, tasting blood and embracing the pain, while wishing she forgot my birthday or that I even existed. *This is just a bad day,* I told myself. *We're having a bad day.* I'd been inexplicably moody since I left Joshua. Cranky since I found out about the refrigerator. What if he didn't come back in to buy his Red Bulls at the convenience store?

Anger at myself and at her flooded my veins. She was trying to be nice, but I told her I was a size four. Repeatedly. A six would never stay on my hips without duct taping them to my waist. Now I had to empty the kitchen in a day and a half; this wasn't the time to talk, not with my emotions in an uproar. Besides, I was only turning seventeen. So what? Eighteen? Now that would be an actual reason to celebrate. Packing up Bennie and driving away forever.

Deep down, I hoped and prayed she understood what living like this had done to me. Maybe buying me stuff— like the jeans—was her way of making amends. I clung to those moments when she experienced full lucidity, when I hoped I was making progress.

Then she pulled a stunt like buying a refrigerator, just to prove how oblivious she was to the house. My shoulders slumped under the invisible burden. Why did I try? Why did I dupe myself into believing this life could change? There wasn't any point in arguing about jeans already on their way—or the refrigerator. Best to say what she wanted to hear and hide in my room.

"Six is fine. They might be a little big."

"You just need to eat more. We should get a cake for your birthday. Chocolate? You love chocolate. I could order one from the bakery that delivers. You know the one?" She shook her head and fished around in the nooks of the chair. "Now, where are those reading glasses?"

"I hope you only ordered one pair of jeans," I cautioned, bringing her back to the conversation. Mom tended to buy in bulk, like the TV shopping channel gave things away.

She smiled as she came up with the glasses. "Oh, there they are." She dropped them on her nose and gazed at me over the rims. "Silly. Of course not. You can't just have one pair of jeans that fits you. Besides, they were on sale." Mom flipped through the busted book, shedding pages of Scarlett's trauma onto the floor. "Oh, no. I guess I need a new one."

Fury blasted up my throat, but I clamped it back down. How much did she spend on the jeans? How many hours would I have to work to make up for the dent in our finances? Plus the added payments on the refrigerator?

"Where did you go today?" Her mind shifted gears back to our original conversation.

I ignored the question. "I might be doing some landscaping work with Titan. I could use the extra money." If Joshua got the bank contract, he'd ask for my help.

Or was I kidding myself and lying to my mother . . . again.

"With the boy?" *So, she remembered Joshua.* She looked up at me over the top of her glasses, disproval coloring her cheeks. "Now, why would you do that? You'll have no time at all this summer."

"It's almost July. Summer's half over, and I like working outside." The lie rippled off my tongue, smooth as silk, covering my true motive for taking the job. I'd get to send more time with Joshua.

She sighed and leaned forward, dropping her book. The binding split in two when it hit the floor, knocking out more loose pages. "Oh, darn it. I forgot to tell you. I ordered pizza *and* a salad for you."

My fists clenched. "Mom, I'm not hungry."

Her gaze washed over me, and she said nothing. I stomped back to my room to dig up enough cash to pay the bill. Joshua said he worked tomorrow night, so I expected some other delivery person would bring our meal.

The afternoon sun flooded into my room as I opened the French doors to the deck. I surveyed the deep green lawn on the way to the pizza money drop and smiled. *Joshua.* He cut my grass because he wanted to visit me.

Well, I wanted to be seen. How long before I needed another trim? The weekend? My heart swelled with hope. He'd be back. He promised.

Grinning, I took my seat on the porch just as a FedEx driver pulled into the driveway. With my emotions plummeting, I tried not to think about what my mother purchased now. *Fifteen Minute Cardio* workouts? A futon? More Harry & David chocolates? A new Alexa to find the old one?

Didn't matter. Just another package to add to the pile.

The driver jumped down from the truck and made her way up the sidewalk. She carried an envelope. A piece of refuse easily hidden in an outgoing trash bag.

"Shelly Frank?" she asked me.

Surprised, I nodded. "Yes. I'm Shelly."

"Oh, good. This has to be signed by you." She typed on a tablet before turning the screen toward me. "Sign here with your finger."

I scrawled my name on the screen and accepted the envelope, my hands damp with anticipation and dread.

"Thanks."

"You bet." She paused for a second. "I just have to tell you, I love this house. It is gorgeous. I bet it's something on the inside too."

I smiled with a wry twist of my lips. "Oh, yeah. It is."

"Have a good day." She waved as she backed out of the driveway.

Shock momentarily paralyzed me as I stared at the Florida return address. Mr. William Frank. It was from my father. I smoothed the cardboard envelope. With shaking fingers, I pulled out a card. Amazement choked me, and I pressed my palms to my cheeks. Several moments passed before I could bring myself to tear into the bright blue envelope. My breath caught. A picture of a beautiful, tropical sunset over the ocean graced the front of the card. Two chairs perched in the sand beneath a lone palm tree with a small birthday cake on a table between them.

I struggled to hold in the sob. He remembered my birthday. Finally, he thought about me.

Inside the card, my father wrote:

Shelly,

I've missed too many birthdays and Christmases. I don't want to miss any more. Open the other envelope and say yes.

Happy Birthday.

Love,

Dad

I covered my eyes with my hand, hanging on to the pain threatening to claw through my chest and spill my heart on the porch. My gaze sought the end of the yard while I struggled for breath.

God, Dad. Why did you leave me like this? Why do this to me now when I am barely hanging on? All those days, weeks, months, years. Ignoring the fact that he had a daughter. Leaving me to live in this house. And suddenly, I should care about him and his cryptic card. I reread his note, resentment bubbling in my aching stomach. *Say yes.* Say yes to what? I slipped my fingers in the package.

Inside the FedEx packet, I located another envelope, this one bright orange. I removed a one-way airplane ticket dated for a week from Monday.

Two days after my birthday.

A sticky note said: Please come.

A trembling breath tumbled from between my lips as the impossibility of his request and his gift slammed into my brain. How? How could I leave my mother in days and go to him, the father who left me? How would she take care of herself? How could I stay with *him*, knowing he abandoned me—us?

I pinched my lip and stared out at the whispering magnolias. A hundred reasons why this was a bad idea popped like fireworks in my mind. A fresh breeze lifted the damp hair at my nape, chilling my skin.

And . . . if I left, how could I ever come back once I was free?

I clutched the envelope to my chest, holding back hope I couldn't afford to feel. Mom couldn't find this. I needed time to think. Then I'd tell her and pray she was with it enough to understand. But that would be later. After I made my mind up about going.

Florida. A thousand miles from the nest.

I'd been there once when I was little. The standard six-year-old Disney trip. I recalled getting sick on some Disney princess's shoes after too much ice cream and not enough sleep. But the main thing I remembered was the flowers. Everywhere I looked were flowers. Bushes cut like Donald Duck, brilliant vines laden with floral trumpets, hanging baskets overflowing with tendrils. The flowers changed me. Made me. I stared out into my perfect, resort-quality lawn, loving every bloom I nurtured. If I decided to be honest with myself, I never wanted anything more in my life than to cash in my father's ticket.

A group of kids rode by on their bikes, carrying swimming noodles, their beach towels draped over their shoulders, the ends fluttering behind them like banners. I'd missed out on being a kid. Having friends and a life that didn't revolve around secrets. At seventeen, I could have a new start, a thousand miles away from the nest. Dad wanted me to come to Florida with him. To live with him. I could stay in a house that didn't reek like mold and spoiled food. I could sit on an uncluttered sofa and watch television. I'd be able to have a life that I didn't need to hide. Go to school. Have friends. A new job, a new life.

But Joshua. I'd leave him behind, too. There was something brewing between us, a mutual attraction. Or was it only friendship? If I left next Monday, I would never know.

A teenager brought the food while I considered my options. I paid and headed back into the house, balancing the pizza and salad, my mind whirling with palm trees and sudden possibilities.

SEVEN

MY MOTHER WASN'T aware I knew all her passwords, which saved lots of arguments and accusations. I logged in to her email when the nest sounds faded into slumber and found the receipt for the refrigerator. With a couple of clicks, I put the delivery off until Friday. Another full day to battle the kitchen hoard into submission.

Shrugging off my exhaustion, I gathered an armful of trash bags and a flashlight.

In the kitchen, I started on the counters, sweeping everything but pots and dishes into the bags. One by one, I hauled them out the back door, waiting to make sure my mother was still asleep before tackling another. My fingers broke through the skin of a slimy, rotten cucumber, and my gag reflex kicked in. I rushed out the back door and retched dark-colored bile and salad onto the grass. When my stomach settled, I wiped my mouth. No time to waste. The clock was ticking.

At just after three, I gave up. The counters and kitchen table were cleared. Boxes still sat stacked in front of the refrigerator and stove. Part of this would have to be done with my mother up and mobile. I had no choice. I dragged my body back to my room and showered before collapsing into bed.

BOOM! Boom! The walls and windows rattled.

What the hell?

I jumped out of bed and ripped the lock off my door.

"Mom? Mom!" I waded through the book tunnel and stopped dead. The kitchen door stood open. So much for her not noticing my cleaning. I gingerly stepped over a single, abandoned roller skate as something shattered on the kitchen floor.

"What are you doing?" My mother stood on two wobbling wooden boxes under the ceiling fan. A shattered bulb lay on the tile.

"The light's out," she said. "Hand me another bulb."

"Really, Mom? That's the biggest problem we've got?" I picked a pack of bulbs off the counter. "You're going to break your neck."

"Just give me the bulb." She snatched it from my fingers and twisted it into the socket. I helped her down off the boxes. "There. Now they can bring in the new refrigerator tomorrow."

"Mom, we have to clear a bunch of this stuff out so they can bring the new one in." I pointed to the stack in front of the refrigerator. "What's in these?"

She stared at me like I'd spoken Mandarin.

"Right. I'll look." I gingerly opened the top box. It was

loaded with paper. Magazines, newspapers, old tax returns, bills, and a full box of petrified doughnuts. My teeth clenched as I picked up a trash bag.

"What are you doing?" she asked, her eyes wide.

Reason. You have to reason with her. "If I get rid of the junk, we can get rid of the box."

"The box is not junk."

"Oh no?" I held up a shriveled pastry. "How long has this been here? A couple of years?" I dropped the box in the trash bag as she rummaged in the paper.

She picked up a 2013 Halloween edition of *Better Homes & Gardens*. "You don't know what's in here."

Frustrated, I pulled the magazine out of her hands and dropped it into the bag, my patience fraying like last month's *USA Today*. "And I don't care."

"Shelly! These are important." She stood in the middle of her shipwreck, wringing her hands.

I patted her shoulder. "Mom? Mom, look at me." Her gaze shifted to my face. I desperately needed her to focus. "Would you go in the other room and look something up for me online? Use your phone."

Confusion clouded her features. My distraction tactic was working. "What?"

"You bought me the jeans, right? Can you find me some shorts? I *really* need new shorts."

Her eyes darted around the room, ricocheting off piles of debris. "Shorts?"

"Yep." I gave her a gentle nudge in the direction of the dining room and her lair. "Can you order some for me?"

My mother's chin quivered. "All right." With a final hand-wringing glance at the mess, she left.

I sagged against the counter. Disaster momentarily avoided. With whirlwind speed, I dumped the contents of the box and four others into the bulging trash bag, flattened the boxes, and hauled the mess out onto the deck. Two more bags joined it before my mother came back, but I uncovered the top of the stove and freed the sink. I turned on the tap and water flowed for the first time in years.

Huge accomplishment!

Mom's inner turmoil spilled onto her face in blotches of color and tears, but she held it together. Good thing. After all, she bought the refrigerator, and I was the one paying for it.

I dropped an arm around her waist and hugged her. "It's okay. It'll be great to have the new fridge." I didn't mention cleaning out the old one. Save the most delightful chore until last.

She said nothing as she ran her fingertips over the counters, lost in her own world. What went on in her muddled mind? Did she remember cooking and cleaning in here when I was little?

I found a bottle of spray cleaner and a new package of paper towels. Removing the accumulations of clutter exposed the filth beneath. I might have to call in sick to get it all done before the delivery. I left my mother rummaging beneath the kitchen table and headed for the deck.

Outside, I dragged the bags to the shed before she noticed. With what I removed last night, the shed was full, but it would be okay until pick-up day. Just in case, I snapped an extra padlock on the shed. I didn't need my mother reclaiming parts of her nest.

One step at a time. One room at a time.

Maybe this refrigerator was a blessing in disguise. A new, clean appliance. A sparkling kitchen. What if cleanliness became the new cancer, eating away at the hoard?

What if?

BY FRIDAY MORNING, the kitchen was clean enough. My muscles ached and my fingers cracked from cleaners. But, with the kitchen trash eradicated, the house smelled . . . decent. The old refrigerator had been emptied of petri-dish-quality specimens, and I wrestled it out of its corner. It sat near the door like a tired old man, ready to head off to his eternal reward. I patted the door. "Don't worry. I've got a dozen bags of your closest friends ready to join you."

The delivery truck parked in the driveway, and I directed the men to come in through the back door. The kitchen still felt shabby with skewed blinds and faded, stained walls, but the room's function returned. With the old fridge removed, a new, shiny one took its place. Stainless steel gleamed.

I couldn't remember being so happy.

Mom stayed in the dining room while I held the door for the delivery guys and handed them twenty bucks as they wheeled away the old refrigerator toward their truck. As soon as the door closed behind them, I called for my mother.

She ambled into the kitchen and frowned. "Where did you get that?"

"What?" I blinked in confusion.

Her hand lifted to point at the stainless-steel fridge. "Where's the refrigerator?"

I sank into a chair, the breath momentarily knocked from my lungs. "Wait a minute. What? You bought this. Mom, you bought it online."

Mom shook her head, her eyes wild and wracked with confusion. "I did not."

"I don't know, Mom! You tell me. Check your email. You placed the order."

Her lips twisted. "You're lying to me."

"Jesus! Mom!" As soon as the words were out of my mouth, her hand whipped out and smacked my cheek. I pressed a hand to the spot as tears sprang to my eyes.

"Don't you dare say that." She leveled a finger at me. "I know what you're doing. You're trying to confuse me." With a disgusted look around the clean kitchen, she stomped back into her nest.

I crossed the kitchen and stood in front of the new fridge, staring at my distorted image in the stainless steel. My fingers grazed the cool surface. She didn't remember. What just happened?

My image blurred through tears. *How much more can I take?* Defeated, exhausted, I leaned my head on my arm.

SATURDAY. Happy Saturday, full of yard work and sunshine after a week of dodging my mother. I loved the smell of fresh-cut grass. Now that I had my own personal lawn servicer? With the face, the biceps, the hair? Those gleaming aviators?

Joshua.

Sigh.

I hid behind the window blinds as I washed dishes in the thankfully still-clean kitchen sink. He rode back and forth across the yard. Earbuds dangled from his ears as he cut perfectly aligned swaths in the side yard. He trimmed around the lilac bushes, careful to clip the wayward shoots spiking up from the ground.

Drying the last plate, I shifted to the right side of the house for a better vantage point. My heart leaped up into my throat. The lawn mower turned toward the trees bordering our property.

My delphiniums. "Oh no!" I dropped the towel and plate on the table.

Yanking the door open, I dashed barefoot across the deck and into the yard, yelling and waving my arms, except he couldn't hear me over his music and the clang of the tractor.

"No! No! Joshua!" I reached my delphiniums just as the tractor cleaned out their bed.

He lifted the spinning blades and slammed on the brakes. The tires sank in the softer dirt of the freshly turned bed. I planted the delphiniums only yesterday, forgetting to mark the spot with the white edging fence I used elsewhere. He yanked the earbuds out of his ears.

"Look what you did!" I cried.

"What? Where?" He hopped off the tractor as I picked

up the one remaining stem of my flowers. The rest had been reduced to mulch. "Where did they come from?"

"Victor's Nursery," I said crossly. A headache bloomed behind my eyes.

"I didn't see it. It wasn't marked." He gestured to the other flower beds, all clearly marked with small white fences. "No fence."

"You didn't see the fresh dirt? There's no grass. What are you mowing?" How could he be so blind? I spent over twenty bucks on those flowers trying to cheer myself up after the refrigerator mess. They were tough to grow, and I finally found the right spot to plant them. Perfectly shaded and not too dry. I threw the stem on the ground.

"I mowed here last time. Look, I'm sorry. I'll replace them, okay." He took two steps toward me and stopped.

"Forget it," I told him and stalked back toward the house. So much for my illusions of perfection.

"I said I was sorry!"

I spun back to stare at him. "Everybody's sorry."

Inside, I found a granola bar, ate half of it, and threw the other piece away. I just needed to calm my churning stomach and my emotions. A bite to stop the shaking in my limbs. A few calories or some caffeine. I sat on my bed, chewing the bar into a gummy paste. The murder of my plants multiplied the throbbing in my temples.

It's not his fault.

I glared at my bedroom door. She was out there, rummaging in the nest. My stomach rumbled, and I ripped the top off a cup of unsweetened applesauce and drank it from the container. It hit my stomach hard, and I smiled, imagining the tiny bit of food digesting and soothing the sore spots. I downed a full bottle of water. It helped ease the pain.

Something thudded against the floor in the hall. What was she up to?

On tiptoe, I approached the door, pausing to listen. Mom was in the hallway, not far from where I stood. Adding or subtracting books from the pile? Maybe it was a new copy of a retired Danielle Steel book she already owned or a tome on ancient alien civilizations. Maybe a dated set of encyclopedias she found on Amazon and just couldn't pass up,

I didn't want to know.

I moved away from the door, startled to find Joshua standing outside my room on the deck, a gallon water jug in his hand. Rolling my eyes, I went to the door and slipped out onto the deck.

"What?"

"I just wanted to say I'm sorry. I didn't mean to kill your plants. I want to make it up to you."

Narrowing my eyes, I studied him. Did he look sincere? Contrite? Maybe.

Amused? Definitely.

"How?"

He lifted a shoulder. "I don't know. Buy you some new plants?"

I crossed my arms over my chest. "They didn't have any more. Sold out."

Joshua frowned. I was acting bitchy, but my throbbing head and my mother in the hall outside my room had that effect on me.

"Then I'll pay for them."

The ground dipped with sudden dizziness. I leaned against the house to hide it from him. "Forget it. They're just plants."

"Well, like I said. I'm sorry it happened." He backed away and headed for the steps.

I sighed. "The yard looks great. Thanks."

He lifted his water jug and disappeared around the corner of the house.

Why are you such a bitch? Why? A cute guy was cutting my grass for free, and I ran him off over a couple of flowers. I buried humiliation in my hands as whatever my mother was doing in the hallway came crashing down.

Ignoring the vertigo, I ripped off my lock and pulled open the door. "What are you doing out here?"

My mother stood in the middle of the hall, surrounded by an avalanche of fallen books. "I was looking for a book."

I waved my hands at the scattered piles of titles littering the floor. "Take your pick. How about picking up what you dropped, so I don't kill myself trying to get out of here?" Her hitting me broke something inside me. I couldn't deal with her. Not anymore.

She lifted one book, scrutinized it, and set it back down. "I'm no good at organizing. You're the one who's good at it."

"Mom, this isn't organized! This is a pile of shit! What are you going to do when I go to college? You need to do something about this mess."

Mom blinked at me as if I turned a spotlight to her eyes. "You are doing online school."

I crumpled against the door frame. *Here we go again.*

"I am. But I'm going to college next year. I'm going to move there."

Her chin trembled. "Why? Don't you want to be home?"

"Yeah, right. Can't leave this, right?"

"We can't afford college," she said.

Always excuses. I was done with the excuses. "Dad can," I told her, and her posture stiffened. Whether or not he would pay my way was another story. But the plane ticket he sent hid in my pocket. If using my father's guilt to get out of this crazy house, even for a semester at a time, was the only way, I'd do it.

She threw the book to the floor. "You stay away from him. He's no good."

"Yeah, so you've told me. As if this is any better."

"I'm going to clean it up," she told me, a hint of desperation in her tone. "I just need to find the time."

"Time, Mom? What do you mean time? What do you have to do all day that's so pressing? Crosswords? *Gone with the Wind?* Get your head out of the book, Mom. Dad's not Rhett, and he doesn't give a damn."

"Watch your mouth," she snapped, her hand drew back.

I bent down to gather up the books she dropped. "You gonna hit me again, Mom?"

Her skin went white as I piled books in the corner. "I'll pick it up."

Closing my eyes, I shook my head, holding on by my fingertips. "No—you won't. Go. Go sit somewhere." I waited until she turned and shambled off into the house, following the path to the sagging corner of her chair.

Books crowded the hallway on both sides. The last thing I wanted to do was return these to the pile. I snagged a trash bag and a sturdy box from my room and rapidly filled them with books, most brand new. Maybe I should take them to the library. Drop them off on their doorstep. I cursed under my breath. New or not, the books were worthless, out-of-date titles no one wanted to read.

Don't be like Mom. Throw them away.

I stuffed the bag to the breaking point and dragged it into my room. Despite my work, I didn't make a dent in the hallway. Maybe four more inches of passageway––a slight thinning of the book walls. But, however small, it was another victory over the hoard. If I added a box or bag of books to the trash pile each week, eventually I'd be able to walk through the hall without fearing a collapse. Someday, I might be able to find the walls.

A cramp doubled me over, and my empty stomach gnawed at me. It was only eleven o'clock, and the applesauce was long gone from my system. Lately, if I ate a little, it calmed the spasms.

"Toughen up," I whispered as I set the bag of books next to the deck door. They'd land in the shed with the other junk. Maybe I should celebrate the book purge by vacuuming my carpet.

I forgot about my spat with Joshua as I ran the vacuum, carefully cleaning baseboards, ceiling corners, under and behind my dresser, and under my bed. I followed the vacuuming up with vigorous window washing until the panes in my two windows and the deck doors sparkled. If only I could chop this room and the

kitchen off the rest of the house, eliminating the conta-
gion boiling just outside my door.

After a shower, I dressed in clean shorts and a fresh
tank and grabbed my car keys from my dresser. Time for
a trip to the plant nursery. I'd find something to replace
my massacred delphiniums. I stepped out onto the deck
and stopped in my tracks. Joshua knelt in the grass
surrounded by flats of plants, next to the flower bed he
mowed over. My chest tightened as I walked toward him.

He looked up at me. "I couldn't find anything like
those other ones. So, I got these." He gestured to the array
of plants. Begonias, Russian sage, impatiens, snapdrag-
ons, and coleus—at least fifty bucks' worth. "I was gonna
plant them, but I didn't want to muck it up."

Defeated and weak, I knelt in the grass beside him,
the fight draining out of me. "You didn't need to do this." I
dropped my hands into my lap and took a deep breath.
"I'm sorry I yelled at you."

"I wanted to do it." Joshua nudged me with his elbow.
"It's hotter than hell out here. Let's get these guys planted
before they fry."

I lifted the pots of perennial sage to the back and set
the begonias in the middle. "These are Russian sage.
They come back every year and get tall, so we can put
them in the back. The begonias can get about a foot tall,
so they're in the middle."

He stared at me. "How did you learn all this stuff?"

"After my dad left, I had to figure out how to take care
of the place. I read all the plant books in the library."

"No kidding." He picked up a trowel. "You want to
teach me?"

We spent the afternoon planting and mulching the bed, finally setting a section of white fence around our work to protect it.

"Don't worry. I know where this is now." He stretched his back. "Looks awesome. I bet the bank people are going to love what you picked out. You should do this for a living. I can mow down people's plants; you can come in and replant. We'll make a fortune."

I laughed as I wiped the dirt from my hands. "You don't think your customers might catch on?"

He wrinkled his nose. "Nah."

"Thank you," I told him, overcome with feelings I wasn't built to handle. My eyes filled, and I looked away, embarrassed by his kindness and my lack of finesse in accepting it.

"Now we're even," he said.

I glanced back at him. "Even?"

He smiled, and my heart crested a hill of rolling emotions. "Yeah. I didn't want you holding a grudge. Look out." Suddenly, he reached out and brushed away dirt on my arm. "You're covered in mulch." My stupid heart stopped dead, halfway down the hill. "I'm looking forward to cutting your grass again."

I returned his smile.

Me too, Joshua. Me too.

EIGHT

I CARRIED the plane ticket with me the next few days, terrified my mother would somehow find it. I imagined the argument and worried about her sudden penchant for physical abuse. Some days, I wondered just how far she'd slip from reality before I joined her. What if I lost it, too? I couldn't let that happen.

While I refilled the bottled water cooler at the Quick-Serve, I let my thoughts play with the idea of boarding a plane and flying away. The clock was ticking. Mere days remained to make up my mind, and I was no closer to a decision.

"Hey, there, where's your Monsters?" A voice boomed from the other side of the store. The only other customer, a young kid perusing the vapes he wasn't old enough to buy, ignored us. Without fail, Joshua stopped in every day I worked this week. Twice, he arrived just at closing, and we sat out in the parking lot talking, slowly inching closer to each other.

Maybe it was the ticking clock heightening my feelings, but I found myself hoping something might be happening between us. Whatever the reason, my heart palpitated as I watched him on the surveillance cameras while he made his selection. Today, he wore jeans and a long-sleeved shirt over a blue tank. Totally overdressed for the current temperatures in the mid-eighties and pushing lawnmowers. He made his way toward the counter and picked a pack of Sno Balls off the shelf as he went. He added two bottles of water to his purchase.

"You actually going to eat these?" I asked, pointing to the cakes. I made my best yuck face.

"Of course. I need my fiber. So, how's business?" he asked with a smirk as he eyed the kid in the back of the store. "Looks like he gave up on the vapes."

Bits of leaf stuck in Joshua's hair. I reached up and plucked them away. "Slow." I gestured to his clothes. "What were you doing today? Aren't you hot?"

"I'm dying. No lawns today. I was cutting brush for my uncle and it's loaded with poison ivy. I'm real allergic."

I once came across a patch of the stuff at the edge of my yard. The welts were miserable. "Yikes." I cringed. "That stuff is nasty."

He glanced around again. "When are you done with work?"

"In an hour. Why?"

Joshua leaned against the counter. "I was wondering if I could stop back then. Maybe grab an ice cream cone to celebrate?" He wrinkled his nose and sniffed his shirt. "I better shower first."

"Celebrate what?"

He beamed. "I got the bank contract."

"Congrats!" We high-fived across the counter.

"I'm psyched. So how about ice cream?" He wiggled his eyebrows.

I laughed and nodded before I could stop myself. "I'd like some."

"Good," he said, dropping his purchase on the counter. "I'll go home and shower, so you don't get grossed out by my stank."

"That's not going to happen." I stared at him, aghast at what flew out between my teeth.

Joshua laughed, flashing his brilliant smile. "Okay. Ring me up, so I can get back in time."

In the lot, he climbed into his trunk, and I hoped my heartbeat would settle back down in this century. *I have a date. An honest-to-God date. He came here to ask me out.*

No, it's a celebration. Not a date. Or was it?

I dug my phone out of my purse and shot a text to my mother telling her the manager asked me to stay. I shut the phone off before she could fire back a feeble protest.

True to his word, Joshua was back an hour later with damp hair and a clean shirt. I clocked out and met him beside my car.

"So, where are you taking me?" The afternoon had grown oppressive, and thunderheads darkened the horizon.

"There's this great drive-up ice cream place. The Caboose. Ever heard of it?"

I shook my head. If it didn't exist between the Quick-Serve and my front door, I was ignorant of it.

"Good. You'll love it. It has a real train caboose you can climb in."

The way he said it, I knew he climbed on the caboose more than once. "Sounds great." I shrugged out of my smock and ditched it on the front seat of my car. "I guess you're driving?"

"Yeah. Hop in. The door is open."

I hurried around the side of his truck and pulled myself into the front seat. The truck was littered with pizza delivery slips and old landscaping invoices. "Sorry. I clean this thing out once a week. By Friday, it's a real shithole."

"It's okay," I told him, brushing aside the papers like they were no big deal. Still the clutter spiked my anxiety, just like walking through my mother's domain. I rolled down the window to get some air.

I gradually relaxed as we sang along to the radio, laughing when I flubbed over some of the lines. Lightning zigzagged in the distance, but the rain stayed away, the storm skirting the edge of our excursion.

"Why are you sitting way over there? I have a perfectly good spot, right here." He patted the center of the bench seat. Unhooking my seatbelt, I slid across the seat and sat next to him while my heart pounded out of my chest. This *was* a date! His arm draped over the back of my seat. In no time, we were pulling into a graveled parking lot. He maneuvered the truck into position right in front of the caboose. "See? This is what I'm talking about!"

Kids jumped and scurried over the train car, leaping from the ends to turn around and climb back up again.

"It's chaos," I said, laughing.

"Nah. It's just fun. Come on."

I followed him up to the window where he turned to me when the man asked for our order. "Vanilla. In a cup," I told him.

"Medium or large?"

"Small is good."

Joshua glanced at me, then shrugged. "I'll take a large with hot fudge, extra fudge, hold the cherry, kill it with peanuts."

The man stepped away from the window to make our orders.

"You can get whatever you want. I'm buying. I invited you," he said with a bemused grin.

"Small's plenty. I ate dinner right before you came in."

He seemed to accept my explanation. "Okay. Next time it's go big or go home."

I laughed at his exuberance. "Sure." Reality slammed into my happiness. If I left for my father's house, there would be no next time. Suddenly, staring at Joshua's profile as he watched the kids play made leaving hurt too much to dwell on.

The man passed our order through the window, and we found a picnic table out of range of the caboose jumpers. Kid after kid leaped the five feet to the ground until finally one didn't stick the landing. He ran for his parents, blood trickling down his leg.

"Ah, that's gonna leave a mark," Joshua quipped. He dug his spoon deep into his sundae. "I have at least a dozen of those. You ever do something not smart as a kid?"

"Me?" I licked vanilla from the back of the spoon and let the icy sweetness coat my throat as a low roar emanated from the pit of my stomach. This was the first thing I'd consumed today besides two unsweetened iced teas and a bottle of water. But the ice cream felt good.

"Yeah, you. You must've done something to piss your parents off."

The only stupid thing I'd ever done was smuggle Pam home, but I wasn't about to tell him about it. The diffusion from my one act of defiance continued to ripple across my life, years later. "I was a pretty dull child. I never caused my mom a lot of grief."

"Lucky for her. I broke both arms and my nose—at the same time—longboarding down our street. That was a hell of a summer. Ended my Little League career." He turned his arm over. A long surgery scar ran from his wrist to his elbow. "A couple of plates and screws later, good as new."

"Wow! How old were you?" I dipped my spoon in the ice cream and licked it clean.

"I was in eighth grade. My mom freaked. But my cousin owned a motorcycle and what he did on it was way worse. Aaron crashed more than he rode."

I studied him, trying to imagine him as a short kid in middle school with two casts and a busted nose. He'd still be beautiful.

"Where do you live?" I asked him.

His spoon stopped halfway to his mouth. "Um . . . I live over on the east side of the river. Collins Drive."

I hadn't been across the river since I was little, but I remembered the houses were not close to each other like in my development. "Is it nice over there?"

Joshua nodded. "Not bad. They have a couple of acres

I get to mow." He grinned and stirred the fudge and melting ice cream into a soupy brown syrup, but sadness darkened his eyes. "It's okay. Living with my uncle and aunt's been great." He violently attacked his sundae, shoveling down massive spoons of vanilla. "So why did you decide to go to online school? Isn't it boring?" He reached for the pile of napkins and brushed my hand. My pulse fluttered. I didn't flinch, but my stomach twisted.

I swallowed hard. *Personal questions, oh how I loathe thee.* "My mom's sick—you saw her. Kids . . . well. They talk about stuff. It's a long story." I took a bite of ice cream to deflect the rest of the question. The confection grated like sand on my tongue.

"That stinks. Not classes online, though. I like going to school every day. But I'm D-O-N-E anyway."

"Yeah, it's okay. When do you think you'll get to college?"

Joshua scooped up another colossal spoonful and wiped his mouth on a paper napkin before answering. "I have a couple of options. I have a decent ride offer at a school down south. Two others up here, but they're pricey. But I have to run for my scholarship."

I shifted closer to him on the bench, our shoulders nearly touching.

My brows drew down. "Run?"

"Oh, yeah. Cross-country. I was on the cross-country team. After I broke my arm and couldn't pitch, I took up running."

I managed another bite from my cup, surprised at how much I'd eaten. Even though we ended up discussing heavy subjects, being with Joshua made me forget about my churning stomach and the anxiety lashing through my veins.

"Cool. I hate running, but you go ahead."

He nudged my shoulder with his.

"What do you want to go to college for?" I asked him, avoiding his gaze. The air thickened between us. Did he feel what I felt? The tug?

"Believe it or not, landscape design. I like what I'm doing. I'd like to have a bigger company someday. But I'd have to move south so I could work all year."

"My dad lives in Florida." I swore I felt the ticket vibrate in my purse.

"Yeah? The school I'm looking at is down there." He scooped up the remnants of his sundae and finished it. "That was awesome. This place knows how to do it." He tossed his cup in the trash while I took another bite and then tossed mine as well. "You didn't need to ditch it. I have lots of time."

"It was getting watery," I explained. I learned when to push my stomach, and when to call it quits. Maybe I should go to a doctor for a stronger antacid.

"Oh, I almost forgot." He fished a bank envelope out of his pocket. "Here, this is your cut."

"My cut?"

"Of the bank work. I told you I'll pay you."

In truth, I completely forgot about our business arrangement. The money was totally secondary to spending time with him.

"Thanks," I told him, smoothing the bills out in my hand. The money would help bail me out of my mother's recent impulse shopping.

"Okay. Want to go for a drive?" His eyes held mine.

"Sure." At the moment, I wanted nothing more in the world.

He took my hand. "Is this okay?"

My heart thumped, and I squeezed his fingers. "Yeah. It is."

We held hands in the truck as he took me north of town into thick wooded areas where cars sat parked on the sides of the road and people carried kayaks through the trees. "What's this?"

"Franklin State Park. You've never been here?"

I shook my head. "No. It's beautiful."

He pointed out the windshield. "There's a lake behind those trees. We're gonna park up further. There's a dock we can walk on."

We hiked through the woods on a graveled path from the parking lot. My heart pounded in my chest. I'd never done anything like this, especially coupled with lying to my mother outright about where I was or who I was with. The effect was liberating, freeing. As I stepped from the tree line and beheld the sparkling lake, I knew what it was like to be lost in the world.

Joshua grabbed my hand. "Come on."

We climbed the steps to the pier and walked out toward the lake. Fish leaped beneath us, and I had the feeling they had been trained well to beg for food. At the end of the pier, Joshua dug in his pocket for change and purchased two handfuls of pellets for the fish from a dispenser.

"Isn't this like cheating?" I asked.

"What do you mean?"

"Well, there are fishermen on this pier. Here we are pulling in the fish with bait." Ducks joined the frenzy as I dropped kernels of food over the rail.

"Most of these big ones are too smart to get caught. I used to fish here with my dad when we visited my cousin. Most of the time I pulled in blue gills."

I shook my head. "You'll have to help me out with details. I don't fish."

"Oh, they're about this big." He held his hands a few inches apart. "Nothing like these guys."

A big, striped fish muscled the others out of the way for the last piece of food.

"This is a beautiful place." A sailboat made its way across the lake, away from us, gliding on the glimmer of early sunset.

"I'm glad you like it. There are a lot of cool places I'd like to show you." He read my wide-eyed reaction. "What? Are you surprised?"

"You don't even know me." I gripped the railing. I never wanted him to *know* me, or my mother.

"So? Doesn't mean I don't like hanging out with you." He gave my twisted bun a playful tug I felt down to my toes. His fingers found mine again, no longer timid.

"I like hanging out with you, too."

"Good. We've got a lot of hanging out to do, thanks to your plant smarts." He tugged me closer.

This was progress. I felt lightheaded but couldn't wait for the next time. "When do we start?"

"Are you working tomorrow night?"

"No. I'm done at three."

"Good. I have four lawns to do tomorrow. After, maybe we can scout out the other banks?"

"Four lawns? That's a lot of grass," I said.

"And a lot of green. They're big lawns. Paying seventy-five bucks a pop."

My eyes flew open. "Seventy-five bucks? To cut the grass?" I did the mental math. Not bad money to ride around on a tractor and tan.

"They're not all perfect like yours. It only takes me about forty minutes to do your yard. These lawns take much longer."

A pair of colorful kayaks drifted by, and a sudden wave of guilt hit me in the chest. Mom. She'd be waiting for me. Someone had to pay for the pizza she undoubtedly ordered.

"I should probably get home. I need to check on my mom."

"Sure." He brushed the back of his fingers over my cheek, his eyes connecting with mine. "Thanks for coming out with me."

"Thanks for inviting." I smiled at him with my entire face and felt the mask I wore for my entire life crack in a dozen places.

NINE

FRIDAY. Almost two weeks since I started spending time with Joshua, and three days and counting until liftoff. The more I thought about it, the more I wanted to explore what might develop with my favorite lawn-care professional. But staying here for him meant another year with mom and another year of fighting the battles I had nearly given up on. I wanted a full suitcase and a seat on the plane.

Knowing I wouldn't be able to stand another year at home, every minute with him was suddenly precious. But I wanted more out of life than scurrying around in trash and pretending I was happy.

I met Joshua at the first of two banks we planned to landscape. The sun burned through my tank top. "We need to work fast today," he said. "It's gonna be a hot one."

"Ready when you are," I told him. His fingers touched my arm. Sooner or later, I'd have to explain the ticket to him. What would he think about me leaving? One-way meant permanent relocation. Dread built up in my chest until I could barely breathe. I didn't want to lose this. Not after I just found it.

He tossed a shovelful of mulch at my feet. I jumped. "Hey, you're a million miles away today," he said.

I smiled. "Sorry. Lot on my mind."

"Like what?" Joshua leaned on the shovel handle while I finished spreading the mulch.

"It's a long story."

"You want to take a break?"

The top of my head felt cooked from the heat burning through my hat. "Yeah, I need a water."

We sat shoulder to shoulder in the cab of his truck with the doors open and the air cranked on. "So, what's up?" he asked, concerned.

I sucked in a breath and blew out my cheeks, preparing for my next words. "Remember I told you about my dad living in Florida? He sent me a plane ticket for my birthday. He wants me to go to his house."

"Good for you. You guys gonna go to the beach?"

"It's not a vacation." I chewed my lip and turned to meet his gaze. "It's one-way, Joshua."

"Oh," he said as the reality of what I meant settled in. "He wants you to live with him."

Nodding, I said, "Yeah."

He played with the cap on his water bottle. "What are you going to do? Does he know your mom is sick?"

I reached across the seat and took his fingers in mine. "I don't know. I wanted to leave. The issues with my mom are . . ." I stopped myself. "When I got the ticket, I was like, *yes*, I can finally get away from my mother's problems." My gaze drifted to our entwined hands. "Now I'm not sure what I want."

He squeezed my hand. "What do you mean?"

"It's complicated," I told him, relying on my favorite excuse. Confession time. "He sent me the ticket for my birthday, but I haven't told my mother yet. She might freak."

"They don't get along, huh?"

"You could say that. It was a bad divorce." I guzzled my water and felt lightheaded. I reached for the bag of pretzels on the dashboard and took a handful. Maybe the salt would help my headache.

"Sorry you have to deal with their problems."

I shrugged. "Life sucks, right?"

Joshua lifted my hand and touched his lips to the back. "Not always."

"YOU DON'T LIKE THE SALAD?"

We sat in Paulie's Pizza after our second landscaping job of the day. I hurt in places I never knew I could. The air conditioning chilled my sweaty shirt as I picked through my Caesar salad.

"No, it's good. It's just . . . I'm tired. I've never worked so hard in my life." I popped a crouton in my mouth.

He considered my plate before retrieving a container from under the counter. "Here. Take it for lunch tomorrow." I reached for the box, but he suddenly yanked it back. "Wait a minute. You said your birthday is coming up. When?"

"Uh, tomorrow?"

His seriousness morphed into a brilliant smile. "Great. I'm taking you out for your birthday."

I was stunned silent for a moment. "You are?"

"Yes. It's Saturday. I can pick you up at, like, eight. I've got a great place to hike. You'll love it. I'll text you when I'm on my way."

I had a shift at the Quick-Serve in the morning, but I could come in late—or not at all. I never called in sick, but there was a first time for everything.

"How about you give me your phone number?" he asked.

My heart swelled with gratitude and disbelief as I exchanged phone numbers with him. No guy ever asked for my number or held my hand. What did I do to make this incredible, beautiful guy want to spend the day with me? Whatever it was, I needed to do more of it.

The idea of a day out of my house with Joshua over-whelmed me, and I burst into tears.

"What? What did I do?" He jumped up, suddenly frantic. "I'm sorry, okay?"

"Everything okay out there?" his aunt called from the kitchen area.

I threw my arms around his neck. I never hugged a boy before, but hugging Joshua felt all kinds of right. "Thank you. I'm just—thank you."

His fingertips traced a tear path on my cheek. "It's all good. We'll have a great day."

"Yes, we will."

He walked me out to my car. We stood in the darkened parking lot, leaning against Bennie's fender and listening to the crickets chirp and hum.

"It's nice out," Joshua murmured, his gaze turned to the sky. Planes blinked on their flight paths, reminding me of the ticket in my purse.

"Too nice to go home yet," I agreed.

Joshua took the container of salad from me and set it on Bennie's roof. I forgot how to breathe as he pulled me around to face him. His arms found their way around my waist, and I followed his lead. Joshua holding me was the rightest thing that ever happened to me. I leaned against his chest, tilting my head back to see his eyes.

"I'm glad you took the job with me," he said.

"Me too." I smiled. The simple slip of my emotions sent a tremor through my body.

"Are you cold?" he asked me.

I shook my head. "Nope."

"Good," he said, his head tilting down toward mine. I closed my eyes. I'd been waiting for this moment forever. Just as his lips grazed mine, I opened my eyes, wanting to see his face. Wanting to witness my first kiss. His hand cupped my chin, deepening the kiss as a new flutter low in my stomach elbowed the constant upset out of the way. My fingers clutched his shirt, and I held on for dear life.

Behind us, a car door slammed. I jerked back from his lips. A teenage guy waved like a maniac from the driver's seat. He peeled out of the lot and laid on the horn for half a block.

"Idiot," Joshua muttered.

"Is that your cousin Aaron?" I asked him.

"Unfortunately."

I released my grip on his shirt. "I have to go."

He brushed my hair over my shoulder, his eyes dropping to the exposed side of my neck. I shivered again but backed away before I lost all control.

"See you tomorrow?" I asked him.

His fingers trailed down my arm. "Text me?"

"Absolutely," I replied.

Joshua grabbed the salad from the top of the car as I opened the door. "Don't forget this."

Forget it? I might frame it when I got home.

I smiled at him, my heart full, blood racing in my veins. "Don't worry. I won't."

TEN

MOM WAS WAITING up for me when I arrived home, and an odd pang of remorse hit me. She spent her nights curled on the couch, reading. Once I let her sleep in my room on an old sleeping bag I kept in the closet. But she'd been so agitated because I separated her from her things that she left before midnight to crawl back into her nest.

A colorful afghan covered her legs, and a fresh copy of *Gone with the Wind* lay in her lap.

The plane ticket burned in the back of my mind. I hated my life. With each day, I hated it more, especially now I saw a way out. But my phone buzzed in my pocket with another text from Joshua, and I clung to the silent promise of hope for a normal birthday tomorrow.

"How was the new job?" Mom asked, her appearance guarded. This is how we were around each other since the college truth dropped the other night. Careful. As if my age was a ticking time bomb ready to blow her world to hell.

I remembered the memes from the movie *Fight Club*. The first rule of Fight Club? Don't discuss Fight Club. We didn't discuss the hoard. We didn't discuss how I felt about the hoard. We didn't discuss anything beneath the surface of our relationship because Mom would run and hide.

"It was great," I told her.

She set the book aside and removed the afghan. Today, she wore a skirt, a rarity. What the heck? The other day, she stepped outside, and now she was fully dressed on the couch. She hadn't worn a skirt since she used to be an elementary school teacher, and before she became a collector of damned and destroyed dreams.

"Why are you dressed up?"

"It's pretty, isn't it?" She smoothed the flounce over her knees. Her feet were bare, her toes painted three different shades of pink. On top, she wore a tattered hooded sweatshirt. "What's in the box? Did you have something good for dinner?" The hope in her voice turned a knife in my heart and flipped my stomach more than normal.

"Caesar salad. It was okay."

"Put it in the fridge. You can have it for lunch tomorrow." She turned back to her novel.

"Mom, I need to tell you something." My brain bounced back and forth between my birthday date with Joshua and my impending trip to Florida. Two very different issues. How would she react to the first one? "Uh, I'm going out tomorrow. A friend is taking me out for my birthday."

Her eyes went uber wide, her smile radiant. "Is it a boy? Where'd you meet him? At school?"

Clearing my throat, I said, "Actually, he's the one who cuts our grass." I added quickly, "You remember? You met him the other day."

Her brows creased, the lines deepening between her blue eyes. Confusion darkened her gaze. "You cut the grass."

I breathed in, calming myself. "No. He cuts grass. I help with landscaping." I lifted the container. "He bought me dinner."

"How nice! You should bring him by so I can meet him," she said as if she hadn't comprehended a word I said. "We could have dinner on the deck. I can make the grilled chicken you like."

I stared at her, aghast. "No. I can't."

My mother frowned like she didn't understand my response. "No? Don't you want me to meet your boyfriend?"

"Mom! He's not my boyfriend." *Wait a minute. Was he?* "Besides, I'm going to be gone for a while and . . ."

"What?" Her nose and lips scrunched up like she was in pain.

My mouth clamped shut, and I blinked back tears. Now I'd done it.

"What did you say?" Her fingers gripped the edge of the sofa as she pushed up into a seated position. An avalanche of mismatched throw pillows crashed to the floor.

"Nothing. It's nothing."

Her eyes narrowed and her old teacher-tone crept into her voice. "You're lying to me."

I took a step back and decided to pull out the lie I gave Joshua. "I'm going to Dad's for a while to look at colleges. He sent me a plane ticket for my birthday. I haven't seen him in years. I've always wanted to see a palm tree."

Rage burned through her features, and a vicious, feral snarl curled up her throat. I didn't recognize the person who lunged at me.

"Bastard! What right does he have to take you? He's taken everything from me! Everything!"

I stumbled back out of her reach, accidentally flipping the salad on the floor in the process. She struggled toward me but slipped in the salad dressing and careened into a pile of old pizza boxes. They tipped over and spilled their moldy, soiled contents on the floor. A mouse dashed beneath the pile of refuse.

She shook a furious finger at me. "Look what you've done! Look at it! You're not going anywhere tomorrow until you put all of this back. You hear me? And you're not going to Florida!"

My body trembled, old wounds tearing open one by one. "Mom, please . . ."

"You think he cares about you? All he does is *lie*! He's down there with the whore! You want to live with her? She took him away from us!" Her voice rose, shrill. "He calls all the time pretending he wants to talk to you." Mom smiled smugly. She shook a finger at me. "I know better. I know how to protect you from him."

My breath whooshed out of my lungs, and my knees

weakened. "He called me? When?" She kept this from me. Kept him from me.

Dad. My dad. He called.

She ignored the question, slipped, and fell to the ground. Surrounded by her hoard, she gathered a smashed china doll against her chest and picked bits of food from the doll's hair, and my heart cracked, cracked, cracked.

She loved her hoard more than she loved me. And now I knew my dad's FedEx package to be a last resort, not a first attempt at contact. She'd been keeping him from me all this time. He hadn't forgotten me. I backed away toward the safety of the hallway and my padlocked room, my own brand of pissed off bubbling to the surface.

"You're not going anywhere," she sneered from the floor. "You're mine."

The words echoed in my brain, slamming into my skull. A possession. Another piece of her hoard. That's what I was to her. That's all.

"You can't stop me, so don't try. I'm an adult—the only one living in this filthy, disgusting, rattrap of an excuse for a house! This crap is garbage, Mom. Trash! You live in a dump! How could I bring someone into this place? After what happened with Pam?"

She got to her knees, the doll clutched in her hand. "She was no good. You didn't need to hang around with that—"

"That what, Mom? She was a kid. Twelve years old. How was she supposed to process the fact I live in a landfill? You want to live like this? Die like this? Because that's what's going to happen, Mom. Just like Randy. One day, your piles of junk are going to grab you and swallow you whole!" Tears coursed down my face, and I wiped my running nose on my hand.

"Get out of my sight." Her voice quieted. Flat, emotionless.

I retreated to my bedroom, locked the door on the inside, and leaned against the solid plank to catch my breath. Guilt strangled me with an iron fist around my throat. *She's sick*, I told myself, but the old excuse was as devoid of life as my will to fight her. Tomorrow, I turned seventeen. My father wanted me. I could leave. I was the adult, whether she wanted to believe it or not.

And I needed to go. Sooner than later. I glanced around my sanctuary and imagined a life without bars. Years ago, when my mother's illness began to metastasize throughout the house, I took over the larger bedroom with its adjoining bath. Even at thirteen, I had to protect myself. My bathroom was as spotless as my room and the inside of my Honda. But clean didn't mean I was free.

I filled the deep, jetted tub with hot water and bubbles and slipped into the foam, closing my eyes against my life while the jets soothed my aching muscles. Outside in the dining room, she slammed and banged, the crashes interspersed with bright curses. I fleetingly wondered if she cleaned up the salad or left it for the mice. My body trembled, icy cold in the hot water.

For the first time in my life, I didn't care what my mother did. I didn't care if she ate pizza for the ninth day in a row. I didn't care if the water heater stopped working tomorrow or the central air conked out.

I'm done, over. Do what you have to do. Get the hell out while I was still sane. But I'd leave Joshua. Our friendship-turned-relationship would be another victim of my mother's nest. Maybe what we had would survive the distance. He said he eventually planned to go south for his scholarship and to work year-round. Maybe one thing would go right in my life, and we'd land in the same place away from my mother. I crawled from the tub, shaking with stress and fatigue, my head pounding like a bass drum on parade, and I began to pack.

I owned one suitcase. Mom bought it at some yard sale when she used to go outside, back before television and internet shopping made leaving the house unnecessary. I pulled it from under my bed and began to fill it, taking all my warm-weather clothes, my hair dryer and straightener, and my shoes. When the suitcase was full, I used my stash of trash bags to collect my favorite winter clothes. I wouldn't need many in Florida, but the thought of my mother adding my precious things to her vile nest was more than I could bear. But I couldn't take everything. Not the box of family keepsakes in my closet. Not my grandmother's quilts and the heirlooms locked in my mother's bedroom closet beneath years of hoard.

I'd rather burn them than have my grandma's hard work abused.

The house quieted, and my mother settled into her nest for the night. I waited another hour to be sure she was asleep before I slipped my suitcase and bags out onto the deck. I visited with my plants—the potted geraniums, the petunias. They would suffer my absence the most.

She'd never water them. In days, they'd wither and die, just like me if I stayed another second.

At just after three o'clock, I crept out the back door and loaded my car silently, hiding my belongings under a blanket in the back. The only problem was Joshua. He promised to pick me up at my house.

What would he say when he found out I ran away from home?

ELEVEN

I DOZED in the Honda until the sun rose over the high school parking lot. Groaning, I checked my watch in the early dawn. 6:34 a.m. A whopping three hours of sleep since I left my house. Happy seventeenth birthday to me. I ran my tongue over my sticky teeth as my empty stomach burned.

Opening my backpack, I located my toothbrush, toothpaste, and a bottle of water. Nothing like brushing your teeth and spitting on the side of your old high school. Not my best moment, for sure. Briefly, I wondered if my mother figured out I was gone. All she had to do was check the driveway. But why would she look for me when she had everything she needed at her feet?

She'll blame Dad for me leaving her. Just like always. I should call my father and tell him I never got his messages, and I hadn't been hiding from him. I'd been a prisoner. Finally, after all the years of blaming him for leaving, I gained a different perspective. I understood. I got it, but I had to work up the courage to talk to him. For me, a thousand miles might not be far enough to escape the foul stench of my childhood. I might go farther to see everything the world offered. Maybe I should go to California. Hawaii. Europe. Anywhere but New Jersey.

After brushing my hair and twisting it into a messy bun on the back of my head, I felt semi-human. I scrubbed my hands over my eyes and nose. Time to find something to eat, which would give me access to a restroom where I could at least wash up.

A new pain wracked my stomach, this one higher up. Maybe I could swallow a banana. Maybe half. I drove out of the parking lot to the McDonald's in town. Inside, I ordered a vanilla ice cream, a small carton of French fries, and an unsweetened iced tea. I dipped the fries in the ice cream and managed to down half the food before I needed to vomit.

I barely made it to the bathroom before breakfast heaved itself against my tonsils. Dark vomit colored the toilet. What had I eaten? Nothing black. Leaning against the stall door, I wiped my sweaty face on some tissue and contemplated my next move. Joshua would meet me at the Paulie's parking lot in a little over an hour. I could leave my car in the restaurant's lot and spend the day with him before I hit the road for the Sunshine State. It was better to head there sooner because Monday was two days away, and I couldn't go home. It would take those two days to drive to my father's house. I hoped my old car could make it, but I'd rather not leave Bennie on the side of the road when I hopped on a plane. Besides, how would I get all my stuff to Florida?

I fired off a quick text and counted the minutes before I could meet him.

JOSHUA WAS PARKED in the lot when I pulled in. He gazed in the car windows at my suitcase and bags and his jaw clenched. I took a pair of sneakers and fresh socks from my suitcase and stuffed them into my backpack along with a bottle of antacids.

"Uh-oh. What's going on Shell?" he asked. "You don't look like you feel good."

"My stomach's bothering me." We stood facing each other; my secret was a dark blob of misery between us. "It's a long story. Can I tell you on the way?"

"Sure. Hop in." He opened the door for me, and I climbed into the seat. The freshly cleaned interior of his truck hinted of cinnamon. Maybe the fresh air would clean the smells out of my nose. A tremor of anticipation hurled through my stomach. An entire day with this boy.

I chucked off my flip-flops and pulled on my socks but left the sneakers on the floor.

He clicked on the radio. Ed Sheeran's "Perfect" came through the speakers. Today would be perfect, I was sure. When we were rolling, I half-turned in my seat to gauge his reaction. "I'm leaving my mother's house."

"Okay." He gave me a sideways glance as he maneuvered the truck onto the highway. "I figured as much by the way your car's packed. Where are you headed? Your dad's?"

I nodded. "My mom and I got in a terrible fight last

night. It's not the first time, but I can't take anymore." Pine forests replaced the stores and houses as we headed west. I breathed in the scent of trees and damp earth, easing my headache and the pain in my heart. It would be difficult to tell him, but somehow, I could trust him.

"What did you fight about? I mean, you don't have to tell me," he added quickly, tapping his hands on the steering wheel before reaching over to squeeze my left hand. "But you can if you want to. I fight with my aunt and uncle, too."

My mouth twisted up into a half-grin, and I took a deep breath. "This is going to sound worse than it is, so don't judge me before I tell you the whole thing."

"Okay."

"I told my mother I was going out with you today. She said she wanted to have you over for dinner. I said no."

He side-eyed me and changed the radio channel to avoid Katy Perry. "Okay. The raccoon eyes are an issue, but I can explain them."

I burst out laughing.

"So, not the raccoon eyes?" he asked with mock sincerity.

Shaking my head, I said sadly, "No."

We were quiet a moment as vintage One Republic sang in the background about the ghosts they couldn't hide from. Talk about waxing poetic.

Joshua shifted in his seat and leaned against his door. "You going to tell me, or should I keep guessing?"

Heaving a breath into my lungs, I expelled it with a whoosh. "No. I'd love for you to meet my mother for real and have dinner with us, but you can't. She can't. No one can come to my house. My mother has a problem. She's a hoarder."

He ran a hand through his hair, confusion on his face. "A hoarder? Like on television?"

I shrugged. "If you say so. I haven't seen our television in a couple of years."

Joshua shook his head as if he couldn't believe what I said. "Jeez, Shelly. I'm sorry. I didn't know. Looking at your house on the outside, I never suspected."

"Because I refuse to let it happen."

He snagged my fingers, sending shivers up my arm. "It's okay if I don't meet her for real. You don't have to leave the state because of me."

"It's so not because of you! Nobody knows what goes on in there except my dad and one kid I brought home from school when I was twelve. Well, after that, every-body knew because she told them. It's why I left school." I pressed a hand to my mouth. The new ache throbbed dead center in the pit of my stomach. "And now you know. It's why I have to leave, and why my dad left and moved to Florida."

"So, what? She keeps stuff?" He shrugged like it was no big deal. "Lots of people are rotten housekeepers."

I shook my head. "Ah, no. This isn't just housekeep-ing. She keeps everything." I shuddered, remembering the mouse. "All those pizzas I told you Paulie's has been delivering to my house . . ."

"Yeah?"

"So, she keeps them. She has about a dozen pizza boxes. She keeps old soda cans because she says some-day, she's gonna recycle them, which she can't because she won't leave the house, and she won't let me take them to the recycler. She has books, hundreds of books. And boxes and crap she buys—" I ran out of steam as I turned toward the window. I couldn't bear to look at him.

"Man, that's messed up."

"You don't know the half of it."

Joshua pulled off the highway and onto a narrow two-lane road. The shadowed dirt track wound through a canopy of trees. "What is she going to do if you leave?"

I lifted a shoulder and dropped it, my emotions raw. "This sounds heartless, but I don't give a crap what she does."

Several miles of silence stretched as we curved deeper into the woods. "I can't believe it. I love your house from the outside. I would've never guessed. Your room is so clean."

"I guess I'm very good at keeping secrets," I said, my voice and resolve weakening.

"But that's not right. Not safe, I guess. Isn't there someone you can call? The health department? The police?"

The practical solutions were always the easiest to consider. I shook my head. "There's a lot of bad stuff in the world. Drugs, abused kids, lost puppies. No one has time for one crazy lady in a house full of stuff."

He was quiet for a while as he drove. Then he asked, "What about a counselor? A shrink?"

"Been there. She refused to go." I inhaled and blew it out. "I can't save her, Joshua. She doesn't want to be saved."

"This just sucks. For you and your folks." Joshua reached over and stroked my hand again.

I laced my fingers through his. "So, you still want to do this?" I asked softly. "Knowing what I come from?"

He lifted my fingers to his lips and pressed a kiss to the back of my hand, causing my heartbeat to stutter. "You're not your parents. You're so not your mother."

I smiled at him, filled with gratitude.

"Besides, it's your birthday, and we have a date."

Joshua patted the center of the seat, and I unlatched my seat belt and slid over beside him. We held hands while he drove until he turned onto a dirt track cutting through the woods. "This is it. My dad and uncle used to bring my cousin and I here all the time when I was little. I haven't been up here in years."

The truck climbed over ruts and deep puddles. "Why did you stop? I wish my parents took me somewhere cool like this."

He parked the truck in a tiny, dirt lot. "After my dad died, I didn't feel like doing a lot of stuff anymore." He shrugged. "And I was hoping you'd like it. You better put those sneakers on now." The truck sat on the edge of a wide clearing filled with summer wildflowers. In the distance, a rocky hill dominated the background.

"It takes about two hours to get to the top. I brought lunch," he said, holding out his hand for me. He slung a backpack over his other shoulder as I lifted mine. I slipped my hand in his, and we set out across the field with our packs.

Joshua told me stories about his trips with his father. "One summer, when I was six, I stepped on a ground hornet nest. That sucked." I grimaced as he continued. "I got stung a couple of times, but my dad got it worse. He picked me up and ran. The hornets chased us for a half mile."

"Are you telling me there are hornets in this grass?" I glanced around anxiously, expecting to see a barrage of furious insects divebombing us.

"Sometimes." He drew me next to the warm length of his body. My skin tingled from head to toe. "Stay close. I'll protect you." His arm slid around my back like it belonged there.

We hiked for nearly an hour before the trail began to incline. "You need a breather?" he asked me. "Your face is bright red."

"Nope. Just need a bottle of water out of my pack." I shrugged out of my backpack and pulled out one of my three bottles of water. "My face always gets red. When I work outside and come back into the house, it looks like I'm going to burst into flames." We laughed at the image I painted while we sipped, our free hands intertwined. I dreaded the moment I'd have to let go.

He waited until I settled my pack over my shoulders. "Is your mother the reason your stomach gives you issues?"

I stopped and stared at him. "What did you say?"

"Look," he said, closing the distance between us. "I'm just worried. You don't look . . . well. You didn't eat much last night. I bet you didn't eat today."

I planted my hands on my hips. What did he know? "I went to McDonald's this morning."

Joshua bit his lip before asking, "Did you eat?"

He had no right to ask this of me. Ignoring my clenching stomach, I told him, "Some ice cream and French fries."

"Now there's a combination." His fingers trailed along my cheek. "A little ice cream in two days. Shell, you're gonna get sick. Maybe you should go see a doctor."

"I'm fine. I'll eat lunch." Eating in front of him terrified me.

"I hope so." His eyes found mine, and I withered under his concern, the joy of my day darkening by degrees.

I slipped back out of his reach, and the walls I created to protect myself from the world slammed into the ground at my feet. "I said I'm fine."

He stuck his tongue out at me and crossed his eyes, fracturing my fence ever so slightly. "Fine."

"Fine!" I returned the gesture but couldn't hide my smile.

TWELVE

AN HOUR LATER, we reached the summit. Joshua drew a red-and-tan plaid blanket from his pack, and we spread it on a rocky outcropping guaranteed to be hornet-free. I leaned back on my elbows and admired the view as the sun warmed my shoulders. Mountains texturized the horizon in browns and greens, and thin clouds scattered across the sky. In the distance a thunderhead spiraled up into the heavens.

He plopped down beside me and smiled, sweeping his hand across the vistas before us. "See? I told you it was worth it."

I breathed in the warm, fresh air. No residue of old food. No rotting garbage. Just air. I could live here, on this hill, for the rest of my life. I wouldn't need a thing.

"Definitely," I agreed, relieved the subject of my mother and my poor eating habits dropped.

He spread out the lunch he packed for us, and I suspected he chose our meal with me in mind. My heart warmed at the attention he'd taken. Cut-up watermelon and cantaloupe, a bag of pretzels, a container of cold, cooked chicken, cubes of cheddar, strawberries, and grapes. For him, he packed two monster sandwiches and a couple of Snickers bars.

Gratitude made it difficult to speak, but I managed a thank you.

"I thought this might settle your stomach." He ran a hand over my back and tugged on my ponytail while I nibbled on pretzels.

"You're the best," I told him. "Why didn't you show up sooner?"

"I wanted to keep you in suspense as long as I could." He rocked forward on his hip until he filled my field of view. "You want to know what else I want?" His voice dropped with a sultry edge. My heart stuttered.

"What?" I whispered, the question a mere breath in my throat. I swallowed hard in the thickening air.

"I want to kiss you. Can I?"

Every cell in my body screamed yes, but I kept my wits about me long enough to fashion a nonchalant answer. Tugging my lip through my teeth, I leaned into him, inhaling the scent of his sweat and his spicy cinnamon gum. "I don't know. Can you?"

Joshua's mouth turned up in a heart-stopping smile, and he removed his sunglasses. "Ooh. I love challenges," he said. His lips settled against mine, tentative then sure. With a sigh, my lips parted, and my blood sizzled in my veins. He deepened the kiss, his tongue grazing my teeth, and I lost myself against his sun-warmed shirt as he pulled me closer. A perfect, indescribable kiss.

I drew back from him, and he snagged a lock of my

hair between his fingers. "We're in this incredible place, and all I can see is you." His other hand grazed the exposed skin of my back where my tank top tugged free. My body reacted, angling toward him.

I wanted this. I wanted him. But I needed him to see what leaving my mother meant; I was leaving him too. "I have something to tell you." His lips found the incredibly sensitive edge of my chin, making me shiver. Who knew this group of nerve endings lived on the cusp of my face, just waiting for Joshua to make them come alive?

"Sure," he said, his brows drawing down.

Putting a bit of distance between us to clear my head, I began. "My mom blew up when I told her I was going to my dad's house. She confessed he's been trying to call me all this time, but she never told me. I'm driving to Florida, not flying," I said.

"Okay. Not a fan of you driving by yourself."

"Me neither. Joshua, I'm not sure if I'm coming back."

He said nothing as he lifted his hand and cupped the side of my cheek in his palm. I leaned into the gesture, closing my eyes while my heart tore in my chest, shredding the fragile hold on my wild mood swings. How could I reconcile this feeling of needing to escape but never wanting to leave? How could I explain how much I wanted him in my life?

His gaze circled my face, from eyes to lips and back again. "You should go, Shelly. You need to get away from your mom for a while."

"But you—" He stopped me midsentence with a finger against my lips.

"I'm not going anywhere. I've got too many lawns to cut," he added wryly.

It was my turn to kiss him. Too soon, I pulled back to catch my breath. "I just found you. Now, I have to go."

"You leaving your mom's issues changes nothing about the way we are together or what this is. You can call me. Get done what you need done." He captured my cheeks between the palms of his hands, his eyes locked on mine. "We'll figure out a way to keep this rolling. Okay?"

I nodded, my eyes tearing. "I will."

We leaned back on the blanket, and he nestled me against his chest. I rested my head on his bent elbow as a wash of security and contentment filtered through me. Where had this been my entire life? Did other kids get this feeling of love from their parents? Did everyone have to wait for someone to come along and fill the void?

An eagle soared on an updraft, wings spread, gliding through the sky. "Joshua?"

"Yeah?" His voice was dreamy and soft behind my head.

I closed my eyes, sealing this moment into the movie screens of my mind. "I need you to promise me you'll keep my secret. I'm not going back to my mother's house, but the world doesn't need to learn what she does."

He lifted up on his elbow to gaze down at me. "There's no way to help her?"

"Please don't tell anyone," I begged him.

"I won't. I swear. I just feel bad for you going through this."

I shook my head, the weight of what I carried threatening to crush me in its fist. "You can't save someone who doesn't want to be saved."

He drew an X over his chest with his hand. "I'll never tell."

"Promise?"

"Promise." He touched my hair, tangling his fingers in a strand. "You have the most incredible hair. The curls just appear."

My thoughts fractured beneath his hands, but I gathered the pieces of myself back long enough to say, "Thank you for helping me escape."

He licked his lips, and I wanted to kiss him again. Every kiss was precious and one closer to our last. "You think your car's gonna make it?"

"I hope so." Bennie would never forgive me for driving him across the country.

"You should fly. I'd feel better about you making the trip. Leave your other stuff here for now. When are you going?"

I sighed, my heart tumbling from the edge of the cliff. I didn't relish the fact I faced a long, solitary drive. "Early tomorrow morning. But my plane ticket is for Monday."

"What about tonight? Where are you gonna stay?" His gaze was serious, but I couldn't tell what he was thinking.

"I'm going to get a hotel room." Being alone on the interstate frightened me, but I wasn't about to admit it. "I have the plane ticket, but if I fly, I need to leave my car somewhere."

"Okay. That's easy. You can leave it at my house. I'll drive you to the airport." He paused. "If you want me to."

Joshua keeping Bennie solved all kinds of problems.

It also guaranteed I'd have to see him again. "Are you sure?" Imagining walking away from him at the airport drove the strawberries to the back of my throat.

His gentle fingers smoothed the breeze-tangled hair out of my eyes. "Yeah. I can't let you go without saying goodbye."

My throat closed. I swallowed a dozen times before I whispered, "It's not goodbye. It can't be." Even to me, the promise sounded hollow. But I wanted to believe this closeness between us would survive, even if I never returned home.

"It won't be," he told me. "Besides, I still have to check out those schools down south." He tapped me on the nose. "Who knows? Maybe I'm destined to cut grass in Florida."

My heart bounded back over the edge of the precipice and slammed into my chest, pumping its fist in the air.

"Is this a promise?" I gripped the front of his shirt like he was a lifeline. In so many ways, that's what Joshua was, even just days into our relationship.

He kissed the corner of my mouth. "Absolutely."

JOSHUA DROPPED me back at my car outside the restaurant, and we lingered, leaning against the side of the car, his arms entwined around my waist. I gathered the moment in my mind, imprinting the softness of his shirt and the warmth of his body within my memories.

I hugged him fiercely. "I'm working tonight at the Quick-Serve. My last shift there. Maybe you should come in. I could give you a discount on a six-pack of Monster."

He pushed off the car to stand in front of me. "Oh, yeah? What if I'm out of cash?" Shivers broke out on my skin as his lips grazed below my ear. "Would you accept another form of payment?"

"We could work out an arrangement," I giggled.

"Good," he said. "What time do you quit?"

"Ten."

Joshua swept a hand down my arm from shoulder to wrist. All this touching might drive me crazy.

"How about I make sure you get to your hotel okay." A flutter buzzed in my stomach that had nothing to do with feeling nauseous and everything to do with the way he touched me. I loved the way he looked at me. Like I was perfect and the only person in the world who mattered to him. Like my mother's hoard didn't taint me. How long had it been since someone cared about me?

"Thank you," I murmured into his lips, inhaling the spicy, warm scent that was Joshua. I drew away from his kiss, breathless. "I have to go."

"I know. I'll see you at ten." With a final brush of a kiss, he jumped into his truck and roared out of the parking lot. A group of customers gaped as I settled into my overheated Honda, my fingers pressed to my lips.

I CHECKED into a Holiday Inn Express near the airport, showered, and changed for work. Joshua texted me a dozen times, checking up on me.

My mother sent one, all caps.

WHERE ARE YOU?

I deleted it.

At five, I was behind the counter at the Quick-Serve, relishing the monotonous sameness of checking out customers, directing harried mothers with small children toward the bathrooms, and making sure the coffee carafes were always full—in between an emoji war with Joshua. About six-thirty, the bells on the door jingled, and he strode in, a fresh glow to his deepening tan, his aviators securely on his nose. This guy took my breath away.

"Hey, beautiful." I loved how he called me beautiful before he checked if we were alone, like he didn't care who heard him. My body warmed from head to toe. "Are those hot dogs any good?" He made a goofy face at me through the glass in the hot dog roller.

Blushing, I said. "They're crappy but hot."

"Just the way I like them. I'll take two." He went to the cooler and came back with a Monster while I wrapped up his dogs. "So about paying for this," he said, his voice heavy with meaning.

"We can work something out," I teased, both thankful and resentful for the wide counter separating us. I wanted his arms back around me like I needed to breathe.

"How about I pay for this now, and we can discuss it when you get off work?" He wiggled his eyebrows, and my heart tripped over itself.

"Five fifty-six," I told him, ignoring the innuendo, but loving it at the same time.

He pulled out his wallet and handed over the cash, brushing my fingers with his. "Is it ten o'clock yet?"

A pool of need burned low in my stomach, edging out the regular dull ache. I missed out on this part of my life. What else had my mother taken from me by keeping me prisoner in her wretched nest? The desire smoldered next to resentment, but the way Joshua gazed at me slowly evaporated the bitterness. Ten o'clock seemed like a hundred years away.

The doorbells chimed, breaking the thread drawing us together. With a wry grin, Joshua picked up his meal. "Later."

THIRTEEN

I FOUND him sitting on the hood of the Honda when my shift ended. I left a note for my boss informing him I would be out of town for at least the next couple of weeks, keeping my options open even though I hoped this trip to my father's house would lead to something more permanent and more stable, far away from the stench of my childhood.

The other, guilty part of me wondered what my mother was doing without me to get the pizza from the porch. How was she surviving? Was she eating? What about groceries? How would she get the things she needed without me to forage for necessities out in the real world?

There are delivery services for everything. Food, pharmacy, you name it. She knew how to work Amazon. She'd figure it out. At least the bills would keep getting paid. I kept the passwords from my mother for the bank and utilities. She wouldn't be able to divert funds to her pursuit of more feathers for her nest.

"Hey, there," he drawled as I walked over to the car, keys in hand.

"Hi." I opened the car door and deposited my bag on the passenger seat, intensely aware of his presence. Every nerve and cell buzzed with life, and my body tugged me toward him as if he were magnetized to the perfect frequency.

I drifted away from the door, and he pulled me against him and between his legs.

"How're you doing?" Without waiting for a reply, his lips sought mine, and he kissed me until my head spun in circles. Finally, I edged back enough to breathe. "You look tired."

"I am. It was a *long* day." His hands brushed over my back, chasing my chills with his heat. I slid my arms around his waist and held on.

"You eat dinner? We could grab something."

My empty stomach churned. Joshua's impromptu fruit salad from our hike sped through my system hours ago, but at least I held it down. I shoved the feeling aside, ignoring the hunger pains because I could. A couple of antacids would make it all better.

"I'm good."

He set his hands on my shoulders. "You're sure?"

"Yes!" I exploded, shoving back away from him. "Lay off the food, okay?"

Joshua held up his hands. "Hey, I'm sorry."

"My stomach hurts. I'll eat when I'm hungry."

"Okay, okay. I get it. Sorry." He pushed away from the hood of the Honda and folded his arms over his chest. He changed out of the work clothes he'd worn earlier. His hair was damp from a recent shower, and he smelled of soap and aftershave. I, on the other hand, felt like a rag doll that had been kicked to the curb.

I shrugged out of my work smock, rolled it in a ball, and jammed it into my bag.

"I said I'm sorry," he said, his eyes flashing with annoyance.

Sighing, I puffed my cheeks and blew out a breath. "I don't mean to take this out on you. You didn't do anything. Let's just go get something to eat." Suddenly, my appetite roared to life like a forgotten dragon released from a dark dungeon. "I want a cheeseburger."

His eyes lit up. "Really? You want to follow me?"

"Yeah."

He kissed me then hopped in his truck. I followed him onto the highway. Ten minutes later, we pulled into an old drive-up restaurant with a neon ice cream cone out front but no caboose. Kids ran from one side of the eating area to the other, most of them wearing Little League shirts covered in melted chocolate.

I climbed out of the car, instantly swamped by the crispy scent of deep-frying and grilling. At least it wasn't pizza.

"Great place. I'm sensing a theme to your favorite dining spots," I told him as his arm slid around my shoulders. I didn't want him to worry about me when I left. I had to do this for him. I would eat even if my stomach burned.

Joshua eyed the menu. "I knew you'd like it. Best burgers in the area. What do you like on yours?"

"The works," I told him. "Fries, too."

"You bet."

We sat at an empty picnic table while our food cooked, and the Little Leaguers cleared out. By the time the burgers were delivered to our table, only a couple of parents and kids remained. Joshua sighed as he lifted his burger, surveying where to begin.

"You won't be disappointed," he said.

I bit into the juicy burger, moaning in delight. "Oh, that's good." It was. Except I didn't eat food like this. Ever. But I had to play along.

Joshua laughed as I licked ketchup from the side of my hand. "It's good to see you relaxing."

"This is why I need to go to my dad's for a while," I said. As the words left my lips, disappointment dug a narrow channel in my heart with a dull, serrated knife. The clock was ticking on my departure.

He seemed to notice my change in mood and said, "It's not forever; I'll still be here."

I wasn't so sure. Not about him, not about returning. "What if I can't come back? I can't continue to live with my mother or even be near her."

Joshua said nothing for a long time. "Then don't. I'll come to you."

My eyes lifted to his, my heart thudding out a rhythm of hope. "We've only known each other for, like, two weeks."

"Thirteen days," he corrected. "But I stared at you for two months in science class. That counts for something, right? You trusted me with your deepest, darkest secrets. You're brave, honest, and beautiful. I've never met anyone like you. What more could I ask for?"

Tears rolled down my cheeks. He handed me a pile of napkins, and I blew my nose.

"This conversation is way too deep for a restaurant with a giant ice cream cone out front," I said, pushing aside my meal. Under my T-shirt, my stomach rumbled and pitched, complaining about the rare quantity of food I forced it to handle. "I'm going to go wash my face. I'll be right back."

He reached over and squeezed my hand as I walked by.

In the bathroom, I leaned on the cool porcelain sink. I'd overeaten. My stomach flopped and heaved. The familiar itch gathered in my throat, and I stepped into a stall and closed the door. Moments later, the meal left me as quickly as I'd eaten it. When I spit into the toilet, the water turned bloody. I must have scratched my throat.

Leaning on the stall wall, my skin clammy, I couldn't linger even if weakness invaded my limbs. I didn't want Joshua to come looking for me like this.

I dug in the pocket of my jeans for a pack of gum and popped two sticks in my mouth before heading back out into the restaurant.

Joshua glanced up. "You okay? You look pale."

"I just finished my cry." I gave him a weak smile. I hated lying to him, but the truth was too much to handle. Besides, the blood freaked me out.

The table had been cleared while I was in the bathroom. "You ready?"

I picked up my bag and said, "Yes."

He paid the bill, and we walked out into the muggy July night. "I bet it's hot down in Orlando."

"I'm sure it is. July in Florida? Isn't that on the equator or something?"

Joshua laughed before asking, "Did you call your dad and tell him you were coming?" When I shook my head, he removed his phone from his pocket. "Here. You want to use mine?"

"No, I've got it. But you're right. I guess I better make sure someone's there to pick me up."

Joshua stared at the phone in his hand. "Shelly, I could go with you, if you want. Make sure you get there okay."

My fingers found his and laced through them. I let him become part of my life. Joshua meant everything. He represented what I imagined about my future: the hopes, dreams, and possibilities.

"Thanks for offering, but Dad and I haven't spoken in a long time. There are things I need to work out with him. Hard things."

He nodded once.

"Besides, you've got the bank jobs to finish." I tugged on his hand, suddenly wanting more than just the use of his phone. "Let's call from the hotel, okay?" Warmth gelled in my stomach.

Surprise deepened the crease between his eyes for a second before he recovered. "Where are you staying?"

I told him.

"I'll meet you there," he said.

WE HELD hands as we walked into the Holiday Inn, just two guests turning in for the night. I fished my key out of my bag, and we rode up the elevator to the third floor. Joshua didn't say anything as I led him down the corridor to my room. The key clicked in the door in time to the hitch in my breathing. In the room, the air was icy. I left the air conditioning on too high. A habit of cranking it at home, I guessed. Cold air kept the odors at bay.

"Wow, frosty in here," he said.

When the door was secured, I turned to confront him with my back against the solid plank. "I bet I could figure out a way to get warm," I said. Something turned in my belly, not the unpleasant gurgle I normally experienced. This was deeper. Darker. More primal.

As if he sensed it, he advanced on me, claiming my lips in a kiss. My arms wound around his neck. He lifted me off the floor, and my legs clamped around his waist.

Teeth and tongues clashed. My head fell back, and his lips trailed fire across my throat. This. This is what I imagined Joshua to be. Desire roared through my body until I lost the ability to think, only feel.

Hands swept over my ribcage, setting my skin on fire.

I gasped against his mouth. The noise seemed to wake him from the daze we succumbed to, long enough to draw away despite my soft cry of protest. He lowered me down, and my legs released their grip so I could step on the floor.

"Come here," he said, tugging me toward the bed. He stretched out our joined hands until only our fingertips were touching.

I followed.

Joshua sat on the bed, watching me. I stood in front of him for several seconds, my stomach twisting on a different kind of upset. His thumb traced lazy circles on my hand.

"What do you want?" he asked me.

"You," I told him. No hesitation.

I fell on top of him, tangling in the blanket as my T-shirt found its way to the floor. His hands burned over my skin, my back, my waist, to the clasp of my bra. He chased his hands with his lips until I writhed with him.

How had I let myself miss this part of my life? The feeling of being totally and completely alive, on fire for another person.

His fingers found the sensitive spot beneath my navel, and a moan tore from my lips. God, what he did to me! My skin turned to flames, torching me from the inside out. Joshua pulled back suddenly to gaze at me, his eyes dark with his own desire. For me. He wanted me.

"If I don't stop now, I won't," he warned.

I bent forward and captured his mouth with mine in a furious kiss. Oxygen tore from my lungs. He rolled me beneath him, my skin on his in an electrical storm of sensations I never imagined I'd feel.

Joshua's weight pressed down on me. But I had no air. I couldn't breathe. My thin, weak body wasn't strong enough to resist his.

Our teeth clashed, but I paid no attention. Spots dotted my vision, and I pushed against his chest. "Joshua," I gasped around his lips.

"Hmm?" he hummed against the side of my neck, his body pressing down on me, preventing my inhale.

I drifted, part with him, part somewhere else, my body desperate for his touch, my lungs screaming for air. My hands slipped from his back and fell on the mattress. My lips airlessly formed his name. "Joshua."

It was a second, maybe two, before he realized I was in trouble. He rolled to the side and air, glorious air, found my throat. I greedily sucked it in, coughed and gagged, my empty stomach heaving.

"Shelly! What's wrong?" He helped me to sit.

My head fell forward between my knees as the spots faded away. "It's okay. I just need a minute." I breathed, opening my lungs to blissful oxygen as embarrassment flooded my face with heat. My first time with a guy, and I nearly passed out.

"Tell me what's wrong," he said, gently stroking my back.

I shivered, the fire in my skin extinguished. "I couldn't breathe. I'm okay now. Just cold."

Joshua found my T-shirt on the floor and held it open so I could drag it over my icy skin. I slipped beneath the covers and curled into a ball.

"I'm sorry," I told him, tears streaming onto the pillow.

He slipped an arm around me, careful to leave space between our bodies. "I didn't mean to hurt you," he said.

I turned to stare at him. "You didn't. I'm fine."

Brushing a finger over my lips, he said, "I feel like you're fragile. You're so little, tiny. I might break you."

"You won't break me," I told him, pulling him down for a softer, sweeter kiss.

We parted, and he tucked his arm over my waist,

holding me close as I grew warm against his chest. The shivering faded as the slow burn returned. Tonight wasn't the night. I wanted to be with him, more than anything, but I was leaving. And finishing what we started wouldn't be fair to either of us.

He reached over to the nightstand and picked up my cell phone. "What's your father's number?"

I chewed my bottom lip. His question cooled the flames burning underneath my skin. I wiggled out of his arm and went to my backpack, removing the journal where I kept important notes. I handed him the page with my father's information. He dialed the number and handed me the phone.

It rang several times. My father's distant but familiar baritone rumbled on the line. When was the last time I heard his voice? How many times had he called, and my mother intercepted?

"Hello?"

In one breath, I said, "Dad? It's Shelly. I'm coming."

Joshua guided me into his arms as I began to cry.

"I hoped you would." My father's voice thickened with emotion. He probably believed I wouldn't come. "Shelly, I'm so sorry. About all of this. I tried to talk to you, but your mom . . ."

"I know, Dad," I managed.

"I'll be at the airport, waiting on you." He paused. "Is there anything you need?"

I stared at Joshua. "No, Dad. I'll see you Monday. Thanks for the ticket."

"Happy birthday, sweetheart."

A moment later, I ended the call and held out the

phone. Without a word, Joshua kicked off his shoes and pulled me against him, cuddling me in the safe haven of his arms.

"Thank you," I told him, closing my eyes. I breathed in his scent and wrapped my fingers around his hands. This time when I drifted, I didn't fight it.

"You're going to be okay," he whispered into my hair.

"Promise?"

"Yeah. Promise," he said.

FOURTEEN

"CALL ME WHEN YOU LAND." He kissed the back of my hand as we stood in the bustling terminal of the Newark Airport on Monday morning. Around us, people from all over the world came and went, dragging suitcases and crying children. I'd never been outside of my hometown or even seen a city. Conversations in languages I couldn't decipher echoed around the terminal. I couldn't believe it. I was leaving.

"I will," I told him as I collapsed into him and held on. Tears streamed down my face. I dragged my sleeve across the moisture.

Joshua leaned down to kiss me. "Hey. You're gonna be fine. You need this, Shell."

We stood outside the security checkpoint, and I eyed the slow-moving lines uncertainly. I'd never been on a plane before. People in the rows across from me removed their shoes and took out their laptops, depositing them in gray plastic bins. I had to figure this security thing out if I planned to make it to the Sunshine State.

"Your flight's boarding in forty-five minutes," Joshua said as he read the overhead screens.

A sudden terror for my mother's well-being gripped me. "How can I leave her? How will she live?" I said.

"You need to worry about you. I'll drive by the house and check on it for you, okay?" He lifted my chin a fraction. "Go. Spend time with your dad." Joshua hugged me until I thought my bones would shatter. "Getting through security is a piece of cake. You have your boarding pass?"

"Yes."

"Hand it to the guy at the podium with your driver's license. Shoes in the bin. Bag on the counter. Easy."

"You've flown before?" I asked him, wondering about all the things we didn't discuss.

"A couple of times commercial, mostly with my parents. I went to Europe once when I was younger. Italy." He glanced at the time on his phone. "You better get going. You'll miss your plane."

"Thank you for staying with me again last night," I told him, meaning those words with every bruised and bloodied shred of my heart. He stayed all night Saturday, his arms around me. Sunday, he'd gone home only long enough to grab a change of clothes. Yesterday, we walked for hours at the state park. I'd never felt so safe, so happy, and now, I was leaving him.

He tucked a wayward chunk of hair behind my ear. "Feel better. Let your dad get you through this."

"You could help me, too," I said. He could. He had.

"Call me when you land," he said again. He kissed me hard and fast before giving me a playful shove in the direction of the waiting TSA line. "I'll keep an eye on your car for you."

"I miss you already." I threw a teary glance over my shoulder before bolting for the line. A smile spread over his face. He stood there until I couldn't find him anymore in the mass of people waiting to get through the checkpoint.

On the other side, I bought a bottle of water and tried not to think about leaving him as I chewed a handful of antacid tablets. I'd see him again. It was a promise I intended to keep.

AS SOON AS WE BOARDED, I stuck my earbuds in my ears and closed my eyes against the first-time-flier nerves. I didn't want to talk to anyone and wasn't interested in the in-flight beverage service or what the ridiculously tanned and weathered retiree next to me wanted to chat about. Thankfully, Dad booked me the window seat, and my heart filled with gratitude as I hid my face against the window and cried myself dry.

I caught how much my dad missed me in his voice. He hadn't forgotten me in the years we'd been separated. He sent me a lifeline just when I was about to go under. The plane roared to life beneath me, and I stared in wonder at the receding earth below. Clouds took over the view as I dabbed at my tears until I fell asleep and didn't dream.

I woke with a jolt as the plane touched down and gazed out at the unfamiliar palm trees flashing past the window. Thin, wispy clouds threaded through a brilliantly blue sky as planes lined up for approach like weightless sentries at the far end of the runway we just traversed.

When I turned on my phone, it vibrated like mad, and I flipped through the texts.

Joshua wrote me one text:

Flowers for Shelly.

Then there were pictures. Flowers from my garden. A single upturned bloom from the magnolia. A closeup of the begonias beginning to bloom. The roses at the side of my deck, framed with Shasta daisies. Tall, spiky foxglove hiding in the shade on the side of the house.

He'd gone to my house and taken pictures of the things I loved best about it. My heart swelled with love for his beautiful gift.

What could I say, after this? Thank you would never be enough. I sent him a line of red hearts in reply.

The plane began to empty. I gathered my backpack and carry-on. Other than my car sitting in Joshua's driveway, the bag was the sum of all my personal belongings from the past seventeen years of my life.

One bag. A backpack.

Deep down, I took pride in my minimalism. My mother well made up for it.

Muggy, thick air hit me as I stepped onto the jetway. Parents huddled waiting for strollers and car seats at the exit. An elderly couple tried to navigate a wheelchair. I scrambled ahead, desperate to be free from the clutter of bodies crowding me. My head spun in all directions, furiously searching for a way past the confining tube until a hand reached out and descended on my shoulder.

"Miss? Are you missing something?"

"How do I get out of here?' I asked a man in an airline polo shirt.

The man smirked like I wasn't the first panicked passenger he rescued today. "Straight ahead. Up the ramp."

Heaving my single-handled, yard sale suitcase, I hated the people around me who sported bags with tiny swivel wheels skimming over the floor. I bumped into a woman walking with her phone pressed to her ear. She shot me an evil look as we cleared the jetway and stepped out into the expansive terminal. Dozens of people walked briskly away from the gate, and I instinctively hurried past the parents and crying kids leaving the state with their Disney goodies.

I followed the signs for the terminal exit, passing through the checkpoint and boarding the escalator down to the first floor, proud of my growing independence. Straining over the heads of the people in front of me, I scanned the waiting crowds for my father.

No easy task.

The last time I saw my father, I'd been twelve with a face full of acne and a bad haircut my mother gave me. Since then, I shed my babyface, grew my hair, and thinned my body. I looked quite different.

Still, I felt a pang when he stared past me not once but twice.

Had we grown so distant in only a few years?

When I tapped him on the shoulder near baggage claim, the shock on his face nearly drove me to tears.

"Shelly?" He scooped me into his arms, and I clung to him for longer than I should have.

"Hi, Dad," I said when he finally released me.

"Happy birthday, sweetheart." He reached for my ancient suitcase. "This all you've got, kiddo?"

I nodded, warmed by the familiar endearment he always used on me. "Yep. And my backpack."

He draped an arm over my shoulders. "God, you've gotten tall. All grown up." A strong hug squeezed my shoulder. "C'mon. Let's get out of here."

I let him guide me through the throngs of passengers and families and out into the parking lot. The summer sun in Florida was like nothing I'd ever experienced—like stepping into a blast furnace. Heat leaped off the pavement in tarry waves, and I instantly wilted. Gone was the humid, chilly dampness of New Jersey. The tropical ovens of the Sunshine State burned away all memory of cool.

Dad smiled at my reaction to the temperature. "Different from home, huh?"

I wiped the sweat from my nose. "About a hundred degrees different," I said. Hot or not, I couldn't hold back my smile. I was here, away from my mother, away from the disaster of our lives. My thoughts darkened as worry for her invaded my happiness. I straightened my shoulders, determined to not let her ruin this moment for me.

My phone vibrated with a text. All I could think about was Joshua and how much I wished he were here.

Dad led me across the street. "My car's over here." He led me to a sporty white BMW.

The luxury car slapped me. I always knew he traveled for work; he had an important job at a pharmaceutical company. But I never considered what his position meant in dollars and cents. He always sent Mom the hefty child support check like clockwork. Now I understood his wealth in tangible terms.

When I turned eighteen, those checks to her would stop. Mom would never be able to afford the mortgage without it. But my father wouldn't suffer. What would he do with his windfall when the payments stopped? Buy a membership to a golf club? Take a cruise? His options remained open while my mother's constricted beneath the weight of the house.

Seeing him standing beside his expensive car, I comprehended we scraped by while my father had a life. A real life after he ran away.

"Nice car," I said, my heart brimming with emotions too volatile to vocalize.

"Thanks. You need a white car down here. Gets hotter than this." He clicked the fob to open the trunk and dropped my suitcase inside.

I slid into the stifling interior as he adjusted the air conditioning and found his sunglasses. Joshua sent me a text, adding a pink heart. I smiled.

"Friend?" Dad asked.

I nodded. "Yes. A good friend."

In no time, we were out of the airport, cruising down a palm-lined street. White sidewalks bordered a huge lake. The surface glimmered under the harsh afternoon sun. Dripping joggers breezed past fishermen beneath a crystal sky filled with towering white clouds. I breathed in and hugged my breath inside my chest, stunned by the unreality of it all. Just two days ago, I'd been living in the despair of my mother's house, holding back the hoard outside my door by mere inches. The beauty of this place threatened the fragile hold I maintained on my emotions, and I swallowed back the tears.

"You okay, Shell?" my father asked.

I nodded, but my voice shook. "I will be."

"I live in Lake Mary. It's not far."

"How far is it to Valencia College from here?" I asked.

"Um, not sure. It's around here somewhere." He paused. "How come?"

I shook my head. "Nothing. It's a college I might be interested in," I lied.

"That's great. We can check it out if you want." Dad ran his hands over the steering wheel. "Mindy will be at the house. I've wanted you to meet her for a while."

My mother hadn't used the kindest terms when discussing my father's new wife, but why should she? Was Mindy the reason my father left? Did he see in this woman what I saw in his plane ticket—a way out? Guilt flexed its grip around my chest, and I dragged my lip into my teeth.

I have to do this. I have to save myself.

"Sounds great," I told him, manually brightening my smile. If I planned to live here for any length of time, I'd better play nice until I understood the rules of engagement.

I dug my phone out of the side pocket of my backpack. Joshua texted again.

I MISS YOU.

All caps. He must seriously miss me.

"Wow. That old phone looks familiar. Was it mine?" he asked.

"Yeah. I found it in a drawer and activated it. I needed something."

"We'll look into getting you a new one. I'll put you on my plan."

I nodded and let the subject drop so I could text Joshua back.

ME TOO.

Dad pointed out landmarks as he drove. Banks and museums, stores and a high school. The car turned through an open gate and down a street lined with sprawling houses. Huge screen enclosures hugged the exteriors. Different types and sizes of palm trees clustered on the perfect lawns—flowering bushes and plants unlike anything I'd ever seen. I counted a dozen or more beautiful homes until he turned the car into a wide concrete driveway in front of a sand-colored house with tasteful awnings the color of Caribbean waters. A skylight sparkled in the early afternoon sun, and a smaller Mercedes SUV sat in the driveway.

"This is it," he said with a tentative smile. "I hope you're happy here, Shelly. I want you to be happy."

"Thanks, Dad."

I followed him through the garage, marveling at the order and organization on display as if it were part of the decor. Tools hung neatly on pegboards and shovels and rakes dangled from hooks on the wall. The floor was swept clean beneath my feet, and bins were clearly marked with seasonal decorations.

Dad pressed a button beside the door, which dropped a screen over the front of the garage entrance. "Right through here. You can drop your shoes inside the door." He opened a door to the main house.

I stopped just inside the threshold, speechless. Inside, the structure was a marvel of open, soaring spaces. Overhead, the ceiling dipped and vaulted following the lines of the roof. More skylights, which had been invisible from the front of the house, opened to the azure sky. The floors were wide sand-colored tile, and the expansive kitchen and dining area were pristine. Nothing sat on the table besides a napkin holder and salt and pepper shakers. The kitchen was uncluttered, and the granite countertops shone. A wide island sat in the middle of the roomy space, and the stainless-steel appliances gleamed in the afternoon sunshine.

"What do you think?" he asked, sliding out of his sandals and tucking his sunglasses into the collar of his polo shirt. I noticed my father's apprehension. He wanted me to accept this; he lived here for years while I lived with Mom and her illness.

"It's beautiful," I told him, which was the truth. "It's clean," I said, which was also the more glaring truth. "Not like home."

He swallowed, staring at me with remorseful eyes. "I'm so sorry, Shelly," he said.

I could say nothing over the tightening in my throat,

so I dipped my chin to acknowledge his late apology. He was so wrong. No one could be sorrier than me.

No one.

He picked up my suitcase as I removed my shoes. "Let me give you a tour and show you your room so you can get settled."

Dad led the way through the house, down a tiled hallway littered with cushy throw rugs and past several more rooms. "This is our room," he told me, opening a door to a huge bedroom with a four-poster bed atop carpeting the color of seagrass.

I stepped inside, unable to conceal my emotions as tears filled my eyes. A ceiling fan slowly rotated overhead, and two skylights hung over the bed to allow whoever slept there a clear view of the sky. The walls had been painted a soothing shade of mint beneath a brilliantly white ceiling. In the corner of the room, a glass block wall hid the huge bathroom. Not a toothbrush was out of place. Fresh flowers sat in the middle of the double bowl sink. I felt like I'd been transported to a magazine photoshoot.

"Do you like it?" he asked, his voice gruff.

"It's very pretty," I told him. My heart hurt looking at it. I imagined my mother's house without all the stuff—the clean kitchen and shiny new fridge. The house could be pretty, too, if we cleared it out. Our yellow house would never be as grand as this, but it could be a home. The house could be happy. Maybe I could be, too.

He pulled the door partially closed as we stepped into the hallway. "Your room is down here."

At the far end of the house, we traveled down a

spacious, thick-carpeted hallway empty of books and clutter. Framed pictures of tropical sunsets hung on the walls. Dad stopped outside a door and opened it. I bit my lip and stepped inside.

Soft coral walls stood above carpeting the color of pristine beaches. The full bed sat high and wide in the center of the room beneath an angled ceiling and the single skylight I noticed from outside. The bedspread was printed with palm leaves in muted shades of green and tan. A dresser and mirror lined one wall, and double doors hid what I suspected was a massive closet. My bare toes sank into the carpet.

"I hope you like it." My father's voice held a hopeful edge.

Swallowing my tears, I ran my fingers over the comforter, relishing the colors of sun, sand, and sky. "It's beautiful, Dad. Thanks." My gaze lifted upward, and I imagined watching the sun fade and brighten through my skylight.

My skylight. This was mine.

His shoulders lifted as he breathed in, and his voice betrayed his relief. "Let me know if you need anything. I can get you to a store. Your bathroom is across the hall. Mindy bought you some stuff she thought you might need."

I stepped across the hall and flicked on the light. The bathroom gleamed like the rest of the house. A cluster of unlit candles and potpourri sat on the counter, adding spicy scents to the air. The bathroom was nearly as big as my bedroom back home, and I felt a swell of emotion building in my empty stomach as I checked the variety of products Mindy provided. Shampoos and body washes, toothpaste, hair dryer.

The clothes I brought with me—T-shirts, shorts, and faded jeans—there was nothing in my suitcase remotely classy enough to wear in this house. But the extra money I earned helping Joshua would be enough to cover some new clothes. "I might need some things. I only have a couple pairs of shorts."

He brightened as if providing for me made him happy. "Do you have a bathing suit?"

My mouth formed a wide O. I never owned a bathing suit, not since my plastic pool days. "No. Do you have a pool?"

His smile spread, crinkling the corners of his eyes. I'd forgotten how handsome my father was. With his hazel eyes, dark hair threaded with gray, and glowing tan, he appeared several years younger than my mother, instead of being three older.

"Follow me."

With one more glance back at my beautiful bedroom, I strolled behind him, acclimating myself to my new surroundings. Walk through the kitchen, through the living room, into the hallway. Past Dad's room. Next is my bathroom, then my bedroom.

My directional road-mapping fled when we stepped out through a sliding glass door to the patio surrounding the pool. A tropical paradise awaited. "Wow," I murmured.

"This is my favorite place. It's why we bought this house. I felt the same way the first time I saw this."

The pool's edge rippled across the patio, curving in

and out until the glimmering surface met a slightly elevated hot tub at the far end. Water rippled from one container to the other, tinkling as it fell into the pool over terraced stone walls. A rich, watery tone of notes drifted in a song I only ever dreamed of.

Lounge and Adirondack chairs perched on the deck, waiting to welcome leisure and enjoyment among groups of potted palms. A dining table sat beneath a patio over-hang inside the shelter of the massive, screened room. Palm trees whispered overhead in the afternoon breeze, dappling the pool with shade. Painted geckos hung on the backside of the house, and strings of light criss-crossed over the table.

I imagined the time I would spend out here, listening to the silky cascade of water and the brush of palms against the air, my feet propped up on an ottoman beneath the tiny white lights. I'd never known it was possible to enjoy a home like this.

"Do you like it?"

So much. I'd missed so much. I pressed a hand to my chest, holding the flood of feeling at bay. "I . . . wow. Can I sleep out here?"

Dad laughed and dropped an arm over my shoulders for a quick squeeze. "Sometimes I do," he confessed as he checked a text on his phone. "Hey, Mindy went for a walk. She wanted you to tour the house without her here." He offered me a seat at the patio table. I sank into the deep cushion, as overwhelmed by this house as I had been by my mother's.

His fingers tapped against the glass of the table. "We don't want this to be awkward for you."

I inhaled, preparing myself to speak truthfully but with restraint. "I don't know what to say about all this. It's a lot to process."

"I figured you might want to rip my head off," he said with a rueful smile.

I stared at him. Had he been reading my mind? "Why?"

"You've been through a lot living with Mom. I didn't do anything about it. I didn't know how to." He fixed his gaze on the sparkling pool.

My anger bubbled to the surface, sprung loose from its cage. "You could've tried, Dad. You knew what she was like."

"Yes. I should have." He swallowed hard. "Mindy told me I waited too long. She wanted me to get you right after we married. I expected Mom would fight me, and I'd have to tell a court what she was like. Her illness would have been public. I didn't want to expose her. Or you."

I sat back, stunned. "You protected her," I said softly.

He nodded. "Yes. I'm not sure it was the right decision. I tried to call you. All the time. She wouldn't let me talk to you. If I had any idea you were using my old cell phone, I would have called you directly."

The old pain of his abandonment stirred in my chest. "She told me you called me before I left. Up until then, she never told me. But the FedEx plan worked,"

We sat in silence. The tinkle and splash of the pool filter filled the gap in our words.

I crossed my ankles beneath my chair. "So, what now? We just leave her up there alone?"

"I want you to know, I tried many times to get her to understand what she's doing to herself and to you, even after I left. She doesn't see her lifestyle as a problem—or won't," he said, his voice turning harsh. "Before I left, I got her to go to a counselor a few times. They said it was depression and started her on medication. It worked for a while, but then she stopped taking the meds and didn't tell me. We even started to clear out some of the stuff. Box it up. Then I went on a business trip for a few days. I came back, and she opened all the boxes and dumped the stuff back on the floor. I didn't have it in me to keep fighting her—not if she wouldn't fight for herself or you." He wiped his eyes. "I told her I was going to take you away . . ." He trailed off, his eyes on the pool. "She told me she'd kill herself if I did. I couldn't do it. I couldn't live with her taking her own life."

Fear clutched my throat. I left, like Dad. "Do you think she'll hurt herself?"

He shook his head. "No. Now, I believe it was a bluff. It took me a while to come to that conclusion, which is why I sent you the ticket now. She's not too far removed from reality. And you're just about old enough to make your own decisions without us having to go to a custody hearing."

Dad hadn't seen the mismatched slippers and the broken china doll. My mother wasn't stable. There were times I believed she wasn't sane. "She doesn't go outside anymore," I told him. "How is she going to live on her own?" Tears dropped over my lashes onto my cheeks.

"It will work out." He grasped my hand in a fierce grip and studied the way our fingers fit together, his tan, mine pale white. "Your parents' problems are not yours to deal with. I've made some calls to people to alert them about her past threats of self-harm. Social service agencies. They're going to check on her and make sure she's all right. They promised to keep quiet about the house."

The pressure in my chest released, ever so slightly.

"I'm so afraid of what's going to happen to her."

"Shelly, Mom is an adult. She's making these choices to live the way she does. You're going to be a senior in high school, a year from being an adult. You need to save yourself. You need a future."

I turned my eyes to his, a thousand accusations bleeding into my tone. "Is that what you did?"

He rubbed a hand over his mouth and averted his gaze. "Yes," he said.

Behind us, a door opened. My body tensed, but I forced myself to turn.

A petite woman of about fifty stood on the patio. Her blond hair was short and stylish above high cheekbones sprinkled with freckles. Her clear, blue eyes drifted to my dad before resting on me. "Shelly? It's nice to finally meet you."

She gingerly stepped toward me as if she were approaching a strange, possibly feral, animal and reached for my hand.

"Hi," I managed, accepting her gesture.

She sat beside my father. I studied her for anything I didn't like—something I could latch onto with both hands so I could hate this woman who had taken my father away from me. But she smiled openly, warmly, as if she was genuinely happy to find me sitting beside her pool.

"How was your flight?" she asked as my dad leaned closer to her.

I forced the corners of my mouth upward. "Good, I guess. I've never flown before."

Her eyes widened. "Oh, we've got to get you going places. There's so much to see out there." She stopped as she seemed to realize she was rushing ahead of herself.

"I'm taking it easy right now," I said. "I have a lot to think about."

She glanced toward my father, her enthusiasm dimming. "Yes. Absolutely. There's lots of time."

My father draped an arm over the back of her chair. "Shelly mentioned she might need to pick up some Florida-ready clothes. That's your department," Dad said with a sheepish grin. He wiggled his eyebrows like old times, and I suppressed a giggle.

"I'm good for a couple of days," I assured him. The last thing I wanted was to end up on an all-girls shopping spree with my father's pretty wife on day one. I already felt like the frump-child from the north.

"There's no rush," Mindy assured me, picking up on my hesitation. "When you're ready, you let me know."

I shifted my gaze toward the pool. Was the water as warm and inviting as it looked? I imagined myself there, floating around on a pool lounger, soaking the sun into my cold, sad bones. "I'd like to get a bathing suit."

Mindy and Dad shared a glance. "Whenever you're ready, Shelly," Dad echoed.

Sudden weariness swamped me, and a familiar ache

settled in my temples. Dehydration. "Do you have any water?"

Mindy stood and gestured for me to follow her into the house. "Sure. I'll show you where everything is."

In the kitchen, she showed me where to find glasses, cups, and dishes. I filled a glass with ice and water from the refrigerator door. "Snacks are in this cabinet," she added, opening the door to reveal boxes of snack crackers and a few bags of different kinds of chips. "If you don't find something you like, I'm planning a trip to the store later today."

"I eat a lot of fruit," I told her. "I like carrots and pretzels, too. Do you have hummus?"

"Nope, but we can get some. Make me a list of what you want. Or you can come with me if you'd like."

I suddenly missed my car. Here, I'd have to rely on Mindy or Dad for transportation. But if I entertained any hopes of making a life for myself here, away from my mother's wreckage, I'd have to learn the lay of the land.

"Okay," I told her. "I'll go to the store with you. Maybe find a bathing suit?"

She brightened. "Great. You settle in for a bit. We'll head out after lunch. I know just the place."

"Sounds good." The reality was, if I stayed here with my father like I planned to, I'd have to accept this woman as part of his life. As part of mine. I tried to superimpose my mother's presence on this house. Impossible.

Why didn't Mom want this: a life of calm, serene existence? Why? The scarier thought was maybe that's exactly what she had living in her nest.

FIFTEEN

ORLANDO SPRAWLED out on both sides of I-4, and I wasn't exactly sure where we ended up. We passed towering buildings, arenas, hotels, and high-rises covered in mirrored glass reflecting the image of the sky. I could live here forever and never explore a tenth of what I glimpsed on a fifteen-minute drive.

"This is my favorite store," Mindy gushed as we walked into a small boutique with wide teal awnings somewhere on the north side of the city. The sign out front read Much More.

Inside, one wall of the shop was painted floor-to-ceiling to resemble an ocean sunset. Lounge and patio chairs sat in front of the beach-style cabana dressing rooms. Belts and accessories were displayed in sand pails. So not Walmart.

"They have great styles. I'm sure you'll find something." She waved to one of the clerks, a tall woman with nearly white-blond hair and sun-weathered skin, who then embraced Mindy like a long-lost friend. She wore a long, flowing maxi skirt over sparkling sandals and a gauzy tank top. Very Bohemian.

Comparing the similarity of her outfit to Mindy's, I suspected Mindy spent a lot of money in this store.

"This is my stepdaughter, Shelly. We need to find her a bathing suit." Mindy beamed at the clerk and then at me. I tried not to squirm. Stepdaughter. The word flowed seamlessly off her tongue. Had she been practicing it? Stepmother sure hadn't passed over my lips.

The saleswoman studied me like, See? Look at the pale northern kid. Do we have anything in here to make her look less dead?

"How lovely. Nice to meet you, Shelly. I hope you'll come by often. I'm Fran, by the way." She held out a thin, ring-covered hand for me to shake. Her wrist jingled from a plethora of wire bracelets.

"Fran is wonderful. You take your time. I'm going to browse," Mindy said with a quick quirk of her eyebrows. She faded into the inner recesses of the store, leaving me alone and exposed.

"Any ideas on style of suit?" Fran asked.

Suit? Do you sell armor? I smiled back and tried to sound enthusiastic. "Uh, not really. I didn't swim much in New Jersey."

"Oh! New Jersey. I have a cousin in New Jersey," she said, as if living in the north meant a person should have their head examined. "Or maybe it's Pennsylvania?" She waved her hands. "Oh, it doesn't matter. Getting you set for swim season does!"

"Uh, thanks."

Joshua's face surfaced from the corners of my mind. I

ached with missing him, a totally illogical reaction to someone I'd known for a couple of weeks. But I missed his cinnamon scent and the way he held me. Most of all, I missed his friendship.

The clerk snapped me back to the present. "One piece? Two? We also have a nice selection of bikinis." She smiled the way women who will never wear a bikini do. "With your shape, it's what I'd be wearing."

My eyes widened in horror. How about no! How about a long-sleeved rash guard to go over the bikini? And board shorts? Leggings perhaps?

"Two-piece. No bikini." The last thing I wanted to do was walk around my father's pool in a bikini.

"Perfect. Right this way." She led me over to a rack jammed with brightly colored suits in every style imaginable. Thick tank-top straps. Whisper-thin, camisole styles that crisscrossed in the back. High-cuts. Boy shorts. Low waist, high waist.

My head spun with the choices.

"There are some nice racerback suits here. Are you athletic? You look athletic. Some of these are designed for athletes." Fran frowned, holding up a suit with a Nike swoosh on the boob.

"I don't think that's what I'm after," I told her as I flipped through the rack. "What about this one?" I held up a two-piece, standard tank in turquoise with a white hibiscus print.

She lifted the suit in front of me, critically appraising my choice. "I like what it does to your eyes. I bet the boys will, too," she said.

My spine stiffened. "I already have a boyfriend," I murmured, but not nearly quiet enough.

"You do?" From out of nowhere, Mindy homed in on us like a missile, her eyes wide and delighted. "Does your dad know?"

I clamped my teeth together in a grimace. Freaking fantastic. I didn't need my father asking questions about Joshua. "No." I turned to Fran to deflect. "How much is this one?"

"Oh, yes. Everything on this rack is two twenty-five."

Stunned, I nearly dropped the suit. "Two hundred and twenty-five?" How could a square foot of material cost so much? I'd been able to store away some cash in my bank account. Exactly enough for eight bathing suits. Good Lord.

"Yes," Fran said. "Would you like to try it on?"

"Do you have anything less expensive?" I asked her. "Maybe, fifty?"

Fran and Mindy looked stricken. Oh, this poor, pale relative from New Jersey.

Tsk, tsk.

"Don't worry about the price, Shelly. Your dad's paying for this," Mindy said.

"I don't need anyone to pay for my things," I told her, my voice sharp.

Fran took the hint and set the suit back on the rack. "Why don't we look in the clearance racks for you?"

"Thanks," I mumbled as I followed her to the back of the store. Mindy had enough sense to stay put.

"What about sizes?" she asked me, eyeing my body.

How did bathing suit sizes run? I didn't want anything too clingy. I liked space. "Six, maybe?"

"These should work for you then," she told me, indicating a section of the rack where my size resided.

I shuffled through the racks, knowing I had to find something in this store. Something told me Mindy wouldn't be into the idea of taking me to Target. Frustration mounted the deeper I dug into the sale section. Finally, a couple of suits appealed to me, and I headed for the changing rooms while Fran and Mindy huddled in the front of the store.

In the privacy of the changing room, I texted Joshua.

Save me I'm in retail hell

What?

I'm trying on bathing suits

Cool! Pictures?

I stifled a laugh and sent him an emoji sticking out its tongue.

"Everything okay in there?" Fran's nasally voice grated through the thin curtain.

"Fine," I called back, making a nasty face she couldn't see and wouldn't appreciate if she did. I stood in front of the mirror wearing a vibrant orange two-piece with enough space to hide my ribs. I lost a bunch of weight since Mom's pizza fetish. Palm fronds scattered over the fabric in delicate swirls added distraction from my waist. Definitely tropical, very Floridian. I smoothed the material over my hip bones. Seventy-eight dollars. Still more than I planned on spending but better than the bank-busting suit from the front of the store.

After I dressed, I returned the other suit to the sale rack and headed up front to check out my purchase.

"Oh, how lovely," Fran said. "It brings out the highlights in your hair. A couple of weeks in the Florida sun and those will shine." Somehow, Fran could find a way to compliment my choice even if I cut a suit from a Hefty trash bag.

She rang up the sale and handed me a bright pink shopping bag. "Thank you," I said.

"Ready?" Mindy asked, her tone light. "I'm feeling like a coffee. Do you want one?"

I swallowed hard. I hadn't been looking for a girls' day, but it seemed to be what I signed up for. I was going to stay until I sorted out my life back home. I had to pretend I was all in. "Sure. Is there a Starbucks?" *Please, God. Let there be a Starbucks.*

"Yes, on the way home. We'll stop."

I climbed into the car and noticed the pink bag in the backseat. "You bought something, too?" I wondered how many hundreds she spent on the tiny bag. Did she have a job or was this my father's money at work?

She smiled secretively. "Just a little thing I picked up," she said.

We ordered coffee in the Starbucks drive-thru, and I sipped the hot, sweet caramel macchiato as I studied the scenery on the way to my father's neighborhood. The coffee burned against my empty stomach, but the taste kept me sipping. Maybe Mindy would stop at a drugstore so I could pick up a fresh bottle of antacid.

As if reading my thoughts, she asked, "Is there anything you need at the store? Special cereal you like?"

"Maybe we can stop for fruit," I said, dreaming of summer peaches. Fresh fruit was one thing I would force myself to eat, no matter how bad my stomach burned. Especially watermelon when it was ice cold.

"Oh, I forgot. We were supposed to stop at the supermarket. I know—the farmer's market is the place. It's on the way home."

Ten minutes later, we parked beside a row of white tents covering a vast array of produce. I was sweating in the midday sun, browsing up and down the rows and picking up peaches, plums, and two massive pink grapefruits while Mindy shopped for peppers and squash.

Did my mother know what a squash looked like? Hah! Only if it came as a pizza topping.

Maybe I could eat the food Mindy cooked if it included all the vegetables she packed into the back of the car. I'd even found a vendor selling organic hummus.

"I'm making chicken on the grill tonight. Is that okay?" Mindy asked.

My stomach gurgled, somewhere between hunger and oh-crap-you're-gonna-expect-me-to-eat vomitus. "Sounds great."

"I throw tons of veggies in there, too. You'll like it." She hesitated for a moment as if unsure of what to say next. "Do you have any favorite meals from home?"

I tensed in my seat, wondering what my father told her about my existence back in New Jersey. "Not really. My mom doesn't like to cook, so we did take out. But I'm not a fan of pizza."

"Not everyone is comfortable in the kitchen," she acknowledged without giving me an indication of what she knew or didn't suspect about my home life. "We don't order out much. I cook most nights at home, so maybe we'll find something you like."

A tangle of contradictions twisted my emotions into something I couldn't recognize. Dinners at home with my dad. It was difficult to conjure up images of him at the table, teasing me about my day. But there were glimpses. Thanksgiving, maybe. A birthday with a white-frosted cake. But most of those joyful flashes dimmed beneath the unbearable weight of the last ten years. I'd eaten alone in my room for as long as I could remember, huddled around my tiny microwave.

When we unloaded the car and stored our farmer's market buys, I headed for my room to hide and spent the better part of the next hour pacing like a caged lion. I didn't want to text Joshua every ten minutes. He was busy. He had lawns to mow and pizzas to deliver for his aunt. At home, I had work outside to do to shield the world from my mother's illness. Here, there was nothing but my thoughts and endless small talk with Mindy if I ventured outside this beautiful, horrible room.

Joshua. I'd love to send him pictures, so he remembered what I looked like and could appreciate my new bathing suit. I wanted him to see where I landed so he knew I was okay. But I couldn't with my crappy phone. I needed modern technology.

I stalked from my room and found my father in the kitchen, snacking on one of the peaches I just picked out. A ripple of bitterness twisted through me, but I tamped it down. He paid for my peach, just like he paid for me to be here. The peach and I shared lots in common.

"Dad? Can we talk about a cell phone?"

"Sure," he said.

"Uh, I'd like to send pictures to my friend, but the camera doesn't work in this phone."

"Is the friend a boy or a girl?" he asked.

"Dad!"

He held up his hands. "Sorry. Need to know. I'll take you to the store tomorrow."

My spine stiffened. Here we go again. Pulling up to the bank of Dad. "You don't have to. I have money. I can buy it."

He set down the peach on a small, blue dish beside his tablet. "Shelly, there's a lot of stuff I haven't done for you in your life. I want to make it right."

I glanced around the incredible house, at the pool and impeccable yard, and shook my head, burning with ferocious hatred. "There's no way to make up for what you did to me."

Dad and I stared at each other for several moments before he relented. "I'll get you your own plan."

"Thanks," I said and retreated to my room.

I sat on the bed for a while to compose myself before I gave in and dialed Joshua's number.

"Hello?"

"Joshua, it's me. Shelly."

"Hey! Where are you? Did you buy a bathing suit? Is your dad cool or a jerk? Can you send me a picture?" He fired off questions.

My breath whooshed out of my body. He sounded happy to hear from me. More than happy. Thrilled. Relieved.

That made two of us.

"It's okay," I told him, glancing around my room. "It's way different than my mother's house. We've got a pool here, and yes, I bought a bathing suit. It's pretty."

"Not as pretty as you," he said.

I blushed, thankful he couldn't see me. "Thanks," I mumbled. "The house is beautiful."

"Nice." His voice dropped a fraction. "I miss you. How can I miss you? You've only been gone part of a day."

Warmth spread across my neck.

"You're blushing, aren't you?"

I hid my smile behind my hand. "Am not," I said.

"Are too. It's one of the things I love about you."

Love? Did he say love? I kicked off my flip-flops and dropped on the bed. "Only one?" Fluffy clouds meandered through the skylight view.

"There are many," he chuckled. "I'm supposed to be mowing grass for Uncle Rob. He's giving me the 'move your butt' glare. Can I call you back later? After I get off work?"

"Sure." My father's offer of a phone suddenly sounded very appealing. "My dad is supposed to get me a new phone tomorrow."

"Okay. But I better be the first person you call on your new phone," he said.

"Don't worry. You will be."

"Talk to you later, Shell."

I sat with the phone in my lap, hope flowing under my skin. He still liked me, and there were things he *loved* about me. What did I love about him? With hours of nothing ahead of me, I decided to make a Things I Love About Joshua list.

Eyes

Hair

Smile

Kissing!!!!!!!

He accepted me

The way he didn't judge my life

He said he loved things about me

He answered the phone

He wanted to call me back

TBD

I tucked the list into my bag. I would add to the list. Every day for the rest of my life as long as Joshua answered the phone.

SIXTEEN

DINNER DESCENDED INTO UNCOMFORTABLE SILENCE—FOR me anyway. Dad and Mindy kept up the chipper chatter throughout while I picked at my marinated chicken, perfectly grilled zucchini, and crisp salad. I managed to swallow a dozen bites before my stomach kicked against my ribcage. I should have eaten a peach earlier like I planned.

"Not hungry?" Mindy asked, concern filtering across her face. She glanced at my father, who shrugged.

"I had some. My stomach's a little upside down," I told her. "It was delicious though."

Dad's narrowed eyes fell on my nearly full plate. "You sure? You want something else?"

"It's fine, Dad," I told him. I didn't need him all over me about what I did or didn't eat.

Mindy came to my rescue just as Dad was about to say something else. "It would be nice to take a walk around the neighborhood. Get you acquainted with the area. What do you think?'

I sighed. I couldn't help but like her. She was smart and perceptive. I wondered if she had kids of her own. There was a lot to learn about my stepmother.

Oops. I said it. "Sure. Sounds good."

Mindy stood and began to gather the dishes. I hurried to help her clear the table.

She shooed me. "It's okay, Shelly, I've got it."

"Please. I want to." My whole life had been about not putting away, not cleaning up. Here, I could fully exercise my obsession with cleanliness. I wasn't about to sit on the sidelines and miss this opportunity.

"Okay then. Will you grab the salad and the bread bowl?" She met my father's eyes and retreated into the house.

Dad edged forward in his seat. "I remember what it was like to finally get away from it. I know what you're thinking."

I stopped, the salad bowl in my hands hovering over the table, sudden rage simmering in my veins. "How could you possibly? Do you have a clue how much it's multiplied since you left? How it *smells*?" The bowl trembled in my hands, and Dad reached out to take it from me.

"It's okay, Shelly. You don't have to go back there."

"Someone does," I snapped. "Someone has to make her understand sense."

"Not you," he said flatly. "This is an adult problem. I want to make sure you're okay."

I laughed in my throat, a harsh, unyielding sound. "Really? I was the only adult left in the house. The other adult ran away." I thumped the bowl on the table and stormed past a startled Mindy toward my room.

Inside the sanctuary of my new bedroom, I curled on the bed, listening to the central air conditioning course through the vents over my head, breathing fresh, unpolluted air enhanced by whatever air freshener was plugged into the wall socket.

Hibiscus? Sunflower? It didn't matter.

It was new. It wasn't home.

I wondered what Joshua was doing right then. I sent him a text.

Hello?

Hey there.

I let out a relieved breath.

It's nice here miss you.

Miss you too want me to call?

I sank into the luxury of the bed, my eyes drifting shut.

Later? napping

Sweet dreams

Exhaustion drove me deeper into the mattress until I couldn't keep my eyes open. I drifted, dappled sunshine flitting against the barriers of my eyelids. I dreamed of my mother, outside on the front porch of her house, laughing as we sipped ice-cold lemonade. But her image slowly dissolved. Mindy's tanned face replaced my mother's pale one. Then Joshua was there, pushing a lawn mower back and forth across our grass, his shirt off, his tan back gleaming in the sun . . .

"Shelly?"

I groaned into the pillow as the door swung open. If only I had a padlock. So much for the nap.

"I ran down to the phone store. I have your phone. I'll leave it here on your nightstand. It's all set up for you." Dad paused while I kept my face buried in the blankets. "Mindy asked me to give this to you. I'll leave it here."

The door closed and resentment surged in my veins. He'd gone to get the phone without me. Why not give me an ounce of freedom to pay my own way?

I waited several minutes to make sure my father was gone before I sat up in bed. A smartphone box sat on my nightstand. I picked it up and stared at the picture on the front, and some of the anger bled away. No one ever gave me such a gift. Mom's presents consisted of clothes and knickknacks I'd throw out the day after I opened them because of what they were: just another brick in the hoard.

This was substantial. The phone was big time.

My gaze fell on the pink boutique bag sitting on my table. I figured out what was inside before I opened it and found the turquoise bathing suit. I brushed my fingers over the thick spandex and threw the bag and the suit into the corner of the room.

I dialed Joshua's number on my new phone, hoping he was finished with work for the day. He picked up on the second ring with a cautious, "Hello?"

"Joshua. It's me."

"Hey! This is a different number."

I grinned into the phone, my dark mood evaporating. "Is it? I guess because it's Florida, maybe. It's mine. My dad got me a new phone. I can take pictures with it."

"Good. What kind of phone is it?"

Not being well-versed in the current cell phones on the market, I figured it was an iPhone by the apple on the box. "iPhone something."

"Good. That's what I have. We can FaceTime."

I rolled onto my back and stared up at the slowly spinning ceiling fan. "I've never done a video call. You'll have to walk me through it."

"I will. It's easy. How's your dad been?"

Good question. I pursed my lips before answering. "He's strange. A stranger who left me at my mother's house years ago. He never did anything to help me." I inhaled and harshly blew the air away. "It's a lot to make up for."

"Is he trying?" he asked.

"Yeah. He says he is. So is his wife."

Joshua paused, and he turned down his music. "You didn't tell me he got married again."

"I forgot to mention it, I guess. She's nice. Her name is Mindy." My gaze shifted to the bag in the corner. "She took me shopping."

"Well, it sounds like she doesn't suck."

Laughter snorted out my nose. "Oh, my God."

"She doesn't suck?"

The fan spun overhead, lulling my anger into something I could live with—acceptance, maybe. "I guess not. My mother never had anything good to say about her, but then she never met Mindy either. I feel like I should hate her. So far, I can't."

"Did you figure out how long you're going to stay? Did you decide if this is permanent?"

"Why? Do you want me to come back?" I teased. The sun angled lower outside, creeping toward evening. Maybe we could go camping under the stars at the outcropping we visited. I'd watch the sun set and rise in Joshua's arms.

"Yeah, I do. But not if you have to go back to the house."

It was mid-July. School started in a month and a half back home. I hoped I wasn't making a promise I couldn't keep to Joshua or myself.

Besides, did my father want me to stay? Could we really have a father-daughter relationship?

"I have to figure some things out," I told him. The list of issues was long. Where to live, how to support myself.

"Like where are you gonna stay if you come back?" he asked.

"To be determined," I told him. I didn't want to look too far ahead into my future. I'd rather lay on the bed and listen to him breathe than talk about my mother and what going home would look like. I'd have to get my own place and figure out how to pay for it. I only had so much plasma to sell.

"Okay. I get it. Figure it out when you get here."

"Exactly," I said.

"So, I can text and FaceTime with you now. At all hours of the day. Send you goofy selfies so you don't forget what I look like." As if on cue, my phone buzzed in my hand. A text from Joshua. His face with full raccoon eyes.

"Holy crap! Awesome. Now one with your sunglasses on."

"Hang on. Let me work on it."

A soft knock sounded against my door. I closed my eyes and counted to ten. Privacy. We needed to have some conversations about leaving me the hell alone for more than five minutes at a shot.

"Someone's at my door. Text me later?" The request sounded foreign on my tongue. I'd have to figure out how to text on this thing. It was completely different from the ancient phone, but how hard could it be? Open the app and type.

"You bet I will. Be happy, Shell." Joshua hung up. The phone buzzed, and I giggled at the picture of Joshua in his aviators with trees and sky reflected in his mirrored shades.

I stuffed the phone in my pocket and opened the door. Mindy stood on the other side looking pensive and wearing white, knee-length walking shorts paired with a coral tank top. "I'm going for a walk. Would you like to go?"

The woman was relentless, but she seemed sincere. Still, I hesitated before I said, "Sure."

We headed out through the garage and onto the street. Across from my father's house sat a sprawling ranch with a huge pool enclosure at the back. A squat palm tree with fronds like a stationary firework stood in the middle of the front yard surrounded by pink and white flowering shrubs with long, thin leaves.

"What kind of flowers are those?" I asked Mindy.

"Oleander. It grows all over down here. It's planted in the middle of the highway, too. Very poisonous." She led me to the next house over, a coral-hued beauty with tall stone columns flanking the entrance. "Those white flowers are African iris," she told me, pointing to a cluster of white blossoms beside the home's mailbox. "Those big leaves will be Bird of Paradise flowers. Have you ever seen those? They're orange and quite stunning."

I nodded. "Yes. In a flower arrangement I bought once. Those fat, shiny leaves look like hibiscus."

She smiled. "Yes! They have a great blend of colors. Some of them are as big as dinner plates when they bloom. I'm always jealous of Ramon's garden." Mindy studied me. "You seem to know a lot about plants."

"I did all the yard stuff at home. I like working in the dirt," I told her with a shrug. My flower beds would have weeds sprouting out all over unless Joshua felt sorry for them when he cut the grass. "I used to help my father when I was little."

"That's great! I do it all here. Your father thinks I'm crazy in this heat, but I don't want to hire someone when I enjoy digging around. He doesn't do much planting anymore. He's in charge of the potted plants now. But I'd love to teach you about Florida plants."

Getting my hands into the dirt, planting and mulching, nearly drove me to tears with hope. "I can help. I want to do this when I graduate."

"You've come to the right place," she said. "In Florida, landscaping is a year-round job."

Joshua said as much about the south. Mindy was right, though. Plants didn't go into hiding for five months of the year like they did back at home. Maybe I could work for Disney World or some other theme park carving characters out of boxwoods. Or a hotel chain, making their properties beautiful inside and out. I read a few magazines back home, and I always loved looking at the spreads about resorts and imagining what I would do differently if I had more money and a better climate.

Maybe Joshua and I could go into business here. The possibility made me smile.

"It's a lucrative career. I bet there are some great schools down here for it. Lots of internships, too." We passed a home set back from the road with a gate at the end of the driveway.

"Valencia College is one," I said with a curious glance in her direction. She sounded like someone with experience in college stuff, and I knew zero about getting accepted. "Did you go to college?"

Mindy smiled as she nodded. "Yes. Law school, too."

My eyes widened. "Wow! You're a lawyer?"

She brushed sweat-dampened hair off her forehead. "I used to be. I don't practice much anymore. I pretend I'm retired. But I do take some work now and then for friends and family."

"Wow," I said again.

Mindy chuckled. "It sounds more impressive than it is."

We walked past a beautiful home with a stone front and a hipped roof made of blue tile. "What's that plant? The one with the white bells on it?" I asked her.

"Hmm," she said, stopping in the street to consider the vine. "Trumpet creeper? Too big to be a painted trumpet." She moved on past the house. "Next time Frannie is at the mailbox, I'll ask her for you."

"There are so many cool plants," I said, taking in the

beauty of the neighborhood. It was like every house tried to outdo the other, and we'd only gone half a block.

"Most of them have professionals taking care of their properties." She paused while I took pictures of the white bell-shaped flowers. "I have some plant books I'm happy to share."

I stepped away, feeling my barriers slide into place. This relationship with my stepmother was too fast, too easy. I needed to throw on the brakes and figure out what being here in my father's house meant. Disappointment sliced into my heart. I'd never have this with my mother —this casual conversation. No quiet strolls through the neighborhood or sitting on the porch drinking iced tea on a warm summer night.

"Uh, thanks," I told her.

If my cautious stance affected her, she kept it to herself. "I'm going to the nursery tomorrow to pick up a new Meyer lemon tree. You're welcome to join me. I can introduce you to the owner. She has a great selection of plants."

"Okay," I murmured. Growing lemons in the backyard sounded fantastical and oh-so-cool.

I said little for the rest of the walk, responding only when necessary, my thoughts as dark and unsorted as my mother's closet. I *liked* my stepmother, and that drove a spike of guilt into my heart. The fact I didn't hate her felt like all kinds of betrayal.

We returned to the house as the sun was setting, and I bolted for my room, only to skid to a stop in front of my father's bedroom. His voice was raised, his tone angry.

"I'm not keeping her against her will. Stop it, Madeline. That's not true." He said nothing for a moment while he listened. His feet thudded softly as he paced away from the door. "You need help. You need to find someone to help you. No. Shelly's not the one you need. You need a professional. Someone who can make you understand."

I stepped into the room, and he shifted his gaze in my direction. Dad pinched the bridge of his nose in frustration.

"Stop, Maddy. Just stop."

"Let me talk to her," I demanded, stepping further into the room.

He shook his head, his gaze full of pain.

"Dad. Please." I held out my hand for the phone. Reluctantly, he handed it over.

"Mom?"

Her breathless voice filled the phone. "Shelly? Oh, thank God. Are you all right?"

I frowned, drawing my brows down. She sounded frantic and out of breath. What was she thinking? *Was* she thinking? "Yeah, of course, why?"

"He can't keep you there. You're almost an adult. He can't keep you prisoner. I'll call the police. They'll come and get you."

I nearly gasped out loud before dropping my voice to a whisper. "Mom, I'm not a prisoner."

"Of course, you are! He took you from your home!" Her voice cracked as if she were on the verge of tears.

My father stepped to the window and stared out at the sparkling pool.

"Mom . . . I left. Dad didn't take me. Don't you remem-

ber? You told me to leave. You told me to get out. I did."
Memories of the nasty fight and her anger pushed bile up
my throat. Not for the first time, I wondered if there was
something seriously wrong with my stomach.

There was silence on the phone for several moments
before her grief swung one-eighty into full-blown fury.
"You're lying. I would never say such a thing to you. Is
that the lie he told you?"

Tears slipped from my lashes, and my shoulders
trembled. "Mom! I was there! You threw me out when I
told you he sent me a plane ticket for my birthday. I left. I
slept in my car."

She said nothing for a full minute.

"Mom?" My heart skipped at least a dozen beats
waiting for her to respond. What if she tried to kill
herself? Made good on those promises from years ago?

"The nice boy was here cutting the grass today. Why
can't you find a nice boy, Shelly?"

Had she heard what I said? She must be talking about
Joshua. Did she try to talk to him? What if Joshua talked
to her and decided she was too crazy to speak to me
again? I sank down on my father's bed while he stalked
back and forth in front of the window.

"Mom, please."

"*Mom, please.* It's never 'Shelly, please.' Always Mom
who has to give up what she loves." My mother's voice
dissolved into a sob shredding my heart. "I'm going to
save you, Shelly. Save you from him. I called a lawyer
today. They're going to get you back."

Horror bloomed in my chest. "Damn it! Mom! Stop it!

I'm not going back!" I spat the words out before I could consider them. Maybe it was for the best to just get it out there, into the light of day. Maybe if my mother understood how I felt, she'd get over it. "Mom, you need to listen to me. You need to talk to someone who can help with what you're going through. A therapist can help you."

Silence again. Then she spat, "You're just like him," and hung up.

I stared at the phone. Now what was I going to do?

"She wants you to go home," Dad said, his voice toneless and tired.

"Yes," I said, drawing in a huge sigh. "She said she called a lawyer. She needs a doctor. What kind of doctor treats people like her, Dad?"

"She needs to be hospitalized and the house condemned. You can't talk to her, Shelly. There's no convincing her."

My voice broke. "Can't we make her go?"

He shook his head. "I've talked to Mindy about this. It's hard to prove she's a danger to herself unless she does something awful. We have few options unless something bad happens." His voice sounded old, worn out, and weathered, like the phone call aged him a hundred years. But his words had been echoes of my own. "She doesn't comprehend what she's doing. She doesn't see anything wrong with her lifestyle."

A sob caught in my throat as I imagined her sitting there all alone surrounded by the nest. How did she even find the phone without me?

"I know. But I can't leave her there." An icy thread of fear wove down my spine. Could some lawyer file a case and make me return to my mother's house? Would I have to tell the court how she chose to live? What court would make me go back when they found out about the hoard? I felt seventy percent confident Mom was lying about the lawyer.

"I tried to have her hospitalized." His shoulders slumped. These were the details of their eleven-year marriage I never wanted or expected to know. "Twice. It's very hard to convince someone in her state of mind to listen to reason. She doesn't understand what she's doing is wrong or strange. She sees it as normal. Necessary for her survival."

By the way he spoke, he talked to many people about my mother's condition over the years. "Was she always like this?"

"Not this bad," he told me. He turned to meet my eyes. "But there were signs I ignored. The house got messy, but she was taking care of you and working. Life got in the way, she'd say. Then we had another baby, a boy."

The floor shifted under my feet. "I have a brother?" I whispered.

"Had. He died four weeks after he was born. His name was Dalton. He never came home from the hospital. You were only two years old. Your mother fell apart. She just stopped."

Lies. Secrets. Piled on top of one another like the unstable stack of magazines next to my mother's ancient chair. "I don't blame her alone," I said.

The corners of his mouth turned up grimly, but his eyes didn't smile. "You also blame me."

Good. He got the hint. "I blame both of you. What am I supposed to do now? Does my brother have a grave? Where is he buried? What about her threats?"

He settled on the other side of the bed. "Dalton is in a cemetery in New Jersey. Not far from the house." Dad picked up my hand. "Look. We both want Mom to get better. Stay here with me in Florida."

I winced. He sensed my indecision.

"Maybe your leaving will make her fathom what she's done to you. What else can I do? I'm at a loss," he said. "I never wanted you in the middle of this."

"I've always been in the middle. You left me there." I drew my hand away from his and smoothed the comforter with my fingers.

His jaw bunched up. "I did what I believed was right. I sent for you when I thought you would come. Would you have come when you were twelve? Fourteen? Would you have left her to fend for herself if you knew what she threatened?"

Those younger years of my life—how defensive I felt about my mother and our situation. My need to protect her and our shared secrets, at all costs. I lifted a shoulder in response.

"Exactly," he said before turning and leaving the room.

I barely made it to his bathroom before the remnants of my meager dinner made a rebound. Later, I crawled to my room, shivering and sweating with a stomach full of pain, and slipped beneath the sheets without undressing.

I closed my eyes on the wreck of my life, hoping to let sleep and dreams of Joshua take me to a place better than the one I knew.

SEVENTEEN

DAD LEFT for the office before I crawled out of my cave the next morning. It was for the best we avoided each other for the time being. I didn't have the energy for another argument. Too many volcanic emotions bubbled inside me, threatening to erupt in a blowout so ugly I'd probably end up back in New Jersey living in my car sooner rather than later. If I wrecked my life here, I'd have nowhere else to go.

Maybe in a few days, I could forgive him enough we could be civil to one another.

Or in a few weeks. Years. Lifetimes.

The bitter, pathetic truth? I was currently living under his roof, and twelve long months needed to pass before I hit the magic eighteen button, which would finally give me control over my life. Control. Ha. What a joke. Where would I go? It's not like I'd be flush with cash the day after my eighteenth birthday. I exchanged one house arrest for another with a better view, shackled to my parents' problems.

The only thing I could control was whether or not I got out of bed before noon. I hauled myself to my feet, shaking and weak. My head swam, temples pounding like kettle drums. I needed to eat something—anything I could keep down without the burning ache forcing it back up my throat. Maybe a yogurt. Or my other peach.

After languishing in the shower for half an hour, I dried my hair and dressed in the only other pair of shorts I owned and a simple navy tank top with tiny white flowers sprouting over it. Good choice for a plant shopping day.

Mindy sat on the patio, sipping coffee from a mug with a picture of the Eiffel Tower on it. Did she get the cup on a trip with my father? A discordant note hummed along my spine as I imagined them jet-setting around the globe while I hid in my bedroom. How much did he experience while I lived with Mom, besides traveling? Glancing around the house, I could pick out souvenirs from other excursions to Hawaii, Venice, California, and Mexico.

The dissenting note turned into a simmering seethe.

I opened the refrigerator and removed a bottle of water and a peach. At least Dad left me one. My stomach sounded like boulders rumbling down a hill. I grabbed a yogurt and two tiny squares of coffee cake, which swiftly disappeared. Licking my fingers, I rummaged through the kitchen until I found a spoon. The sugar hit my system like rocket fuel.

Mindy smiled brightly as I stepped outside with the second course of my binge. She wore faded jean shorts and a white tank with hibiscus flowers embroidered around the neckline. Very Floridian. If Dad told her about our fight last night, she hid it well. I was dying to figure out what he shared with her, but it had to be done delicately.

"There you are. Did you sleep well?" Mindy asked.

"Yeah, thanks." I sank my teeth into the peach and nearly drowned in the juice.

"I'm glad. I was worried you'd have a hard time adjusting."

My eyebrows lifted as I wiped my chin. "Why?"

She set her cup on the table. "You've never been without your mom. The separation has to be tough."

Fortunately, or unfortunately, the physical act of being away from my mother was the easiest thing I'd ever done. But knowing how she must be suffering back home? The mental anguish was in a whole different league.

"It's different," I told her, refusing to say more. Tiny birds flitted through the hedges. I focused on them instead of offering her my eyes.

"Well, if you need anything, please just ask away. I'm thrilled you're here."

I shifted my attention to her hopeful face. "You don't know anything about me."

Mindy studied the coffee in her mug. "I'm listening if you want to tell me."

My lips pressed together. I said nothing.

She nodded after several seconds of silence. "Okay. I'm heading to the nursery in a couple of minutes. Do you still want to join me?"

I skimmed my teeth over the naked peach pit. If I

hesitated, she might wonder if I was trying to beg off. Instead, I said, "Yeah, if that's all right."

She gathered up her cup and newspaper. "It's great. I'll meet you out front in ten?"

Back in my room, my stomach rolled, and I barely made it to the bathroom in time. I rinsed out my mouth and closed my eyes as a wave of vertigo made me grab on to the sink for support. It was getting harder to keep food down, and the dark bits floating in the toilet worried me. The more I thought about eating, the sicker I felt. How long could I live on nothing? A sip of water? A spoonful of yogurt?

I opened my suitcase, found a couple of Pepto tablets, and chewed them into a sickly pink paste. Ugh. Surviving on this stuff was getting old real fast.

Joshua sent me a good morning text with a dozen smiley faces, and I quickly responded.

Hi!

Do you want to FaceTime?

I dragged a hand over my face and through my scraggly hair. My eyes were bloodshot from getting sick and dark circles shadowed the thin skin beneath them. I came to my father's house to have a better life. How come I looked worse?

going to the plant store with step monster. later?

:(later <3

A frowny face and a blue heart. What's a blue heart supposed to mean? A red heart meant love, and pink maybe like. But what's with the blue?

I slapped my cheeks to bring color back to my skin and found Mindy in the car out front. Sunglasses covered my eyes, and I ignored the inquisitive look she shot in my direction. True, I didn't eat much, but she couldn't know about the puking. I'd only been here for a day.

My stepmother chattered about places we passed on the way. Her hair and nail salon. A coffee shop with the best doughnuts in town. The local library housed in a small pink bungalow. The beachy house might be a good place to hide in my new life.

"Here we are," she announced as she pulled into the lot. Flowers in every shade imaginable exploded from pots, hanging baskets, and meticulously attended beds. Palms, shrubs, and full-sized trees rimmed the perimeter, and numerous lawn service trucks sat in the parking lot.

I felt for my phone in my pocket. This might be a good time to try out my camera.

Mindy grabbed her purse from the backseat. The cavern-sized Dooney probably cost more than my car. "Come on. I'll introduce you to the owner. She's a friend of mine from school."

Humidity sucked the air from my lungs as I followed Mindy into the forest of plants, snapping pictures of varying colors, textures, and leaf shapes. In minutes, my sweaty tank top stuck to my skin.

We found her friend talking to an older woman and a man I suspected might be her grandson. He didn't look much older than me.

"Mindy! I have your plants!" she called as soon as she saw my stepmother. Her gaze drifted to me standing beside her. "Who's this? You have a helper?"

Mindy laughed. "This is Bill's daughter. She's come to

stay with us. She loves plants. She had to see your place, Beth."

"Great. I'll be with you both in a moment." Beth swiftly finished her conversation with the older woman before dusting the dirt off her hands. She peeled off her gloves, stuffing them in her back pocket. "Nice to meet you. What's your name?"

"Shelly," I said.

She gripped my hand in a solid shake. A wide, honest smile dominated Beth's face. This was a woman who didn't shop in fancy boutiques or carry designer purses. She wore knee-length khaki shorts and a fanny pack I suspected doubled as her cash register. Her skin was flushed from the sun, and stray wisps of blond hair twisted and curled around her face. She had kind eyes, and by the earth embedded in her hands, she didn't keep a regular manicure appointment like Mindy did.

"Shelly," she said, nodding her head. "Got it. Important to remember names when you're in business." Beth set her hands on her hips. "So, what kind of plants do you like?"

"I'm not sure. I'm from New Jersey. These are different, so I don't know the names."

"I bet they are. Why don't you wander while I get Mindy squared away? Then we can chat about what you like." She whisked my stepmother toward a small trailer I guessed served as an office.

I strolled up and down the rows, snapping pictures, studying the jagged edge of aloe and interesting textures of tall, spiky plants, and thinking about my favorites from back home. I loved summer impatiens when they took off and filled shady spaces with color. And petunias. Something told me both of those plants would struggle in the Florida heat. Maybe sunflowers? I wondered if they would make it. I'd have to ask Beth.

She found me photographing a Bird of Paradise flower from multiple angles. "Ah, that's a good one! You've probably seen these before."

"I have in bouquets. But there's so many I've never seen," I admitted. "What about sunflowers? Do they grow here?"

She nodded. "Yes, but don't forget, our growing season starts in February, sometimes earlier. Technically, we grow all year round. I've grown some beautiful spring sunflowers. You should be able to get some to go in the fall as well if the weather stays hot and we don't get a hurricane." Beth studied me for a moment. "How long are you staying with Bill and Mindy? I could use some help around here. Especially if you love plants and are a fast learner."

"Really?" An incredible pressure built inside my chest. A job meant putting down roots and admitting I wasn't going back. The possibility of saying goodbye to Joshua permanently emphasized the ache in my stomach.

Beth held up a hand. "No strings. If you head back north, there's no problem. But it would get you out of the house if you know what I mean." She inclined her head toward my approaching stepmother.

I stifled a chuckle. "Thanks."

"Good. You're hired. See you at eight tomorrow morning." My new boss dashed away to wait on another customer.

"You ready to go?" Mindy asked.

I nodded, then stopped. "Yeah, uh . . . Beth just gave me a job."

Mindy gushed. "She's a great gal. You'll love it here." The way she said it told me she most certainly had a hand in my hiring. But Beth's gesture told me she understood I needed some space from my stepmother. Maybe Mindy figured I needed space, too.

Masking my resentment at her meddling, I dropped my sunglasses over my nose and said nothing on the ride home.

WE EMPTIED the car of the dozen or so plants she purchased. I looked around the yard and the flower beds. "Where are you going to put these?" There didn't seem to be a spot left for another bloom.

"Back by the pool," she told me as I followed her with arms full of flowers. "Some are for the planters. The others are filling in a bare spot. A couple of things got frosted this spring. I hoped I could save them, but you can't save them all," she said with a shrug.

Sure enough, Mindy stopped in front of a section of flower bed devoid of life. "This spot only gets afternoon sun. We had a morning in the twenties in February. I lost everything."

I studied the space and glanced at the plants she'd chosen—two fern-like plants with prickly leaves stood a foot tall in their pots. "Those should go in the back," I said. "And this yellow flower would look great mixed with those purple spiky ones."

She smiled. "You have a good eye. You're going to love the job."

"You didn't have to ask her to take me," I said with more sharpness than I felt.

"All I did was notice her help wanted sign and mention you might want a part-time job. She wouldn't have hired you if you didn't impress her." Mindy knelt in the grass and began to arrange the plants, leaning back on her heels to get a better look.

From the stiff set of her shoulders, I saw I hurt her feelings.

"Thanks." I dropped down on the grass beside her.

She regarded me for a moment, and I tried to read the emotions flashing through her eyes. Hurt? Anger? Disappointment? Yeah, those were familiar to me. The problem was, I cared I put those feelings there.

"What do you think about these pink ones?" she asked.

I instantly recognized the narrow leaves as summer favorites from my flower beds at home. "This might be a butterfly bush, but the buds look strange." I checked the tag. "Yep, that's what it is. It's called Orange Sceptre. I have a bunch of the purple ones at home. They get big. You should probably put the bush somewhere else." Suddenly, I couldn't wait to see the plant bloom. An orange butterfly bush!

Admiration dispelled the upset in her gaze. "See what I mean? You know your stuff."

An hour and a half later, we set all the plants and watered them. Sweat soaked my shirt, but the dirt under my nails felt right. I couldn't wait for tomorrow and my first day on the job. I gathered up the empty pots to return to the nursery in the morning while Mindy retracted the garden hose.

"Let's go clean up. I hear lunch calling."

I jumped up. "Oh! I was supposed to call my . . . Joshua."

Smirking, Mindy brushed the dirt from her knees and picked up the gardening tools. "Go ahead. I need a shower first."

In the garage, I slipped out of my grimy flip-flops and dashed to my room to text him.

I fired off, Hello? Anyone out there?

Seconds later, Joshua replied, and my heart began to beat again.

YEP, ALMOST DONE MOWING SOON CAN I SEE U?

I sat on the edge of my bed, staring at the phone and counting the minutes. Finally, it buzzed, and I clicked to accept the video call. Joshua's sunburned visage smiled back at me from the screen. I nearly dropped the phone, I was so happy to see him. A thousand pounds of weight drifted from my soul.

"Hi!" I waved at him.

He lifted his sunglasses off his nose and took a deep drink from his water bottle. "Hi, yourself. You look like you were outside. You're all pink and freckly."

"Sweaty, too. I was planting some stuff. Are you cutting grass?"

Joshua wiped the sheen from his skin with a towel. "It keeps growing so, yeah. How's Florida?"

"Beautiful. Hot. I miss parts of New Jersey," I told him.

"Oh, yeah? What parts?"

"The part you're standing in."

He smiled at the camera. "Good one. You decide how long you're staying?"

There it was. The hard part got harder every day I stayed away. "I'm not sure just yet. I have to figure out where I can go if I come back."

"If?" Joshua snagged one word out of the sentence and held it up to the light. The left corner of his mouth drew down.

"I meant when," I quickly amended.

"But you said if." He made an exaggerated frown at the screen.

"My life's a wreck right now." I stopped, collecting my courage for the next question. I didn't want to put him in a bad situation, but he was my only source of first-hand information about the condition of my house and, ultimately, my mother. "Have you been by my place? To cut the grass?"

"I'm supposed to go there on Friday. You want me to take a look around?"

So, my mother hadn't seen Joshua cutting her grass. She either made it up in her mind or lied outright. "Please," I said, relief rushing through my veins. "Can you water the plants?"

"Sure."

I stared at his handsomeness, trying to keep the scraps of my heart in one place. With a violent rumble, my stomach demanded food. If I ate something, anything, I would feel better about all of this. I knew it.

"You still thinking about going to school in Florida?" I asked him.

"More and more," he replied with a conspiratorial wink. "I have to get back before my customer hunts me down. I'll talk to you tonight?"

"I'll be here," I promised.

EIGHTEEN

THAT AFTERNOON, I tried out Dad's pool for the first time and decided there was nothing better in the world than floating on my back and staring up at the sky. Endlessly blue and expansive, no clouds dared to disturb my view of the relentless stream of planes departing or arriving in Orlando. Water trickled into the pool at the far end over a rock fountain, giving the impression of a solitary lagoon in the middle of a tropical oasis. With the birds calling in the background, I figured the description fit well.

From the edge of the pool, I admired the plants Mindy and I set earlier. When they bloomed, the petals would fill the rock garden with color. Would I still be in Florida or would I give in to the guilt eating me up? I wondered what my mother would say if I showed up back in New Jersey. If she'd be happy and forget about her fantasy abduction theory.

I imagined posters with my likeness on them stapled to the telephone poles in my neighborhood, next to a younger photo of my father. But wait—she'd have to go outside to hang the posters.

On the patio just outside the kitchen, Mindy was cooking something on the grill. Every once in a while, a whiff of sweet and spicy floated by. Whatever it was, I hoped she made a lot of it. I needed to eat in quantity and feel the expansion in my stomach drive out the deeper need.

The weird thing was, some days I wanted food, like today.

Dad's car door thumped in the driveway as I crawled out of the pool and wrapped myself with a huge green towel. I hoped Mindy wouldn't tell him I was short with her earlier. If he asked, I'd be thankful for the job and appreciative of their generosity, even if it choked me. I had one rule while I stayed here: behave, until you don't have to.

"Do you want me to do something?" I asked Mindy.

"I've got it, but you can grab the salad out of the refrigerator."

My hungry gaze swept over the table. The sweet barbeque scent belonged to the steaming plate of chicken. Beside the plate sat a bowl of browned potatoes and a dish of asparagus, something I'd always wanted to try just because it looked cool. A fruit salad and a pitcher of iced tea made the meal. "Do you guys always eat this way?" I asked her.

She seemed pleased. "Most nights," she said. "Tomorrow will be leftovers, but it always feels special when we eat out by the pool."

Kind of like me eating on the back porch to avoid the

rank of the nest. How many nights had I huddled out there in January or February, not caring how cold I was, as long as I didn't have to go back in the house?

I hurried inside to grab the salad and to avoid sinking into bad memories. Those times seemed a thousand birthdays ago, but Mom was still living in a debris field. Cue stomach flop. Great. So much for my appetite. The memory of her sitting in a pile of shredded *Gone with the Wind* novels set my stomach churning as I returned with the bowl of salad.

Dad came out of the house, dressed in shorts and a clean T-shirt, his hair damp from his quick shower. "Here are my girls," he said happily, as if our earlier argument never occurred—one big, happy family. He sniffed appreciatively. "Wait until you taste those potatoes, Shelly. I don't know what she puts on them, but they're irresistible."

I readjusted my towel and ground my teeth behind my smile. "They smell fantastic," I told him, a twinge of resentment filtering past my control.

"Is that the new suit you bought?" Dad asked, glancing at Mindy.

I specifically dressed in the one Mindy bought me, even though the strings attached to the scrap of fabric choked me. "Yeah. Uh, it's the one you bought. Thanks," I said.

"Oh, I forgot the extra barbeque sauce," Mindy said as she sat.

"I'll get it," I told her. I stood to head back to the kitchen. My beach towel snagged on my chair and yanked away. Mindy gasped and covered her mouth with her hand.

"Oops!" I quickly unhooked the end of the towel.

"Shelly, my God," Dad whispered.

I looked at them like they were crazy. "What?" Jeez, they were touchy about stuff. It's not like I was naked under it. The bathing suit was a two-piece, after all.

He grabbed my wrist as I walked by, his fingers swallowing the narrow bones. "When's the last time you went to a doctor?"

"I don't know. When I was a kid? Why? I don't need one." I caught Mindy's horrified stare. What the hell was up with them?

Dad released my wrist, and I headed to the kitchen. The barbeque sauce sat on the counter. Flustered by their reaction, I grabbed it and headed back outside. Dinner was quiet as I heaped my plate twice, packing away all the foods I never had the chance to eat before until I couldn't fit another bite. They observed me—Dad outright, Mindy more surreptitiously. What was up with them?

"Mindy said you got a job. I'm happy for you." He sipped his tea, his eyes never leaving my face. He wore the most confusing expression—one of fear and worry blended with anger. What had I done?

"Oh, yeah. I forgot. Beth wants me to start tomorrow," I said with a grimace. "Eight o'clock in the morning. Ugh."

"Okay. I can drop you off on the way to my office."

"And I'll pick you up," Mindy said as she began to clear the dishes.

"I'm going to go change so I can help with those," I told her, my insides starting to churn. They were going to have to run me back and forth to work, another burden to their life. At least I could do the dishes. Mom never washed a dish in her life. Was it wrong to look forward to the chance?

"Sounds good," she said, her eyes sad.

I rushed to my room and into my bathroom, turning on the shower in case I got loud. More black stuff. What the heck was wrong with me? When my stomach was empty, I washed my face, feeling faint. A new symptom. Normally, I just threw up and went on with my life. This was different, a profound weakness filtering to the ends of my fingers. I leaned against the sink, my eyes closed.

Breathe, I commanded my lungs. I dragged my body to the bed and collapsed in a shivering ball. *Get up, Shelly. Before they come looking for you.* Light-headed, I dressed in a baggy T-shirt and shorts and found Mindy starting to load the dishwasher. I scraped plates while she rinsed, and I learned where she kept the leftovers containers. If she noticed how shaky I was, she didn't say.

"I'm going to take care of some laundry," Mindy told me when we loaded the last dish. "Your dad's out back." The nudge in his direction might as well have been lit up in neon for all its subtlety.

He stood over the pool, using a long pole and hose to sweep the bottom. I sat on the edge with my feet in the water. "I'm glad you took the job, Shell. It'll be good for you."

I chewed my lip. "I like having my own money."

"Good. You're responsible." He paused while adding

chlorine tablets to the skimmer. "Maybe we should talk about a phone call I received today." He lifted the dripping vacuum from the pool and began to wind the hose.

"Uh, okay." I inhaled, filling my lungs with the clean scent of chlorine. Whatever he wanted to say wasn't good news.

"Your mother did call a lawyer about you. I got a phone call at the office. They're going to try to have me arrested." He shook his head.

"Arrested? For what?" Anxiety wrapped boney fingers around my burning throat. "What did you tell them?"

"For kidnapping you. I said, go ahead. I've done nothing wrong. I'm not keeping you here against your will. You came on your own. If you would've ripped up the ticket, I would've left you alone. But you're here, and I'm glad." His eyes met mine with worried anger. "Mindy warned me this could happen, but I don't care. I would do it again in an instant."

Crap, crap, crap. Mom lost it. Completely. Why would she do this? She imagined Joshua cutting her grass. There was only one explanation: her fragile hold on reality had slipped further. "Do you want me to talk to this lawyer? And tell him the truth?"

He tugged at his sweaty T-shirt. "It might come to that. If Mom and her lawyer do call the police, it will definitely come to that."

"Then everyone will know what she's doing," I said, horrified. What if it made the news? Joshua would see it. His aunt and uncle, too. Would I be the subject of an Amber Alert?

Dad sighed. "That's not what I wanted either. I wanted to give you a way out."

I nodded once, my gaze moving around the breathtaking backyard. Sunlight sparkled on the surface of the pool, and palms rustled in the afternoon breeze. Sudden terror raced through my veins. What if they made me go home?

"Dad, I don't want to live in that house. But I'm afraid of what's going to happen if she doesn't get what she wants."

"Me too." He heaved in a breath and exhaled as if the experience left him winded. "We'll see where this goes. Maybe nothing will come of it."

I imagined all the things that could go wrong, from the air conditioning giving out to the floor caving in under the weight of her nest. "Dad? Why don't you work in the yard? Mindy said you don't."

"It was our thing, you and me," he said. "When I came here, I didn't have the heart to work in the yard."

I blinked back sudden tears.

He dropped down beside me and slipped his feet into the pool. "Let's talk about you. I want to get you a car."

"I have a car, Dad. A friend is keeping it for me until I come back." Our eyes met. The longer I stayed here, the greater the chance I'd never return to New Jersey.

"Is your friend the boy?" he asked, wagging his eyebrows at me. I giggled in spite of the heavy mood. This was the Dad I remembered.

"Maybe. He's waiting for me to call him."

He slipped an arm around my shoulders. "Okay. Dad

can take a hint. But if you want your car, we can send for it."

I splashed my toes in the water, suddenly reluctant to leave the first meaningful conversation we'd been able to have. "Dad, what am I going to do? I don't know where I belong anymore. This feels like I'm invading your five-star hotel. I need to do something to help her."

He patted my knee. "Let me talk to my attorney. Those friends of mine at social services are working on it, too."

"Mindy is an attorney. She doesn't handle your stuff?"

"She is. But not this kind." He pulled me up from the side of the pool.

"Thanks," I told him, my chest tight.

"Bill? Could you give me a hand?" Mindy called from the house.

"Duty calls," he said and pecked me on the cheek.

When he was gone, I dried off my legs and headed for my room, my mind swirling with what-ifs. What if I stayed here? What if Mom got some counseling and straightened out her life? What if Joshua came to Florida for college? There were so many things we could do, places we could go. The beach, Disney World, Key West, Cape Canaveral. The list grew and grew.

Back home? Not so much. The grasping tentacles of the nest would never let me live.

I opened the FaceTime app and dialed Joshua. He answered after a couple of moments. His truck engine rumbled in the background. "Hey there, beautiful!"

He called me beautiful. Again. "Where are you going?" I asked, jealous I didn't know where he was headed.

He smirked. "Out delivering Paulie's passionate pizza, what else."

"I miss you," I blurted.

"I miss you, too. Everything okay?" He laid on the horn and waved at someone.

"Yeah, fine. Don't crash. This probably isn't safe."

"It's okay. I pulled over. How's your dad? He's not being a dick, is he?" The phone moved, and I caught sight of the insulated pizza delivery bags. I wondered if one was headed to my mother's house.

"No," I said, laughing. "He's been great, actually. He said we could bring my car down here. I told him I had a friend keeping it for me."

"A friend? Ah . . . that's what I've been reduced to."

"A very good friend," I teased.

"We'll see how you feel about my friendship next Friday," he said casually. "I'm coming down to look at Valencia College. I figured it might not be a bad idea to start in the spring."

"You are?" I flopped back on the bed, my heart bursting in my chest. Joshua was coming!

"Yep. Ready or not."

I held the phone closer to my face. "You see this smile? I'm ready."

"Good! We'll figure out the details. I gotta get to my next pizza drop." He pulled on his ball cap with a pizza slice on the front and gave me a wink. "Talk to you later."

"Bye," I said as the screen went dark and light burst into my world.

Joshua was coming to Florida. I wanted to run up and down the street doing cartwheels.

NINETEEN

AT SEVEN FORTY-FIVE the next morning, I reported for work at Beth's nursery wearing the only pair of jeans I brought and my other clean T-shirt, which instantly sweat-welded itself to my back. Mindy promised to take me shopping at a regular mall on the weekend. Until then, I would do a lot of laundry.

"Hi, Shelly!" Beth waved me over, her face already rosy with heat. "Is that your lunch?"

I held up the bright yellow insulated sack I borrowed from Mindy. "Yeah."

"Come into the office. I'll show you where the refrigerator and water cooler are. Make sure you keep drinking, especially if you're not used to this weather. Take it easy these first few days until you can handle the heat. Take breaks, as many as you need, no questions asked."

"Okay, thanks." I stored my lunch where she told me to. The office felt icy compared to the furnace outside. "What time do I need to have Mindy pick me up?"

"Three. Oh, don't worry. I'll text her." She handed me

a folder of papers. "Fill these out so we can make sure you get paid. After, come on outside. You're on watering duty today."

I filled out the application and tax information as fast as I could and headed outside to find her. She stood beside a small ATV fitted with a trailer. A plastic cube filled with water sat on the bed. My eyes widened. The cube had horns, brown floppy ears, and two big, bulging eyes.

Beth noticed my amazement and laughed. "We call it the water buffalo. The kids get a kick out of it." She pointed to the back end. "See? It's even got a tail. We call him Bob."

I covered my giggle with my hand. "Bob the water buffalo?"

She smiled at me. "Can you drive one of these?"

"Yeah. I've driven one before." The Quick-Serve purchased one to make trash pickup around the property easier, until someone stole it. But who needed an ATV when they had a Joshua?

"Good!" She explained the layout of the nursery. "We irrigate every night, but I've got a couple of rows that never seem to get enough and get shocky in this heat. Also, some newly dug palms need some TLC. Those will be your responsibility." Beth pointed to the left toward a shell-and-gravel path between towering potted palms. "If you follow this path, you'll get to the end of the nursery rows I'm most concerned about. They're marked with orange flags. Start watering there and work your way back. Be generous. In this heat, we need to water heavily. I usually water twenty feet down and repeat to make sure they're soaked. You should use at least five containerfuls of water on this one row."

The cube was taller than I was. It had to hold fifty gallons. Times five? "Where do I fill it back up?"

"This way." She gestured for me to follow. We stopped beside a huge greenhouse. "Right here. Set both garden hoses in the cube and take a bathroom and drink break. It takes a while to fill. Make sure you fill your bottle, too."

I held up my insulated bottle. "Got it."

"When you finish this row, I have eight other rows needing water. We rotate, two rows a day, so everything gets extra water at least once every four days." She checked her phone. "I have a call I have to take. You get started. Watch out for snakes. If you find one, steer clear."

"Snakes," I whispered as she walked away. I was used to the little striped garter snakes scaring the heck out of me in my flower beds back home. But this was Florida, and they had the dangerous kinds of snakes. Venomous nasties. Pythons that could swallow me whole.

I hopped on the ATV and pressed the start button. I engaged the throttle and puttered down the row, amazed at the length of the path and the variety of plants Beth sold. No wonder it took all day to water one row. There had to be a half mile of thirsty plants.

"Come on, Bob. We've got a job to do," I said and patted the buffalo between the eyes.

It took fifteen minutes for me to figure out how to make the hose spray, but after Bob decided to cooperate, things moved swiftly. By the time I returned for my third cube of water, I felt confident in my abilities as a water bearer. *Here I am! The Age of Aquarius!*

I lifted my gaze to the sky. The sun fiercely beat on my head and sweat trickled down my back to soak the waist-band of my jeans. Mid-morning, Beth appeared out of nowhere with a wide-brimmed straw hat, which I grate-fully accepted.

Swarms of gnats and mosquitos followed me later in the day. Heavy-duty, industrial bug spray—that's what I needed. Something with a dead bug on the can and a money-back guarantee. By lunchtime, I was shaky and starved. I filled my water bottle and retrieved my lunch bag. Beside the office sat a picnic table, and I lounged in the shade, picking at my sandwich. At least the fruit salad tasted good. The few bites I choked down tumbled around in my gut. Better go light on the food. With only one bathroom for all her employees, I didn't need to get sick in between the rows and have to answer questions.

I was filling my water bottle when Beth walked into the office, fanning her face. "Bugs are getting bad out there today. I bet we're in for some rain tonight. Good for the plants, bad for us." She pointed to a shelf. "We've got some stuff to keep them off you. Have a spray before you head back out." Beth removed her hat and sprayed under the brim.

"Thanks," I said as I stored the remnants of my lunch in the small refrigerator.

Like Beth had done, I sprayed the underside of my hat, my neck, and my arms.

"Long pants are a good idea, but make sure you don't overheat. You might want to switch to a lighter material."

"I'll go with shorts tomorrow," I told her.

"You're doing a good job. I checked the row. Things look good and wet." She patted my arm as she left.

I smiled and headed back out to wrangle my buffalo. The humidity hit me in the face and sucked the air out of my lungs. How did Joshua mow in this all summer? But Jersey heat and Deep South heat were two totally different things.

Pride filled my chest. I couldn't wait to tell him about my first day on the job.

By two thirty, I finished my row. Beth told me to clean up the yard, and I organized the long, low shopping wagons and picked up the occasional piece of trash. When Mindy pulled in to get me, I was relieved and ready to go home. My arms and legs shook from the physical exertion.

"Same time tomorrow, Beth?" I called.

"Yes! Great job today!" She waved and took off after a customer whose small children played hide-and-seek around the potted palms. Didn't they know about the snakes?

"Well, you look like you had a fun first day," Mindy said, laughing.

I glanced down at my clothes and joined her. Mud smeared my jeans, and I was soaked from the waist down thanks to the splash-back from the watering cube.

"You look hot, too," she added.

I pulled off my sweaty hat and fanned my face, glad to sit in the air-conditioned car. "Yeah. It's brutal today. I'm not used to it. I feel like a wimp." I turned the vent to point it directly at me. "I can't wait to jump in the pool."

"It takes a couple of years to get used to it. I used to

live in the Midwest. St. Louis area. By August, I'll be ready to head up there and visit my sister for a break." She pointed ahead. "I'm going to pull into Starbucks. Do you want anything?"

"Yes. A black tea lemonade," I said, fanning like crazy. "Unsweetened. Lots of ice."

WHEN I SHOWERED and felt human again, I called Joshua to video chat, but there was no answer. I frowned at the phone as I texted him.

Hello?

Joshua:

Knock, knock

Joshua:

Where was he? Had he been to my mother's house to deliver pizza or cut the grass? Did he buy his plane ticket yet? There were so many questions I wanted to ask him, but they would have to wait until he called me back.

I lay back on the bed and watched the ceiling fan spin, glad to rest after my first day, and wondered what it would be like to have him here for a while. Where would he stay? Maybe my father would open the guest bedroom. How awkward would it be for Dad and Mindy to have my boyfriend here? In truth, I was as much of a stranger to them. But I'd eventually fit in here. So would Joshua.

Raised voices in front of the house drew me out of my room. Dad's and another male voice. My heart sank. A police car sat in front of the house. Mindy observed the scene from the front window, her eyes dark with anger.

She'd actually done it. Mom called the cops.

"What happened?" I whispered to Mindy.

She shook her head. "I don't know. They asked for your dad."

When I opened the door, Dad yelled over his shoulder, "Go back inside, Shelly." His scarlet face frightened me. I had never witnessed him this way, this furious.

Still, I ignored him and walked up to the police officers, a male and a female. The woman looked way more agitated than he did.

"Are you Shelly Frank?" she asked.

"Yes, why?" I glanced from one officer to the other, planting an annoyed hand on my hip and pretending my heart wasn't thundering in my veins. What if they made me leave? Took me back to Jersey?

I won't go, I won't go, I won't go.

"Would you like to come with us?" the woman asked, her wary gaze on my father. One of my father's neighbors decided this was a good time to go walk the dog.

"Not really. Why?"

The officers exchanged a surprised glance. "Your mother has reported you missing."

I laughed in my throat. "Is that so? Did she tell you she threw me out, and I had to sleep in my car until I could get here?"

The last comment shut them up. "She reported you abducted in a child custody matter," the male officer said.

"Well, she's lying," I told him.

"Shelly, you don't have to say anything," Dad began,

his voice threaded with warning. I shook my head. This ended here and now. My mother didn't get to do this to me anymore.

"Dad. It's okay. They need to know what's going on." I stuffed my shaking hands in my pockets. "Well? Did she tell you she tossed me out?"

The man, a tall mountain of a guy with a tattoo of a lion on his forearm, checked his clipboard. "No. I bet she didn't."

"I figured. My father sent me a plane ticket for my birthday and invited me to come here for a while. I told my mother I wanted to go, and she threw me out. So, I came here by myself. I didn't have anywhere else to live." My voice ended in a strained choke.

The officers exchanged a weary glance, and the woman sighed. "Wait here," she said as she returned to the car.

"I'm sorry about this," I told the police officer, holding up my hands and drudging up a truly repentant expression. "I didn't have anywhere else to go."

He narrowed his eyes. "How old are you?"

"Seventeen," I said.

The officer nodded. "This stuff happens all the time."

We waited while the woman spoke to someone on the phone. When she ended the call, she came back. "Okay. Someone from social services will be out to talk with you. Right now, I'm going to call this a domestic misunderstanding pending investigation." She leveled a look at me. "Do you have anyone who can confirm your story?"

"Yes. My boyfriend." I pulled out my phone and gave

them Joshua's number. "He helped me out when my mother told me to leave. He's keeping my car for me."

The male officer handed me his clipboard for my signature. "Okay, folks. We'll get in touch with them and wrap this up. Someone will call you," he said before they retreated back to the car.

Mindy stepped out onto the porch.

As they pulled away, my father's ire erupted. "She's gone too far this time."

"Bill," Mindy protested as he threw up a hand.

The police car rolled down the street, and the dog walker decided the show was over.

"Dad, please. Don't make it worse." In his current state of mind, I worried he'd call the police back home. Then, they'd go to the house. Shame burned acidly in my stomach while the need to protect how I survived all those years sank its claws in my back. "If you let people know what she's like, they'll believe the same about me." My body shook and weakness flooded my limbs. Spots burst like the Fourth of July in my vision, and I swayed on my feet.

"Shell?" Dad grabbed my arm.

"I'm okay. I got overheated today. I just need to sit down." I leaned on him, my legs suddenly liquid.

He and Mindy hustled me into the house and deposited me on the couch directly under the ceiling fan. The earth dipped and rolled along with my stomach. The only thing in me was my lemonade tea, and it was coming up. I pushed off the couch and staggered to the hall bathroom.

Outside the door, I found them waiting for me.

"I'm okay," I said again.

"You're white as a sheet," Mindy said. She pressed a hand to my cheek.

"How long have you been having these stomach problems?" Dad asked, his anger deflated by his concern for me.

It was on my tongue to say, "since you left," but I held the retort in check because it wasn't true. I stopped eating the pizza Mom bought, which began this mess with my stomach. The pizza fixation began a little over a month ago, maybe two. "A while," I said.

"I want you to go to a doctor." He touched my forehead as if feeling for a fever.

I shoved his hand away. "Enough with the touching. I'm fine. I didn't eat a lot today, and it was blazing hot." I gestured to the street. "That didn't help." A subtle tactic, dropping the blame back on my mother, but it did the trick. Dad backed off about my puking and refocused on dealing with what she'd done.

"Go lay down until dinner," he told me. "I have something I need to take care of."

Behind my door, I listened to the hushed but heated conversation in the hallway. My name was mentioned several times, but they never came back.

Good. Leave me the hell alone.

I lost track of the days while I'd been here, and it took me a few minutes to figure out whether it was Wednesday or Thursday. I decided it was Wednesday. Joshua didn't deliver pizzas at Paulie's on Wednesday. We'd be able to talk without a delivery coming between us.

But when I picked up my phone, I found a dozen texts

from him, telling me he'd been invited to spend a couple of days at a friend's lake house before he left to head south. Another text told me his cell phone service would be sketchy.

I sat on my bed, holding the phone in my hands as tears dripped off my chin, unrealistically fuming since he was out of contact. Would there be other girls at the lake? What if he changed his mind about me?

My chest constricted until I could barely breathe. Suddenly, I missed my mother so violently, I could barely stand it. Without thinking, I dialed our home phone number. She picked up after twenty or more rings.

"Hello?" Her voice sounded pensive.

I closed my eyes. "Mom? It's Shelly."

"Shelly! Where are you? Are you all right? Why didn't you call me?"

It would do no good to remind her she hung up on me the last time I talked to her. I lay back on the bed, fighting the spinning sensation in my skull and the relentless thump behind my eye sockets. If a bottle of pain killers suddenly appeared, I'd eat them all.

"Yeah, Mom. I'm fine. I'm still at Dad's. You know this, remember?"

"I don't know what you're talking about. Why are you there? Why aren't you here?"

Fresh tears smarted in the corners of my eyes. How could she forget? I cleared my throat. She didn't need to hear me upset. "I'm fine. I wanted to make sure you're okay."

"Don't you worry about me."

I gripped the phone. "Mom, I'm staying here for a while."

"What do you mean, staying?"

"I'm spending time with Dad. I told you this. The other day." I left out the part about her attacking me. No reason to add fuel to the fire.

There was a moment of shuffling on the other end of the phone. "He can't keep you. I sent some people to get you out of there. They'll rescue you. You'll see. He's got no right to keep you there against your will!"

Breathing in, I struggled to calm my voice. "Mom, they were here. The police came to the house. I sent them away." Silence on the line. "Mom? Did you hear me?"

"Why? Don't you want to come home?"

My heart cracked through my ribs, making it difficult to breathe. So many things I wanted and needed to say battled for control of my voice. *I want you to clean up the house. I want you to be normal. I want you to take me to Starbucks, not some woman I just met. I want you to care about me more than you care about the dump pile you live in.* "I can't come home. Not until things change."

"Change? What do you mean change?"

There was no easy way to say it. "I can't live in the house the way it is. It's making me sick. It's got to be making you sick, too. It needs to be cleaned out. I need it to be normal, like a normal house." Mom might not have a lot of money to spare, but poverty didn't mean we couldn't clean the house up. Especially if I kept working two jobs. We could paint, buy new rugs, a dumpster.

"There's nothing wrong with this house, Shelly. You're just a spoiled brat," she snapped.

I sat up so quickly, the room tipped to the left. I held on to the edge of the bed. "Mom, it's full of garbage. You can't live this way."

"I can live however I like, and you're my daughter. I can make you live here. You're not eighteen." Her threat hung in the air, swirling around my head like the stink of her four-day-old pizza. It was hollow, empty. She couldn't make good on it, and I wouldn't let her. I'd send the cops away every time they showed up. Worse, I would eventually have to tell someone why I wouldn't go back to my mother's house, and the truth was the one threat I could wield.

"Mom, listen to me. If you keep sending the police here, I'm going to tell them how you live. They'll come to your house and take you away."

She gasped. I hung up.

For several minutes, I sat on my bed grappling with the truth—my life with my mother was truly finished. I'd never go back to New Jersey—never again live in the sunny, yellow house with the cancer growing inside of it. If I had to, I'd return long enough to get my car and transfer schools. I wondered if I would ever be able to speak to her again.

I found my father sitting at his desk in the office, staring out the window at the backyard. I knocked gently on the doorframe. When his gaze turned to me, I asked, "Can I come in?"

He nodded.

"I talked to Mom." I scrubbed a hand over my eyes and nose. "I told her I wasn't coming back. I told her if she sent the cops here again, I would tell them why I left her."

Dad took my hand and held it. For a long time, neither of us spoke.

"I'm sorry, Shelly. I really am." He released my fingers, removed his glasses, and set them on the desk, then pinched the bridge of his nose as if his head wanted to explode. "This is out of control."

"I can't make her see sense."

"You have to know how hard I tried, Shell. I wanted our marriage to work. I loved your mom and you more than anything." Dad wiped his eyes. "I am so, so very sorry I left you there. I love you so much. It wasn't right. I'll never be able to say I'm sorry enough."

It was my turn to squeeze his hand. I struggled for words. "There's more to it. She's worse, Dad. She doesn't remember things she said a day ago. Like she doesn't remember telling me to leave or talking to me the other night." Tears fell on my cheeks, and I sucked in a sob. "I'm afraid for her. Really freaking afraid."

Dad stood and gathered me into his arms. I cried into his fresh-smelling shirt until the linen was damp. He smoothed my hair with his strong hand as the hole in my heart tore wider. This was what I lost all those years ago when Mom's illness forced him out of our lives. My father, my protector.

"So, now what?" I asked him when I cried myself out. I never had anyone I could say that to—an adult who could make the decisions I didn't want to face when there was no one to act as a buffer.

"We'll make it official. I'll start transferring your school records here. We'll get your car picked up."

"Maybe Joshua could drive it down," I said as a sudden spark of hope burned through the pain.

"Joshua, huh?" He smiled down at me while I wiped the tears away.

"Yeah, that's him. He's coming down next Friday to look at a school. He's thinking about going to college near here."

He smirked, the wry kind of lip twist I associated with kids conniving behind their parents' backs. "Well. That's convenient. Maybe he'll drive your car down. If not, we'll make other arrangements." Dad stared into my eyes. "Does he need a place to stay while he's here?"

Hope flooded my heart. "Maybe. I could ask him."

"Tell him he's welcome here. We've got the room," he said.

"Thanks, Dad," I said around the tightness in my throat. I didn't need to start crying again, but I wanted to.

He gave me a quick squeeze. "Let's go tell Mindy. She'll be thrilled. Someone else to cook for."

TWENTY

ON THE FOLLOWING MONDAY, I just finished my first watering row when Beth paged me to the office. Towering, white thunderheads gathered on the horizon, and the afternoon promised to be stormy. Bugs swarmed around my head as the ATV bounced and the half-full cube sloshed behind me. Even Buffalo Bob's tail looked wilted and ready for rain. It was perfect timing to head in. I had to pee, and my water bottle was skunky warm.

Brassy air scorched my skin as thunderheads collided and morphed in the distance, thousands of feet above the endlessly flat terrain. Could it be getting hotter? Was I hallucinating from heatstroke? Maybe it would rain soon, and I wouldn't have to water the other rows.

"Hey, Beth. What's up?"

She slanted her head toward the office. "There's someone to see you."

"Uh, okay," I said and climbed the steps.

Inside the icy artificial atmosphere of the trailer, a professionally dressed woman waited in one of Beth's quaint, mismatched wooden chairs. She wore a pale coral dress beneath a long, navy sweater. A sweater? On a day like today? She half-smiled at me with kind but suspicious eyes.

"Are you Shelly Frank?" she asked.

I nodded and glanced around. "Yes. Do you need help loading your car?"

Her right-side dimple deepened with amusement. "No. I'm here from the Florida Department of Children and Families about your situation."

My boss picked an unfortunate moment to open the door and step inside. "There you are. I see you've found each other." Her eyes took in the scene, drifting from me to the social worker.

"Uh, yeah." Did she know why this woman was here? The lump in my throat tried to choke me.

"Is there somewhere private we can talk?" the woman asked me.

"Can I use your office, Beth?" I asked, my voice as stiff as my spine. "It's okay," I assured her. "It'll only take a minute. I can stay later to make up the time."

My boss waved the idea away. "That's all right, Shelly." She turned to the woman, and her eyes were suspiciously appraising. "Sure. You can use the office next to the water cooler." The set of her lips told me she didn't want to leave me alone with the woman, but I turned quickly and led the way back to the open office. The fewer questions Beth asked, the better. She'd likely text Mindy the second she could.

I opened the door and flicked on the lights. Landscape design plans and ordering catalogs lay scattered across the conference table. The woman sat waiting while I brushed them into a pile.

"What do you want?" I was hot, tired, and cranky. Not at all in the chatting-about-my-mother mood.

She held up a hand. "Shelly, I'm on your side. Remember that. In all of this. Your mother contacted the local police, and they contacted me." The woman pulled a card from her quilted, leather tote bag. Her name was Tricia Benson. Her title, Investigator.

"I know what she did. The police came to our house last week. I told them I didn't need their help." I shivered in the air-conditioned chill as my shirt turned clammy.

She removed a pen and notebook from her bag. My name and address were written on the top of the page. "Sit down, please. You look like you need a rest. Do you want to tell me what's going on? Why would your mother report you abducted from New Jersey?"

Cold sweat dripped down my back and I sighed. *Here we go again.* I dropped into a seat, grateful for the break. If I had to tell this woman my life story, I might as well get something out of it.

"I told the police all this when they came to the house. My mother threw me out the day before my birthday. I slept in my car. My dad sent me a plane ticket. Now, I'm here."

Tricia wrote in her notebook, then shifted her gaze to mine. "Why did your mother ask you to leave?"

I shifted my aching feet under the table. "We had a fight," I told her, wondering how much detail I had to give her to get her to leave.

"About?" Tricia leaned forward expectantly.

I bit the inside of my cheek. "A lot of things. We weren't getting along."

She tilted her head to the side. "Lots of teens argue with their parents." Tricia paused before adding, "Are you aware your father has called our sister agencies in New Jersey with concerns for your mother's well-being?"

"Yes."

"Why would he try to help her?" she asked.

"Ask him. I don't know." I stared at the door, willing Beth to come in and check on me.

Tricia lifted her eyebrows. "You lived with your mother for many years after your father moved out of state. Yet, he called social services for your mother now that you are living with him. How would he know something was happening with your mother unless you told him?"

My heart hammered in my chest as I stared at the cracked tabletop. "I need to get back." I moved to rise, but Tricia stood to stop me.

"Not until we're done here. You're still a minor, and I have to make a determination about whether or not you should be returned to New Jersey to your mother's care. Your parents' divorce decree gave your mother custody. As of right now, your father is interfering with a court-ordered custody agreement." She let the threat hover in the air. "Now, do you want to explain to me why you're here?"

She backed me into a corner so tight, the walls towered over my head and shut out the sun. "I can't live with my mother," I stalled. "It's difficult."

Tricia took out her phone. "I'm going to record this conversation."

A light blinked on the front of her phone. She stated my name, hers, the date, and the location of our conversation before passing the phone toward me.

"Now, explain the complications of living with your mother. Please."

I swallowed, feeling the blinking light pulse with the blood in my veins. "My mother is a hoarder."

Tricia appeared stunned. "A hoarder?"

"Yes," I whispered. "It's why my dad left. It's why I left."

Her pen scrawled across the notebook. "Your mother has hoarding disorder."

I shrugged. It didn't matter what she labeled it. It was as awful as it sounded.

"How bad is it?" she asked me gently.

Licking my lips, I struggled with how much to tell her. "Is this confidential?" I gestured to the phone recording my secrets.

"For now. It may become part of a court record later if we must go that route. It depends on my recommendation." This statement felt less like a threat and more like a nudge. But what choice did I have?

"It's bad. Horrible bad. I can't . . . the smell. I can't live there." I leaned across the table, anxiety battering the inside of my stomach with baseball bats. "Please. Please, you have to understand what it's like."

After a drawn-out moment, Tricia reached for her phone and clicked the recorder off. "Your father has set some things in motion in New Jersey. He seems to believe your mother is a danger to herself."

Stomach acid bubbled beneath my rib cage, eating at the sore spots. "He's right," I said softly. "I talked with her, but she didn't make sense, like she didn't remember recent things. She didn't remember the fight or asking me to leave." My fingers brushed aside the tears.

Tricia sighed. "All right. My recommendation will be for you to stay here until we sort more of this out. I've got some calls to make. Maybe get your mother some help."

"Please don't let her know I told you." Panic bled into my voice.

You told. You're going to be the reason Mom loses the house. Where will she go?

"You're planning to stay in Florida indefinitely?" Tricia's gaze pinned me to my seat. Was she looking for lies?

After my call to my mother last night, and my betrayal of her secret, I was left with little choice. "Yes. Dad's going to enroll me in school here for my senior year."

"And you have a job? How long have you worked here?"

I shook my nearly empty water bottle. "I started last Wednesday."

Tricia reached for her bag. "I'm sorry about coming here. I hope this doesn't cause problems for you in your new job."

"It will be okay. My boss is a friend of my stepmother."

Her eyes narrowed as she paused. "How's your relationship with her?"

"Fine. Mindy's been great." She's everything I wish my mother was to me.

She closed her notebook and slid it into her bag. "Good. It sounds like you're going to be fine here. Hang on to my card; if you need anything, I'm a phone call away. We'll monitor the situation until you turn eighteen."

"Thank you," I replied. The day couldn't come soon enough.

"Once you're a legal adult, you will be able to make your own decisions on these matters." She shook my hand and left.

I filled my water bottle and sat shivering in the frigid office, dreading hours of toil in the tropical murk. The weight of what I told the social worker pressed me into the chair with a flat hand of betrayal. I wanted to go home and hide in my sweet-smelling room, in my father's beautiful house, and stare out the skylight at the clouds. I wanted to talk to Joshua, but he was out of touch. Maybe I should tell Beth I didn't feel well. I could call Mindy to come and get me.

Don't be a wimp. Two hours left on this shift. I could do two more hours.

My boss was on the phone in the outer office when I headed for the door. "Hey, Shelly. Wait a minute." I stood quietly while she wrapped up her call. "Everything okay? You looked upset. Do you want me to call Mindy? Or your dad?"

"I'm fine. Thanks for letting me use the office." I wasn't about to offer her information about my messed-up personal life. Hopefully, my stepmother kept the details to herself and did not share them with my boss.

"You didn't take lunch today," she chided me. "You should take a break and get out of the heat."

"I'm all cooled off now. And I have some snacks with me," I lied. "The heat kills my appetite." I smiled and shrugged.

She shook her head and patted her ample thigh. "You young girls. I don't know how you do it. I used to be thin, but that was twenty years ago."

"I've got half of a row left to water," I told her.

"Sounds good. I filled up the cube, so you and Bob are ready to roll. Unfortunately, those storms passed us by."

"Thanks. I'll finish up."

I drove the ATV down a row of short palms, barely up to my shoulders. I longed for the tall trees I watered last week. At least I'd been in and out of the shade. Adjusting my hat, I unwound the hose and watered one side of the row and then the other.

In the relentless heat, I quickly depleted my bottle of drinking water. Under my hat, small gnats refused to be thwarted by the generous spray of bug repellent. Hot, sticky, and miserable, I shot a spray of water over my back until my T-shirt stuck to my skin. A sudden wave of dizziness hit me, followed by a blast of chills, and I gripped the edge of the trailer. Maybe I should head back to the office. Beth had been right about my lack of food. But how could I eat after meeting with Tricia Benson?

My empty stomach clenched, and I vomited all the water I drank. Except this time dark globs of blood peppered the ground. I wiped my mouth on my hand and stared horrified at the crimson stain. *Crap. That's not good.* The ground swayed like the bucking deck of a ship, and I staggered up the path. Chills raced up my arms, and I dropped to my knees, heaving up nothing but blood and mucus as I crawled toward the ATV, sharp gravel ripping into my knees.

Buffalo Bob stared at me with his sappy eyes.

Strength failed as my vision went white, bright as the center of the sun. I grabbed for the seat of the ATV, begging my arms to pull, to lift me one more time, long enough to land in the seat, but my fingers wouldn't grasp. Drawn into ineffectual claws, they slipped from the seat, and I fell back ... back ...

Onto the ground. My hat lost, I stared up at the unforgiving sun as my body finally and completely revolted.

TWENTY-ONE

I WOKE UP—THE first thing that amazed me.

The second? I wasn't hot anymore.

My sticky eyelids unpeeled a lash at a time, and I tried to make sense of what I saw and felt. Pale-gray walls, a blind-covered window. Cool sheets beneath my rough fingertips caught on my frayed cuticles. The soft hum of air conditioning. A television on the wall, switched off.

I rolled my neck toward the right. Stark scenery told me where I landed.

A hospital. Fuzzy memories vied for space in my cluttered, exhausted mind. IV fluids dripped into my arm. A small bouquet of flowers sat beside the bed, and my lips lifted a fraction. A vase full of flowers with a single Bird of Paradise blossom.

I didn't need to read the card to know Mindy had a hand in those. Beside it sat two dozen roses in a glass vase and a tiny white teddy bear.

How long had I been asleep since I collapsed at the nursery? My body moved in spasmodic jerks as if each finger and toe were weighed down against the bed with boulders. What was wrong with me? I felt disconnected. Upended. Memories returned in scattered, jagged bits, but before I could fully understand their significance, they melted like ice chips in the palm of my hand.

I remembered being at the nursery, watering in the sun. I remembered Tricia Benson coming to see me. The unbearable heat and the ATV. Then I got sick and lost all my water.

The blood. A groan escaped my throat. *Not good.*

With clumsy fingers, I fished around in the bed. There had to be a nurse call button somewhere, but my fingers didn't want to cooperate. So tired. I dragged the remote to my lap and used two hands to depress the switch. *Somebody help me . . .*

Minutes later, a young, pretty nurse with glowing brown skin breezed into the room. "You're awake. It's about time!"

I blinked as I brushed my thick tongue over my cracked lips. "How long," I croaked out, "was I asleep?"

"Two days," she told me as she reached for my wrist. "The doctor is on her way to check on you. I'll call your folks and let them know."

"My dad," I whispered. "Just my dad."

She nodded as she checked my pulse. "Okay. I'll be back," she promised.

"Can I have water?" I pried my tongue from the roof of my mouth.

"Some ice chips maybe. We'll take it easy for a bit, okay?"

She hurried out of the room but left the door partially

open. Across the powder-blue hall, a woman slept in a dark brown chair beside another patient's bed.

My mind whirled. Two days. I'd been out so long? At least Joshua was at the lake and not trying to reach me. I glanced around, but my phone didn't seem to be in the room.

How would I explain all this to my father? My sudden illness. My vomiting. Did my mother know what happened? What about the social worker? Did this change whether or not I could stay with my father?

Anxiety wrapped its claw-tipped fingers around my throat, but I was too weak to bat them away. I was just about to hit the call button again when the door opened, and a woman I suspected was the doctor entered. She wore a floral-patterned dress beneath her white coat. Her long, dark hair was gathered in a twist at her nape, and dark, intelligent eyes betrayed her relief I was finally conscious.

"Shelly? I'm Doctor Peters. It's good to see you awake." She handed me a cup of ice before she checked the IV and my pulse. "How do you feel?"

"Tired," I said. I slipped a chip between my lips and closed my eyes. The water trickled down my throat but felt funny on the way down. "Thanks." My voice came out raw and hoarse.

"You suffered heatstroke. Dehydration and malnutrition caused by a perforated stomach ulcer. It's why you've had trouble eating and keeping food down," she said.

"An ulcer?"

"Have you noticed blood when you've vomited? It might have looked like coffee grounds."

I nodded. "Can't keep it down," I rasped. "I can't."

"How long has your reflux been going on?"

"A couple of months." When *was* the last time I kept a full meal down? Or allowed myself to eat more than a few bites, worried the outcome would be less than stellar?

Dr. Peters pulled over a chair and sat beside me. "I have to ask you some serious questions, and I need the answers to help you get well. You're not eating, and your weight is dangerously low as a result. Do you also purge?"

I stared at her. What was she talking about? "Huh?"

"Purge? Do you force yourself to throw up?"

Forced vomiting was how this mess started. I swallowed thickly. "No. It just happens when my stomach hurts."

"Do you eat every day?"

"A little. I try." Tears collected at the corners of my eyes. At home, I usually ate pretzels to settle my stomach if I went to the Quick-Serve, where I could be sure what I consumed hadn't passed its expiration date by a few centuries. But on days I didn't work, meals were another story. Some days living in my mother's house, I ate nothing because I couldn't. Days when the reek of pizza turned my stomach inside out, and I couldn't force myself to heat up a can of soup. I hid my illness in my room from a mother who no longer saw me.

Here, at my father's house, I'd been able to eat a bit more, but my stomach refused food like poison. Every time I put something foreign past my lips, the remembered stench of fouled pizza clogged my throat. "What's with the ulcer?" I asked.

"It's been repaired. You have some stitches, but we

were able to repair it with a patch, laparoscopically. You'll have to take it easy for a while. We'll have you on a liquid diet for a while until we're sure you can tolerate soft foods."

My brain swam. I suspected I would have fainted if I weren't lying down. "How did this happen?"

"Ulcers are caused by bacteria. It's kind of like a sore that doesn't heal. Over time, and with the disruptions to your diet, it got worse until the ulcer caused a hole in your stomach. That's the blood you've seen." Dr. Peter's expression turned grim. "You are a very sick girl, Shelly, but very lucky. Bleeding and perforations like this can be life-threatening. And your weight loss is a factor. You were ninety-seven pounds when you came in here, but you've gained a few thanks to the replacement fluids. You should be thankful you woke up at all. Right now, you're at least twelve pounds underweight for your height. Your body mass index should be a minimum of seventeen point five. Yours is somewhere in the fifteen range. You have esophageal damage due to the vomiting. It's not pretty down there, and I can understand why you're having trouble keeping food down."

Shocked into silence, I said nothing.

The doctor leaned closer to the bed and dropped her voice. "There's no easy way to say this. Now that we've fixed your ulcer, we need to fix your eating."

I tried to make sense of what she said.

Her brow furrowed into deep ridges over her chestnut eyes. Dr. Peters leaned in even closer, resting her forearms on her thighs. "You're seventeen. I had your previous medical records faxed to me from New

Jersey. You haven't been to a doctor in almost five years. Why?'

She flipped through my chart when I refused to answer. "Your school records show your height and weight in three of those years. You've grown almost four inches, but not gained an ounce. When did you start to lose weight? I'm trying to get a sense of when this started."

"I started having pain a few months ago. Antacids made it better for a while. I took ibuprofen to help."

"Ah, that's a problem. Pain relievers like ibuprofen make ulcers worse. It's going to take a while for you to get back on your feet. We've given you a temporary feeding tube." My hands went to my stomach, but nothing protruded. Dr. Peters shook her head.

"Not that kind. It's in your nose."

I reached for my mouth, bumping the thin tube in the process. It pressed against the inside of my nostril. I gagged as I felt it brush the inside of my throat, suddenly aware of its presence. My fingers grasped the tube, prepared to yank the foul thing from my body.

"Take it easy, Shelly." Dr. Peters gently moved my hands away from my face. "Just breathe. That's it. Deep breaths."

I closed my eyes, choking and retching.

"Try not to think about it. Just swallow normally. There you go," she said as the panicked sensation subsided, and I slumped back against the pillows. "Do you feel nauseated?" she asked, her gaze narrowed on me.

"No," I lied. I wanted to puke everything I'd ever eaten up. I had a piece of plastic jammed in my stomach.

"I need to ask you some questions about what led up to your perforation—the hole in your stomach. Did you take a lot of over-the-counter pain killers?"

If there was one thing my mother excelled at, it was headache generation. I lived on pain meds to dull the pounding behind my eyes. "I took some," I said.

"Daily?"

"Sometimes."

"Do you smoke? Use alcohol frequently?"

I shook my head.

"That's good. But you're under a lot of stress from what I understand."

"You could say that," I murmured.

"That could be how this started. Add in overuse of NSAIDs, stress, and poor diet, and you have an outcome like this. We're giving you some medications to ease the discomfort, as well as to help regulate your mood and heal your ulcer. The liquid diet you've been on has been tolerated better than I hoped. You'll continue liquids for a few more days, then we'll remove the tube. I want you to try to take some clear foods—gelatin, things you can easily digest. Then we'll move on to yogurt and some nutrient shakes. Maybe even some bland fruits. If there's something specific you want, we'll check with the dietician." She paused as she stood.

"My mood? What mood?"

"Depression. Anxiety. They're big parts of your illness."

"Where's my dad?" I asked her, my throat thick with tears. I wouldn't cry in front of her. I wouldn't.

"He's on his way. And your stepmom." Dr. Peters

replaced the chart at the end of my bed. "Your mother lives up north?"

I nodded.

"I believe your father contacted her."

"Great." I licked my lips, wincing as my tongue brushed the tube.

"Not a good relationship there?" Dr. Peters asked.

"No." A blanket of grogginess threatened to take me down. How could I be tired? I'd slept for two days.

The door opened and a young woman with a thin face and slight build entered the room. She was dressed in a pale-pink sweater and faded jeans with an ID badge clipped to the edge of her shirt. The doctor smiled at her and warmly shook her hand in greeting.

"Marie, this is Shelly Frank. I'm hoping the two of you could get to know each other today." She turned toward me. "Now that you're awake."

"Hi, Shelly," Marie said. I tried to decide how old she was, but I couldn't tell. From the slight crinkling in the corners of her sparkling green eyes, she was older than I was. Her blond hair fell in a pale curtain around her shoulders, and her skin glowed with tanned health.

Exactly the opposite of how I felt: worn-out and bleached of color, barely able to move. "Hi," I replied, instantly suspicious. Was this another social worker? Someone new from family services?

Dr. Peters gazed down at me. "We've also set an appointment up with a dietician for you."

"How long do I have to stay here?" It was Wednesday. Or maybe it was Thursday? It didn't matter. Joshua would arrive in a couple of days. I couldn't let him visit me like this, lying in a hospital bed. Bad enough he knew about my mother. If he found out about this, he'd run out of my life and never come back. I couldn't let that happen.

My doctor paused at the end of the bed and patted my foot. "Discharge depends on you. When you're stabilized and your stomach is healing, we'll talk. Let's get you off the feeding tube first."

A nurse opened the door and motioned to the doctor. They left, leaving me with the blond woman.

"So, who are you?" I asked her. We sized each other up for a few moments before she spoke.

She sat in the chair Dr. Peters vacated. "Someone who's been where you are, lying in a bed with a tube stuffed down my throat, so I didn't die."

"I'm not dying," I murmured, weary. Lead weights tugged at my eyelids.

"Oh, yeah? Looks like it from this side of the bed." She crossed her legs and pulled her lip through her teeth. "And you know what's the worst part? Everyone knows now. The secret's out. They all know you're not eating. Maybe it started with your stomach eating itself, but now it's different. Your parents are going to freak out; everybody's gonna start paying attention to what you put in your mouth and trying to figure out if you're eating enough." She smiled wickedly. "Cat's out of the bag, honey. No going back now."

My body chilled. "It's not that. I have an ulcer. If I eat, I get sick."

She snorted and rolled her eye. "Maybe that's how it started, but now you're in trouble because you're not eating much at all. You're underweight, but I'm sure the doc went over that already. What do you think you're doing? A long, protracted suicide. Could take months, could take years. In your case, I'd bet it's much less." She leveled her gaze at me. "A slow lingering death is what you've chosen for yourself."

"Shut up. Leave me alone," I spat, then turned my face toward the golden glow of the window. I was tired, bone-deep tired, hollow, and empty. I wanted to sleep, not listen to some fanatic who had no idea what I lived with.

"No can do. You've been alone for a long time, kiddo. That's why you're lying there."

"I don't have to talk to you," I told her, backing up my weak words with my fiercest glare.

She smiled again—a knowing, rigid smile that lifted the corners of her mouth but didn't reach her eyes. "Here's the thing. You do if you want to go home any time soon. Because if you don't, you're going to an inpatient treatment facility until you get your act together. You want the tube out of your nose? You need to talk to me, and you need to talk to the doc. There's a reason you're in this mess. Maybe more than one."

"Leave me alone."

"Did the doc explain your situation? Ulcers start from bacteria. Maybe you didn't eat right, maybe you couldn't. Whatever the reason, those bacteria made a snack of your stomach lining until they ate right through. That's why you couldn't keep anything down."

"She said it was pain killers."

Marie studied me, but I refused to give her my eyes. "What are you hiding from? Who are you hiding from?"

I wrinkled my nose. "You're crazy," I murmured.

She laughed aloud. "Ha! I was once, right? What sane person tries to starve themselves to death? For what? Because my butt's too big? Because I can't fit into a size zero anymore? Bull. Had nothing to do with why I didn't eat, and your ulcer turned into your excuse."

I rolled my eyes. Fatigue flattened me to the bed. Maybe if I pressed hard enough, I'd disappear. "Please. Leave."

"Okay, fine. That's it, then. You're worried about the size of your ass. Why? Got a boyfriend?"

I tensed in the bed, silent and still.

She smiled knowingly. "Ah, so there's a guy out there. What does he know about your habits?"

Joshua brought fruit on our picnic because he hoped I'd eat it. He'd been worried even in the short time we spent together. What would he do next week when he came down? With the stress of my mother's interference, I dropped at least five more pounds since I'd been in Florida. The loss had to be the reason for my collapse. That's what made my ulcer bleed—those five pounds. If I gained them back, everything would be okay. I'd feel better, and Dr. Peters and Marie would get off my case.

"I'll eat," I told her. "I'll eat whatever they want me to eat."

She leaned in with a look that telegraphed she wasn't buying my story. "What then? Some laxatives to get things churning? Or the old-fashioned two fingers down the throat? How about we check your hands for calluses?"

"No! I'm not bulimic," I insisted. "I can't keep it down. I've tried. It's the ulcer."

"The ulcer is patched up. You have to learn how to eat food again. Your stomach doesn't know what the hell to do with it!" Marie waved her arms, and I caught her title on her ID. Therapist.

I squished my eyes closed. Maybe if I kept them closed, she'd disappear. "What kind of therapist are you? You're psycho."

"You think so?" A loud crash made me look. She kicked the chair over, spun in a circle, and hopped on her right foot, her head thrown back, laughing.

"Frigging psycho," I said, grabbing at my blankets, trying to find the nurse call button. What did Dr. Peters think this whack job would do for me? Entertain me?

She snatched the call button out of my fingers and dangled it by the cord just out of my reach. "What's the matter? You want someone to come in here and talk about your feelings? Maybe ask you to journal about your sucky homelife? Maybe pat you on the back and tell you it's gonna be okay?" Marie tossed the call button out of my reach. "That's bullshit, and you know it." She crossed her arms over her chest, regarding me with a clinical eye. "You're a smart young woman, and from what I understand, a survivor. It took a lot of guts to leave New Jersey like you did, and your father's given me some of the details, but I bet he doesn't know them all. Am I right?"

I said nothing and turned my eyes to the wall.

"Am I?" she demanded, slamming her hand on the bed.

"Yeah," I said, my voice a tired whisper. I didn't have to look at her to answer her, and I didn't have the strength to fight her.

Marie dropped back into her chair. "Then fill in the blanks."

I drew in a ragged breath around the tube. "I promised my mother I'd never tell anyone. I don't want anyone to know." But my promise had been another lie. Another broken oath. I told people. People knew. Dad. Tricia. Joshua.

"Well, she's not here, so go on." She made a motion with her hands, signaling to get on with it.

"Fine!" I snapped.

"That's more like it," she said with a satisfied grin.

"My mother is a hoarder. Our house . . ." The words caught in my throat, grating against the tube. "It's a pretty house on the outside. I took care of it. Planted flowers and kept the grass cut." I shuddered with a near sob.

"Sounds lovely," she said, her tone cynical. "You cared about what people thought. What about inside?"

"Inside . . ." I drew up my courage, remembering the garbage-strewn path from the living room to the kitchen, the piles of dishes and pots with stuff growing on the insides. The book tunnel. The rotten fruits on the countertop, fuzzy and buzzing with tiny flies. The reeking stench. "Inside, it was a disaster. Except for my room. The rest of the house . . . I couldn't live in it. She did. I called it her nest."

"Appropriate," she said with a nod. "When did she start hoarding?" The therapist picked at a cuticle like this was some coffee shop girl chat about buying new shoes.

The words tumbled from me, picking up speed. "When I was little. My dad worked out of town a lot. I remember him being gone for long periods of time. She'd get bad when he was gone. When she knew he was coming home, she let me clean up a little, but I couldn't keep up with it."

"How old were you?"

Resentment burned a hole in my chest and rasped through my voice. "Nine? Ten? She never helped me. She just sat there reading her stupid books. Then my dad left for a business trip and never came back."

"What a sweetheart," Marie said. "He left you there. Did he try and contact you?"

"I found out recently he used to call, but my mother never let me talk to him. She said if he wanted to talk to me so bad, he could come home." Tears slipped over my cheeks. "After he left, she just stopped caring. The stuff took over, and I started hiding in my room." I left out the parts about her threatening suicide. If Dad wanted to share those details, that was up to him.

I reached for my ice chip cup with shaking fingers. The melted ice sloshed onto the bed.

Marie dabbed at the drips with a wad of tissues. "How'd you keep her from going into your space?"

"I bought a couple of padlocks," I told her between sips. "One on the outside for when I went to school and one on the inside when I was home."

"That was smart." She sounded impressed with my ingenuity.

"I needed to keep her out."

Marie seemed to consider this for a bit. Finally, she asked, "How did she feel when you locked her out?"

The day she tried to get into my room and found it shuttered against her—the argument went on for hours until I cranked up my stereo loud enough to drown out her yelling. She pounded on the door with her fists. "It was bad. Then she didn't talk to me for a couple of days."

"After?" Marie clasped her hands in her lap.

"She ignored the locks, just like she ignored everything else in the house."

"Including you?"

Stony silence filled the gap between us.

"Isn't that the way hoarders operate? They decide protecting their stuff is the most important thing." She scowled at me. "This goes a lot easier if you answer, Shelly. How about this one: did she have a favorite item? Did she buy too much or just not throw stuff away?"

I swallowed, the guilt of what I told Marie pressing me to the sheet. "Both. She would get on these kicks. For a while, it was books. She has so many books. Piled all over the house, it's like a second skin on some of the rooms. She only reads *Gone with the Wind*. She likes to keep the other books around."

She laughed without humor. "Ah, Scarlett and Rhett. Sweet. What about recently? Any new 'kicks'?"

I wiped my eyes with the corner of the blanket. "Now, I guess it's pizza."

The therapist's eyebrows lifted. "Pizza? Like food pizza?"

"Yeah. She gets take-out pizza every day. The boxes are stacked in the dining room with the old slices still inside. Smells like dead things."

She pursed her lips but didn't comment. It sounded crazy. There were no words to describe what fifty molding, damp pizza boxes smelled like. None.

"Well, that explains the stress and not wanting to eat. There's this myth about eating spicy foods causing ulcers. That's not the way it works, but a diet of pizza would aggravate one. Okay, so we know living at home sucked. What about your dad? You never talked to him all this time. He told me you were out of contact. How did you end up living with him?"

A miracle. "I got an envelope from him with a birthday card and a plane ticket." My chest tightened. "He knew how we were living. He'd been calling. My mother never let me talk to him."

"Why?" she asked.

I shook my head. "I don't know. I guess she was afraid."

"You were living in these terrible conditions. So, your dad suspected it was bad and offered you a way out?"

"I couldn't live with it anymore. I told my mother about the ticket, and she went nuts, just like when I installed the lock. Started screaming at me and wanted to rip it up. I wouldn't let her have it, so she told me to get out." I paused, struggling to confess the truth. "I wanted to leave."

"Did she get physical with you?"

I held out my hands, hoping she'd understand. "It was my only chance. The only way I could escape, and my stomach hurt so bad." My body shook, and I dragged the blankets up higher, tucking them under my chin as the words flooded out. "I packed my stuff. When she fell asleep, I left. I slept in my car that night."

"And you came here?" she asked.

My throat felt desert dry. I drank down a sip of the melted ice water.

"Your escape took a boatload of courage. How do you feel about leaving?"

I licked my cracked lips. "Like I abandoned her."

She drew circles on her thigh with her pink nails. "Have you talked to your mother since then?"

"Yes. Twice," I said and sucked in a deep breath to steady my voice. "Last time it was like she lost it completely. She called the cops and told them my father kidnapped me." I shook my head, remembering the ugly scene. "I talked to the police, and they left. I told her she was wrong about this, and I came here on my own. She told me my father was lying to me." A sob ripped from my throat. "I'm so afraid she's going to die in there! And it's going to be all my fault. I left her. She can't even go outside anymore. How's she going to get groceries?"

Marie reached for the box of tissues.

I ignored them and wiped my nose on my blanket. "She can't pay the bills. All she does is order more junk online. I had to trick her to get the electric bill paid."

"You're not the parent," she said flatly.

"Someone has to be!" My chest heaved, and I felt a strange flutter in my heartbeat. "Oh!" I pressed a hand to my chest until it evened out.

"What you're feeling is because you were so dehydrated," Marie told me. "Your electrolytes are off. Add in the near heatstroke, and you're lucky you didn't lie there long. Your heart could've stopped altogether."

"That's ridiculous. I'm only seventeen." Still, the feathery, off-canter beat scared me. My heart twittered like a fluttering bird trying to figure out how to use its rusty wings.

Marie gazed at me, her thoughts unreadable. "You think so? I had a heart attack at twenty years old. I was in college, in class, and just keeled over. Good thing they kept an AED outside the room."

I stared at her in horror, my hands covering my fluttering heart. A heart attack. Not possible. Just because I didn't eat enough?

"It's the truth. The dietician will give you all the gory details about why something like that happens, but here's the basics from someone who knows: your body eats itself when you don't feed it, going after your muscles. Guess what? Your heart's a big muscle."

Revulsion made my mouth drop open.

"You got better, right?" I whispered.

"Not right away. Eventually I decided I didn't want to live like this, so I worked hard to get better. Still do. Every day. It's a process, not a cure. You recover, or you don't. How you live is up to you, just like it's up to your mom to make changes in her life. Lucky for you, your food issues are medically induced. They should be easier to fix once your stomach heals."

It was my turn to give her a skeptical look. "And now you're a therapist?"

"Yes. I specialize in family counseling and eating disorders. I have a shiny license and everything." She smiled at me and held up her badge.

"You don't act like a counselor." Not at all. She was more like the mean girl who sat behind me in tenth-grade biology and pulled my hair. Julie had been her name.

"Thanks," she said.

It hadn't been a compliment.

Marie stood and walked to the window. "When I was lying in bed for the fifth time, I didn't want to hear any fluffy bullshit. I had a big problem. I was dying an ounce at a time. I wanted to know how to fix it, what I needed to do so I didn't die. That's it. Don't try and make me feel all rosy about myself. The belief has to happen in here," she pointed to her head, then her heart. "That's the work *you* need to do."

"This won't happen again," I assured her.

She shook her head, a knowing smile playing over her face. "Just because they fixed your ulcer, doesn't mean your life doesn't still suck. Of course, it will. Saying so almost assures it." Marie plopped back down in the chair, crossed her legs, and let her sandal dangle from her hot-pink-painted toes. "Here's what's going to happen. The dietician will be in to talk to you. Take notes. You obsess over what you eat so it doesn't mess with your gut, right? Well, obsess over everything he says. Learn it, deal with it. Make sure this doesn't happen again." She held up a finger. "That's first. Second," she said, brandishing a second digit, "you're going to start group therapy."

Group. More talking. More people knowing how we lived.

"And tomorrow, *if* they take the tube out of your nose and let you have some soft foods, we're going to have dinner. Together." She smiled brightly.

"I can't eat in front of you," I said, my hands trembling

beneath the covers. The times I'd eaten with Joshua had been a struggle. But the ulcer was gone. Why should I be afraid to eat now?

"We'll see. What's your favorite food in the world?"

"Fruit," I said after a long pause. "I like peaches."

"Fruit? Not enough calories to help you much. You need protein in your body." She drew aside the top of her shirt to reveal a small device taped to her skin. "This little baby is my constant reminder of why I better keep my demons at bay."

"What is that?" I stared in horror.

"A pacemaker—you know, the things they give seventy-year-old grandparents?"

Terror held my tongue in a vise.

"Now, food. Do you like chicken, turkey, beef, or fish?"

Images of the dinners we had when my father lived at home flashed in my memory. Thanksgiving. "Turkey," I told her.

She nodded. "All right. Turkey it is." Marie glanced at her smart watch. "I'll be back at dinner time."

As the door swung shut, I relaxed back against the mattress, trying not to dwell on the tube in my nose pumping whatever slop they could get into my stomach. The idea made my guts clench, but instead of lurching for my throat, they gave a soft gurgle and settled back into place.

Progress.

My fingers sought the bandage covering the hollow concave of my abdomen, the hard outline of my hip bones, the distinct lack of flesh over my hips. What did other people see when they looked at me? I remembered

Dad and Mindy—how they reacted when my towel slipped.

As if on cue, the door opened, and my dad entered with a tentative smile and frightened eyes. "Hey, there. They said you were awake." He settled in the chair, and his gaze left my eyes to fix on the tube. "You scared the hell out of me, Shelly."

I nodded, tears leaking from the corners of my eyes and into my hair. "Yeah, I know. I'm sorry."

For a long time, we just looked at each other, the things we'd never say to each other hanging in the air between us. I blamed him. He also blamed himself.

"Does it hurt?"

"Only if I move too fast," I said. "How long do I have to stay here?"

Shaking his head, he said, "I don't know. They said you're stable. They're worried about your kidneys because of the dehydration." He stumbled over the sentence, emotion thickening his words. "They said you have to gain a bit of weight before it's safe for you to leave." He wiped a hand over his eyes.

Though I was exhausted, I dragged my body up to protest, wincing when my mid-section stretched. "But Joshua's coming on Friday! I can't be here when he arrives. I can't let him see me like this." I waved my hands down the front of me. I'd lose him before I had the chance to be with him.

My father's next words horrified me more than the therapist's predictions about my heart or kidneys giving out. "He's here. I flew him down the day you collapsed. He's been here every day. Even slept in this chair."

Pointing at the roses, he said, "Those are from him. He's a good friend to you."

I stared at the roses and imagined him sitting there, watching me sleep, wondering when or if I'd wake up. "Oh, my God," I murmured, and the fight drained out of me.

"He cares for you, Shelly. A lot. I like him." Dad's eyes crinkled in amusement. "He's handled all this like a champ. How long have you two been together? A year or two?"

A half groan slipped from my lips. I'd have to tell Joshua. He suspected something was going on with my eating, but I never told him the truth—the wretched, horrible truth. Still, he came when my dad called him. "Not long. A couple of weeks?"

Dad chuckled. "For a couple of weeks? I say he's hooked."

"What do I do now, Dad?" I asked him, my voice broken. I'd have to deal with Joshua myself. Soon. "Did you tell Mom?"

"Yeah. I called her. She accused me of lying about you being sick and slammed down the phone." He took my hand, smoothing his thumb over the thin skin. "What do we do? We fix you. Then we'll work on Mom, okay? I'll help you figure it out. We'll find a way to help her. One thing at a time, Shell. You first, okay?"

Fresh tears crept into my eyes. I squinted the waterworks back. It seemed like all I did was cry lately. I wasn't sure if tears were a good or bad sign. "Okay."

"Joshua's in the waiting room. I'm going to send him in," he said as he stood.

"Dad! He can't come in here. I'm a mess."

My father threw up his hands, exasperation bleeding into his tone. "Shelly, he's been here for two days. There's nothing he hasn't seen." He disappeared out the door as panic clutched me in razored talons, tearing through my healing stomach and racing my fragile heart.

I smoothed my blankets and ran a hand over my tangled, unwashed hair. Gah! What I must look like.

Moments later, the door opened, and emotion welled up in my throat at the naked relief on Joshua's face. "You're finally awake. Jeez, Shell." He sat on the edge of my bed and reached for my hiding fingers before echoing my father's words. "Your hands are like ice cubes. You scared the shit out of me. And your dad."

"I can't believe you're here," I murmured, awestruck by his presence. His skin was a darker tan than when I last saw him. He wore a polo, blue as the deeper edges of the sunset sky. The hue turned his eyes from pale aqua to stormy blue.

He drew endless circles on the back of my hand. "How did this happen? I thought things were going to get better for you here."

"They got worse, I guess." I explained what my mother had done—the police, the social worker, the lawyers. Everything. "Living here was supposed to be easier. It's not."

His thumb brushed once more over my hand, and he kissed the back, a brief, tender brush of his lips that drove my heart wild with the gentleness of it.

"Forget about your mother. Let her be batshit crazy if she wants to. Who cares? You've got to get better, you hear me? Don't let your parents screw you up like this." His eyes turned hard, and some of the resentment I harbored was mirrored there. "It's them, isn't it? All this is because of their messed-up lives?"

I shrugged. It didn't matter anymore, who did what to whom. All of that was behind me. "I guess. Maybe? I don't know how it happened. It just did."

He didn't say anything for a long time. It hurt that he didn't smile. He always smiled.

"What happens now? When will they let you go home? Your dad told me some stuff. Not everything." His gaze was expectant. He didn't want me to keep anything back. But I had to. Some of it.

Exhaustion swamped me in a stealthy wave. I yawned, wincing because of the feeding tube. "I've got to talk to people. A counselor, a dietician. I need to eat more. I have to gain weight." I didn't mention the heart damage. He didn't need to carry my burden, too.

Joshua grimaced and gestured toward the tube. "Does it hurt?"

"Not unless I think about it." I swallowed over the pressure in my throat.

"I'm staying at your dad's." He rubbed the back of his neck. "He's been cool about all this. I'm trying not to beat the hell out of him for doing this to you."

I never told Joshua the truth about why Dad left me in New Jersey. Maybe it would make a difference if I tried. "It's not all his fault . . ." I broke off as his expression hardened. "My dad had his reasons. In a roundabout way, he was protecting me."

He made a crude noise in his throat and gave me a

look that said he'd sit there until I fessed up. "Care to elaborate?"

I sighed, sinking into the mattress and wishing the bed would swallow me whole. "My mother threatened to kill herself if Dad tried to take me away. He believed her." Did I want to burden Joshua with more of my secrets? It wasn't fair to him. None of this was.

Joshua sat silent while what I told him settled in.

After a few moments, I asked, "How did he find you?"

"They called me on your phone," he said as his eyes roved over my face, the naked fear he felt brimming in his eyes. "I would've walked to Florida if I had to." His voice deepened. "Come here."

I gingerly lifted off my pillows and into his arms. He held me while I cried, stroking my back with his fingers, working gently through the worst tangles in my hair. "I can't believe you're here," I sniffed, wiping my eyes with my hands. "I can't believe it."

He breathed into my hair. "I'm not going anywhere, Shell."

"You barely know me," I told him. For a long time, he stared at me.

"I know enough," he said gruffly. "I know I'm not happy without you around."

"I'm so sorry, Joshua. I'm so sorry." The incredible pressure building in my chest had nothing to do with my struggling heart but everything to do with the way I felt about this boy. "What about your bank contract? Aren't they going to be mad?"

He smiled. "My cousin Aaron owed me some money. He's currently working it off." He drew back and kissed me gently on the mouth, holding onto my upper arms. "How long are they going to keep you hooked up to this?"

"They said they'd take it out tomorrow. I'm supposed to start on real food."

"You need to. I'm worried. This isn't just being thin. This is terrifying. You never told me you were in pain." Concern darkened his eyes, and a slight tremble quirked at the corner of his jaw. He continued, "You're going to do what they tell you, right? We have a lot to do when you get out."

"Like what?" I laced my fingers through his and bumped his shoulder with mine.

"Like living. Like going to visit my school. The beach. It doesn't matter."

"As long as I'm with you," I told him.

His gaze held mine. "Yes." He stood, and I clung on to his fingers with what little strength I possessed. "Promise me you'll get better."

"Where are you going? You're not leaving already." Overwhelming sadness closed my throat, made it hard to breathe around the tube.

With a frown, he glanced toward the hallway. "They told me I could only come in for a few minutes. They said you had stuff to do."

"Look around this place. Do you see stuff?" My temper flared, and I clapped a hand over my mouth. "I didn't mean to snap at you."

He squeezed my fingers in his strong, calloused hand. "It's okay. Relax. Take a rest. I'll be back later."

I brushed away my never-ending supply of tears. "What about your other jobs? Your truck?" He gave up a lot to be here. I was afraid to ask what his aunt and uncle thought about his leaving them.

"It's covered, Shell. I've got it."

My throat closed, but I managed, "I'm in love with you."

Some of the fear in his eyes dissipated. "I love you, too. Now take a break, okay?" He kissed the top of my head before retreating into the hall.

Weak with relief, I leaned back against the pillows. Joshua was here and not freaked about all this—well, not completely freaked. Gratitude spilled over into more tears. I wiped them on the edge of my hospital gown.

A month ago, I lived in hell, trapped in my bedroom. Now, I had Joshua and a beautiful place to live. My hand accidentally brushed the tube running into my nose. The gag reflex came roaring back up my throat. I breathed through the spasms, my eyes closed, until I could open them without puking.

I couldn't lose him. Not when I finally found him.

TWENTY-TWO

THE NEXT DAY, I clicked through every channel on the television and found old reruns of *Criminal Minds*. Now there was an uplifting show. Dark, twisty, and terrifying. At least it was better than *Judge Judy*.

A nurse tentatively opened the door as I snapped off the television. "Good news. We're removing the IV today." She also carried a bag of whatever nutrient goo they were feeding me.

"Does that come in piña colada?" I asked her.

She chuckled as she clamped off the IV tube. "Nope. And you probably wouldn't want to taste it either. But it will help you get your strength back much quicker." She gave the nutrient bag a gentle squeeze. "This is the last one the doctor has scheduled. That means we'll be taking the tube out later tonight."

I lifted my gaze to the ceiling and breathed in, keeping my eyes from her removing the IV until she taped up my hand. Another hurdle crossed.

The nurse finished and turned to leave.

"What's in the mix?" I asked her, my gaze on the bag of goo.

She stood beside the bed and smiled down at me. Her name was Pattie. So far, she was my favorite nurse. Whenever she came in, she always had an icy cold can of ginger ale in hand. "A little of this, a little of that. Vitamins, high calories. Your IV contained some medication to settle your stomach so all this good stuff stays put. Now, you'll be able to just take a pill." She drew back the covers to check my bandages. Her fingers probed my abdomen. "How do you feel? Any nausea?"

My stomach had become a non-entity since I bumped the tube earlier. I barely noticed its flops and twists. "No. I'm okay."

"Good," she said, gathering her supplies. "Drink your soda. I'll fill your water bottle for you."

Marie breezed in the door behind her, carrying two cafeteria trays. "Now, if you want gourmet, this is what you're after," she said, dropping the trays down on the small table with a brilliant, white-toothy smile. "Here you go. Turkey slice and mashed potato. Applesauce cup and a nutrient shake. Is that heaven or what?"

I froze in the bed, staring at the food and imagining the upset stomach to follow. If I got sick, would my ulcer come back?

"Looks like a good lunch." Pattie finished her duties and closed the door on her way out.

"I can't eat with this thing in my throat," I told her as a means of escape. How would I swallow? I imagined the tube moving every time I tried.

She pulled the plastic wrap off the tray and wadded it

into a ball. "Oh, yes you can. I checked. Dr. Peters said you could eat 'as tolerated.'"

"I was supposed to talk to a dietician," I said, stalling. I waited all afternoon for some jerk to come in with a list of what I could eat, but I'd been left alone. I suffered in silence through a full hour of group discussion where I gave no information about my past to anyone. But the waiting for the dietician aggravated me. I mentally prepared myself for hours.

"Looks like the appointment will be tomorrow, same with your second group meeting. Dr. Peters said you're doing better. Your bloodwork looks good. Pulse and blood pressure back to normal. No more dehydration." Marie dressed more in line with how I expected a therapist would. Linen pants emphasized her waist, and a flowing, multilayered tank top made of a gauzy mint material hung longer in the back than it did in front. Her long hair was up in a more reserved ponytail, and tiny silver sand dollars hung from her ears. "I bet they'll take the tube out sooner if you eat your dinner."

"Good. Then I can get out of here." If I went home, Joshua would be there. We could get back to normal, although I wasn't sure what that was anymore.

She smiled without mirth. "Not so fast. You've got some weight to gain back. Three to five pounds, and we need to make sure you're keeping the food down and your stomach is healing. No more puking it up." She pushed the tray toward me. "So, we begin. This is your journey back, a hundred calories at a time. It'll be as long or as short as you make it. You're going to go along great, then you're going to crash. But you're going to make progress."

I stared at the tray. I hoped she didn't think I would be able to eat all of this. Maybe in a week—certainly not in one sitting with a messed-up gut.

"You won't believe the difference in how you feel once you start eating again. Your skin will glow. Your hair will grow; your nails won't peel off. Go ahead. Trust me," she prompted when I puffed my lip out.

I picked up my fork and stabbed at the turkey like a petulant four-year-old told to eat her peas or no pony ride. I was conscious of Marie's scrutiny. With my fingers, I tore a bite off the turkey slice and put it in my mouth. I stuck out my tongue to show her. "See? I'm eating." The meat was a foreign sponge stuck to the roof of my mouth.

Marie frowned, her eyebrows pinching together as she layered tomato slices on her sandwich and spread a thin stripe of mayo on the underside of the bread. "That remains to be seen. Open your shake and try it out. Tastes just like the real thing."

The real thing? The Quick-Serve, Paulie's, and Joshua's burger joints—the total of my restaurant experience. "I've never had a real one."

Her eyebrows shot up in a *you're kidding me* gesture. "Good. Then you can't call me a liar." She bit into the corner of her sandwich and gave a tiny moan of delight. "You know what this needs?" She dug in the bag at her feet and pulled out two snack-sized bags of potato chips. "Chips!"

I took the bag she offered, wondering how she expected me to consume this in addition to the feast she supplied. Still, I used to like chips. Once. A decade ago. "I can't remember the last time I ate a chip. Maybe in elementary school. Am I supposed to be eating these?"

"Well, that's way too long. One isn't going to kill you. Try another bite." Marie popped open her bag and stuffed a chip into the middle of her sandwich.

"That's gross," I told her.

"Have you ever tried it? Don't judge me. I won't judge you."

"Yeah, right," I said, rolling my eyes.

"It's my job *not* to judge you, okay?" She rolled her eyes back and chomped on a chip as I laughed.

The turkey felt dry as sand on my tongue, and the plain potatoes sucked the rest of the moisture out of my mouth. I managed to swallow around the tube, but it was not very comfortable. I opened and sipped the shake, overwhelmed by the intensity of the vanilla. "This is good," I told her, savoring the sweetness.

"Told you you'd like it. Sip. Don't chug. Don't overdo it."

I nibbled on a crunchy slice of apple without the peanut butter. Marie dipped hers in the spread with gusto.

"Did you have an ulcer?" I asked.

"No. I dodged that bullet. I have enough issues to work through."

"I never meant to stop eating. It just kept getting worse."

"I know. But the fallout of not eating due to the ulcer is that eating becomes difficult. You had a medical reason not to want to eat. It's going to take some time to get past the fear of eating equaling pain and stomach upset. You've learned those lessons the hard way. Now we have to make sure you learn it's not going to make you sick if you eat."

"How long did it take for you to be able to eat normally?"

She made a face like that was the one question she didn't want me to ask her. "A while. Months of back and forth, but I was seriously sick for years longer than you. I'd do great for a couple of weeks, then just stop, land in the hospital, and the cycle would start over. I missed half of my freshman year in college. Luckily, the school let me work remotely when I couldn't get to classes." She uncapped a huge bottle of Evian water. "Dr. Peters told me you haven't been ill that long."

"Not really. It got worse recently."

"Because of your mother?" she asked over the top of her water bottle as she sipped.

"Why else?" I finished a cup of applesauce—a huge accomplishment. I couldn't hide the smile. Maybe I could do this.

"We'll talk about her later. Let's talk about you. You're going to be a senior. That's a big year."

Taking another mouthful of the shake, I nodded my agreement. "Yeah. School's another reason I came here to Florida. A couple of kids in my class found out about my mother's issues. It got around school, so I ended up doing school online. Here, I can go back to school. Nobody knows about my mom."

I stopped. Why should I tell her this? She didn't need to know about the humiliation or the constant abuse I suffered since Pam's grand announcement in seventh grade. She didn't need to know about the kids who broke into my locker and dumped their lunch trays all over my books and coat, or the HOME SWEET HOME sign they taped to the door.

She attacked the second half of her sandwich after layering it with chips. "Well, if you don't have to go back there, another stressor is off your plate."

Relief flooded my system. "Yeah. Exactly." I'd never again walk in the back door of the house to avoid speaking to my mother. Never wait on the front porch for another pizza delivery or smell the fumes of a hundred moldy slices.

After she finished her sandwich, she moved on to a small container of salad outfitted with an oily dressing. "Your dad's going to enroll you here? And you're going to finish school?"

"I figured I would keep doing online school from here. Now with this," I said, sweeping my hand around the room. "I don't know what's going to happen." To graduate or not to graduate. I had no answers. I chewed on the last of the turkey, surprised I finished without feeling sick. My stomach felt snug but not uncomfortable. More progress!

"If you keep eating and drinking, you'll be out of here in a couple of days. It doesn't take long to gain the weight when you've been restricting for so long. An extra five hundred calories a day will do incredible things to your body. But we've got to get you involved in groups. They told me you refused to talk today. You need people you can talk to about how you're feeling."

The four other teens in the group varied between sullen and outrageously happy. I hated them all. "Why can't I just talk to you?"

"Ah, flattering your therapist. Nice try." She shook her finger in my direction while I swallowed. "Who is the cute guy hanging around in the waiting room?" Her food-covered tongue stuck out, and I laughed. "Where did you find him?"

Not in this place. "Yeah, he's Joshua. He's amazing."

"Is he from back home? How did you meet him?"

I suppressed a giggle. "He went to school with me, but I didn't know him then. He used to pop in at my job, and he's recently been cutting our grass."

"Ha! He cut your grass."

It was easy to laugh with her. "How messed up is that?" Had she talked to him while I slept? What did he say about me? "He might be planning to go to school down here. He'll be a freshman."

"Good. I hope he does. You'll have support there." She paused as I drank more of my shake, her gaze appraising my progress. "There's another group you might want to talk to. I can put you in touch with some other family members of hoarders. They might help you deal with your feelings about your mother."

I rolled my eyes and shook my head. The last thing I wanted to do was to share horror stories with a bunch of people. *My sister collected dead cats,* or *my mother bought every American Girl Doll there was on the television shopping network.* I could imagine the scene. I would raise my hand. *Hi, I'm Shelly. My mother collected partially eaten pizza.*

I shuddered. "I'm not ready for that. Not now."

She cocked her head to the side. "Okay. Maybe later on. It would be good for you." She nudged my tray. "Are you finished?"

I felt like I might pop, although my dinner only included a couple of forkfuls of potatoes and few slurps of vanilla goodness. "Yeah."

"You did good. That was a fine first meal." She gathered up her sandwich wrapper and tossed the plastic in the trash.

"Can I keep my shake?" I asked her, suddenly possessive of the small blue bottle. The vanilla danced on my tongue. If I sipped it, I could make it last.

The therapist looked pleased at my request. "Sure. If you want another one later, just ask the nurse. They have other flavors, too. Strawberry was always my personal fave." She headed toward the door with the trays.

Somehow, during the meal, my bad mood moved on. "Will you be back tomorrow?" I asked, suddenly sad to see her go. I never had a female friend. I didn't trust them, especially after the Pam incident. But Marie possessed most of my secrets. They had been hers as well.

She nodded with a comforting smile. "Yep. I'll be here every day until you check out of this deluxe accommodation. After, we'll continue to meet every week to check your progress. Okay?"

"Thanks, Marie," I said.

"You bet. Rest. See you later."

TWENTY-THREE

AFTER THEY REMOVED the feeding tube, the next couple of days felt like wash, rinse, and repeat. Dr. Peters always arrived while I was eating breakfast, as if her presence alone might encourage me to eat more as they moved me on to solid foods. I *was* trying. Every day, I forced down another slice of apple. Another piece of grilled chicken. Another mouthful of scrambled eggs. I went to physical therapy and group sessions to talk about the peace I needed to make with my mother.

Mindy came to visit and brought more flowers from Beth. We watched home decorating shows and drank Starbucks. I began to envision a future with my stepmother in it, superimposed over the places my mother used to live in my mind.

I let go of the guilt because I had to.

Marie visited at least twice a day, and she never arrived at my room without a new treat for me to try. Gooey chocolate chip cookies, fresh mango and pineapple, and smoothies in every color of the rainbow. The food went into my stomach and stayed there, the ulcer healed, and I got stronger.

Every day I walked another five circuits around my floor as strength flowed back into my legs. Joshua often walked with me, with his glowing, dark tan catching more than one nurse's eye. Since I couldn't work, he had gone to Beth at the nursery and offered to fill in until I was back on my feet.

"You look great," he said. "You don't look like you're going to break into a thousand pieces. You look like you."

"And what does me look like?" I teased him. A bathrobe and scuff slippers weren't haute couture, but at least my hair was clean, and the dark circles faded under my eyes after eight days of treatment.

"Happy. Strong—inside and out. I knew you were tough when I met you. You had to be to deal." He twined his fingers with mine. "That's what I liked the most when I met you. You did an amazing job on the outside of your place. You worked your butt off. It mattered to you. That's what I loved. The way you glowed when you looked at the house."

"It is a pretty house," I agreed. "Someday, I'll have my own house, and I'll treat it right." A soaring one-story like my father's home, filled with sunshine and gleaming tile. I pored over the magazines Mindy brought in, tearing out pages of houses I loved and arranging them like the puzzle pieces of a perfect life.

He lightly squeezed my fingers. "So, you're staying here in Florida. I'm glad. I don't want you to go back home." Concern bled into his tone. He stopped in the hall and pulled me around in front of him. "You're better here. You will be, right?"

"If you're with me, I will be." I leaned up on tiptoes and kissed him in the middle of the hall with nurses walking by and doors to patients' rooms wide open. I didn't care. Joshua was mine. The brightest burning light in my dark and dismal life.

"I'm glad the tube's gone. It kind of freaked me out," he said against my lips. I smiled, and our breaths caught together.

"Not very romantic."

We held hands as we finished the lap and headed back toward my room. "How many is that today?" he asked, swinging our joined hands.

"Thirty-five," I told him. "And I'm not even tired. Want to go again?" In truth, I hadn't felt this good in months. My stomach didn't roll; my hands didn't tingle. My body felt like it belonged to me again.

"I gotta get to the nursery before Beth fires us both," he murmured ruefully against my lips. I ached for more than just chaste kisses.

"You know we're going to the beach the minute I get out of this place?" I said.

"I can't wait."

Dr. Peters waited at the nurses' station across from my room. Even she relaxed her worrywart role over the past few days as she assessed my progress. "Out for a walk?"

"Yes. I did thirty-five laps today."

"Very good," she said, straightening her glasses. "And

you've gained another half-pound. That's six and a half, total."

Joshua gave me a high five.

The doctor folded her arms across her chest and smiled, a real smile. "It's time you went home."

"Whoop!" Joshua yelled, then quickly covered his mouth. "Sorry," he murmured as patients appeared in their doorways.

I didn't care if Joshua woke up the world. *I was going home!* I had one question for Dr. Peters. "When?"

"Tomorrow. I want you to eat breakfast here. Then I want to talk to your father about making sure your nutritional needs continue to be met at home. I want you in my office every week for the next month. We'll keep track of how you're doing. You keep making progress and meeting with Marie, we'll be able to extend the time between visits a bit, but I want to know if you have any pain. I want you on the phone if you even have a hint something's wrong." She pointed a cautioning finger at me. "You're not out of the woods, Shelly. You've got a long way to go. I want steady increases in your weight. I want you at a hundred and fifteen pounds by the end of the year. Then it's on to maintenance. This is a marathon."

A hundred and fifteen pounds. Twelve more to go in just over four and a half months. "I can do it."

"I hope so." Dr. Peters turned her attention to Joshua. "Are you staying in the area?"

He nodded and tucked an arm around my shoulders. "Yeah. I'm enrolling at Valencia this fall. I'm going to stay at Shelly's father's house."

"And you?" She turned her attention to me. "What are your plans? It's important you have continuous goals outside of your health to keep you grounded."

"Dad's going to sign me up for school. I need to finish my senior year." I pulled my bathrobe tighter around me as an elderly patient shuffled by leaning on her walker. "And I want to go back to work."

"Good. Keep focused on your goals. I don't want you back in here unless you're stopping to say hello." She reached over and squeezed my shoulder affectionately before turning back to the nurses' station.

A twinge of emotion tangled in my throat. Maybe she wasn't such a hard-ass after all.

Joshua followed me into my room and swept me into his arms. He kissed me until my head spun, then picked me up and set me on the bed. "You're coming home. I can't wait."

"I guess I better call my dad," I said, my face hot from his kisses. How was I going to live in the same house as him and not get into serious trouble with my father? With the pool and bathing suits and sunbathing and Joshua . . .

"I have work this afternoon. I'm going to stop at the house to change. I'll tell him to call you. Do you want me to have him bring you anything?"

Clearing the visions of a shirtless Joshua from my brain took serious willpower. Our relationship was still so new, with lots of ground to cover. "Just the car, so I can go home."

He leaned over and planted a feather-light kiss on my

nose. I reached up and grabbed him, holding him in place above me. "Thank you for being here. You gave up a lot to come."

"I would've given up more if I stayed in Jersey." His crooked smile turned my heart molten.

TWENTY-FOUR

I WAS PACKED and ready when my father arrived to take me home the next afternoon. Pattie hugged me as I walked down the hall. How many laps had I accomplished here in the past six days? Two hundred? More? The pale-green tile bore the weight of my guilt like a champ, taking my secrets in my steps and housing my heartache when I couldn't bear it anymore. I was leaving more of me behind than I took from this place. Guilt, fear, and the vicious self-loathing for leaving Mom alone.

As I followed my father out the front doors into the brilliance of another Florida summer day, I could have sworn the echoes of my steps warned me not to get too smug.

"The car's over in the parking garage," he told me. "You okay to walk that far?"

I breathed in, my head clear, no hint of dizziness. "I'm fine, Dad."

We slipped into the BMW and blasted the air conditioning. The short walk left us both sweaty. "It's a good thing we have a pool," he said. "I don't know how we survive summers like this one."

I texted Joshua as Dad paid the parking fee and pulled into traffic.

I'M FREE!!

He sent back a smiley emoji with two thumbs up.

"How's Mindy with all this?" I wanted to know. Even though she visited the hospital, I worried my situation upset her.

"Mindy's a trooper. It's one of the things that drew me to her. Her strength." He shifted in his seat. "I wish Mom had some of her tenacity."

"Yeah, me too." I didn't look at him when I asked, "What's Mom's take been? Does she understand what happened to me?"

Dad puffed up his cheeks and shot out an exasperated hiss. "So far, she's accused me of intentionally starving you and holding you hostage for ransom. She called the police twice, but they didn't come out to the house. I talked to them on the phone." He shook his head as we turned into the driveway. "She's in some serious trouble. The police are notifying the authorities in New Jersey."

The news hit hard, but I didn't cry. The tears I reserved for my mother and her issues dried up while I was in the hospital. I still loved her. But I couldn't let her ruin me.

"Mindy's been cooking since this morning," Dad said with a conspiratorial wink. "She's happy you're home."

To my surprise, my stomach rumbled, not with upset but with hunger. "She's nice, Dad. I like her a lot."

His eyes shone as he glanced at me across the car. "I'm glad, Shell. She likes you, too."

"I mean it. And for Joshua. Thanks, I mean. For letting him stay here."

Dad turned off the engine. "He's a great kid. You picked a good one."

"Yeah, I know."

He carried my overnight bag into the house. Mindy met us at the interior garage door with a fierce hug. "So good to have you home!" She smelled of garlic and Italian spices. "I'm making lasagna. Do you like lasagna?"

"I do," I told her.

"You relax. Dinner will be later, when Joshua gets off of work," Mindy said.

They stared as I headed for the refrigerator. "What? I'm hungry," I said sheepishly. Dad's eyes glittered with tears. "Guys. Lighten up, okay?"

Mindy was the first to recover. "There's a bunch of your shakes on the bottom shelf. And a container of homemade mac and cheese if you're interested."

"Thanks." I grabbed a vanilla shake, scooped a helping of mac and cheese onto a plate, and popped the leftovers in the microwave.

Dad leaned in and kissed his wife on the cheek. "I'm going to run to the office for about an hour. Do you need anything?"

She shook her head and wiped her hands on her blue denim apron. "Us girls are fine."

When Dad left, I sat at the counter with my food and

phone, surfing the internet for planting ideas while she finished layering the pasta and cheese. "Smells good."

"Thanks. This was my mother's recipe. She made her own noodles, though. I'm not that ambitious." She held up a package of fresh lasagna pasta. "These taste almost as good."

"I remember when I was little, my mother used to cook. I used to stand by the stove and watch her. She kept a recipe box my grandmother gave her. I remember it had pink roses on it. All her recipes were in there."

"Is it gone?" she asked as she set the oven controls and joined me at the counter.

"No, actually. When things started to get bad, I took it and hid it. It's in my closet, way in the back on the shelf. Mom just figured it was gone in the piles. She stopped looking for it eventually. She didn't cook much anymore anyway." I downed the last bite of my macaroni and cheese snack and rinsed the dish in the sink.

"Too bad. I love how the house smells when I cook. It just feels loved."

"I want to learn how to cook. I'd like to get the box from my house." There would come a time when I had to go back to New Jersey to get my car and the rest of my things. I wondered if my mother would let me inside.

"Give it time. Maybe in a few months things will settle down between you and your mom."

My phone buzzed with a text from Joshua. "Maybe." I grinned up at her. "I'm going to head out to the patio."

Mindy narrowed her eyes, smiling. "A little privacy, I'm guessing."

"Yeah. Thanks for the food."

Outside, the air hung heavy and moist beneath the pool screen. Thick clouds built off to the east where I imagined the ocean to be. Maybe Joshua and I could go find it. I never vacationed near the ocean, never walked on the sand or picked up a seashell.

When are you off of work?

Leaving in about an hour. Mindy let me borrow her car.

Joshua was driving the Mercedes? Not a picture I imagined.

She's nice.

Yeah. You home?

Clouds reflected on the surface of the pool.

On the patio soaking up rays.

See you soon

With my heart full, I moved my chair so the sun warmed my pasty legs.

"Looks like you need a pedicure," my stepmother said as she came through the door.

"Yeah. They need some help." I wiggled my naked toenails.

"Maybe next week we'll go get one." She carried a watering can over to some potted palms and drenched them.

The front doorbell rang. Mindy looked up from her watering, but I waved her away. "I'll get it," I told her.

I slipped into the kitchen and headed to the front door. A police officer stood on the other side.

"Not again," I growled as I yanked it open.

"Is William Frank here?" the officer asked.

"He's not home," I told him through the screen,

bristling. There was only one reason this guy stood on our front porch. Mom.

"I'm from the sheriff's office. I have some papers for him." He glanced down at the envelopes in his hand. "And for Shelly Frank."

The ground dipped beneath my feet. "That's me." I opened the door and stepped onto the porch.

"These are official court summons, so I'll need an adult to sign for yours. The other is for William. He your father? And you live here with him?"

I nodded mutely.

The deputy handed me a pen. "You can sign here to accept then."

After I signed, he passed the envelope to me.

"Who is it, Shelly?" Mindy appeared behind me. When she saw my face, she stopped in her tracks. "What happened?"

"My mother happened," I told her.

"Ma'am, I'm here to serve an official court summons on Miss Frank. Could you sign for her? She's a minor." Mindy accepted the clipboard and signed for the summons.

"Thanks. Have a good day," the officer said as he turned and headed back to his car.

I snatched the envelope addressed to me out of Mindy's hands and tore it open.

Must appear in person on August 3rd at 9:30 AM. Superior Court, Family Division, Trenton, New Jersey.

"Dad must have to go, too."

She took the summons and scanned it. "It's a family

court hearing. She's challenging your dad for interfering with custody. I need to make some calls."

As she hurried away to the office, Joshua pulled into the driveway. I met him at the car and handed him my copy of the letter. "What's this?" Understanding dawned as he finished the page.

"I have to go back," I said, my voice flat, my body shaking. "She's making me come back."

TWENTY-FIVE

ON AUGUST 2ND, we landed in a misty afternoon rain. Dampness soaked through the thin sweater I wore over my new dress. This time, when Mindy took me to the boutique, I accepted the suggestions Fran offered about styles and cuts. When the trying on was over, I purchased two sundresses suitable for court and a navy blue linen sweater to match both. I never even asked Fran what they cost. I no longer cared.

All I cared about was my mother found a way to get what she wanted.

Me. In New Jersey.

Dad rented a car, and Joshua helped load our bags into the trunk. "We'll drop you at your house," Dad told him. "Do you want us to pick you up in the morning?"

"No. I've got my truck." To me he said, "I'll be there." Then he kissed me and was gone, leaving me cold and oh-so-alone.

We checked into a hotel not far from the courthouse. Neither of us said much as we waited on our dinner at the hotel restaurant. For the first time in weeks, food made me ill, but not vomit ill. This was a different sort of heartsickness, driven by my inability to escape. I never wanted to come back, and I certainly didn't want to talk to my mother.

I blocked her number on my phone after Joshua showed me how.

"Did you call Marie?" Dad asked me.

"Yeah. She told me to toughen up."

My father chuckled and took a long drink from his foamy glass of beer. "Smart woman."

I picked through my salad, eating around the croutons but making sure to eat all the chicken and cheese. I washed it down with a chocolate shake. "What do you think is going to happen?"

Dad stared off into space for a moment before refocusing. "My lawyer says nothing. Mindy agrees with him. But you have to tell the truth. This time, we need to make them understand what's been happening inside the house. It's the only way to end this nonsense."

I swallowed and shoved the plate away. Another shake later would make up for the rest of my uneaten meal. "Yeah, I know." And shame was the root of the heartache—finally letting the world into my mother's nest.

"This is the only way to help her, Shelly." He leaned back in his chair, weariness deepening the lines on his face. "There's something else we need to talk about. Is there anything in the house that you want? If there is, we need to let the court know. They can order her to let you inside to get your stuff, but this will probably be your last chance. It's likely to be condemned."

"There's a couple of Grandma's things in my closet." I smoothed a hand over my dress. "I don't want anything else out of there."

"Okay. I'll talk to the lawyer. Let's see if we can make it happen."

When I left New Jersey, my mother had been home-bound, unable to leave the house. Unable or unwilling? Perhaps my presence kept her from leaving. If she had me, why bother getting dressed in the morning. If she planned to confront us in court, she'd have to leave the house.

"How will she get to the courthouse?"

"Her lawyer? Who knows? She's also suing me for legal fees." Dad rubbed his neck. "I'm beat. Tomorrow's going to be a hell of a day."

"Yeah," I agreed. Weariness flooded my veins as I stood up.

In the room, Dad dozed on his bed while I ran a bath and soaked for the better part of an hour, loosening the kinks from our flight and sipping a vanilla shake. I missed Joshua. Having him around all the time these last few weeks had been awesome. I wanted the quiet companionship we settled into at Dad's house. Lounging by the pool. Working in the flower beds and eating ice cream sundaes. Walking on the quiet beach we found together on one of our road trips.

Calm. I craved the serenity of the Florida lifestyle.

When Dad went to take his shower, I called Joshua. "Hey," I said when he answered.

"Hey, there." He sounded sleepy, like I woke him.

"Were you sleeping?" I smiled into the phone, imagining him curled up beneath the covers.

"Not yet. Close. How are you doing? Hanging in there?"

"Hanging in and on." I lay on my back and crossed my knees, admiring the blue nail polish on my toes. I even sported a flip-flop tan, my first.

"It's gonna be okay," he assured me. "Wait and see. No court's gonna make you live with her in her screwed-up house. No way. You have a new life. You have to fight for it."

Deep down, I knew he was right but knowing didn't cut through the fear something could go horribly, terribly wrong tomorrow. "Yeah. I'm still dreading telling them the truth, though."

"Your dad's told people. It's out there, Shell. You're not betraying your mother at this point. You're telling them what they already know."

I stared at the ceiling and imagined the sky floating by my skylight at home. "I know. It's just hard." In the bathroom, my father switched off the shower. "My dad's going to be back soon. I just wanted to say I love you without an audience."

"I love you, too. And I don't care who knows."

A warm flush rushed through my body from head to toe. "I'll see you there in the morning," I told him. "Wear something nice."

"Don't worry. I'll be presentable."

TWENTY-SIX

JOSHUA WAS MORE than presentable when he met us at the courthouse just after nine. He took my breath away dressed in a dark navy sport coat over sharply pressed khakis, a white button-down shirt, and a thin navy tie.

"You look great," I told him as he leaned in to kiss me. "Smell great, too."

He removed his sunglasses and tucked them into his jacket pocket. "Oh? Does that mean I usually smell skunky?"

"Oh, shut up," I said, laughing.

"You kids ready?" Dad strode over to us with a grim but capable-looking man I suspected was his attorney. The man wore a dark navy suit and polished brown wingtips. My dad confirmed the man's identity when he said, "Shelly, Joshua. This is my attorney, Richard Doyle. He's representing us today."

I politely shook his hand.

"We have a few minutes. I need to go over today's testimony with you." We followed him into the courthouse to a small conference room. "Joshua, can you sit outside for a few moments?" he asked.

Joshua dropped into a chair in the hall.

I took a seat across from the lawyer and my dad.

"Your mother has made some accusations, Shelly. Most of them have already been proven false through the intervention of the Florida Sheriff's Department." He glanced over his notes and laid the police report on the table.

"Is that from when the police came to the house?" I asked.

"Yes. It was obvious to the sheriff's deputies you weren't kidnapped or being held against your will." He paused and studied me. "There are other accusations of a more subtle nature. Your mother contends your father manipulated you into leaving, and more recently, he is responsible for your illness."

I shot out of my chair. "That's not true!"

Doyle smiled. "Exactly the reaction I was hoping you would have. You need to make sure the judge understands just how ill your mother is—how bad the home environment is at her house. It's my hope they recommend her for family counseling. Possibly inpatient services."

"You're talking about putting her in a hospital?" I asked.

The lawyer nodded.

"And if they don't?" my father asked him. He clasped his hands on the gleaming tabletop.

"That would be unfortunate. We have lots of good, solid documentation she's losing touch with reality." He rubbed his lips with a finger as his bushy brows dipped above his eyes. "And, with what you've told me about the condition of the house, we should move to have the home condemned as well."

Condemned? The pretty yellow house didn't deserve death.

"But where would she go?" My voice broke as I imagined my mother forcibly removed from her nest. "The house is her whole world. It just needs someone to clean it up."

Our attorney straightened in his chair. "From what I understand, the house is beyond help. There have been some recent complaints in the neighborhood about odors. Flies. Garbage lying in the yard. I have all of those right here." He tapped the file in front of him.

"Sounds like she's gotten worse," Dad said.

My hopes for a good ending to our story plummeted.

"Who is the young man in the hall?"

"Shelly's boyfriend," Dad informed him.

"Is he aware of the condition of the house?" the lawyer asked, jotting notes.

"Yes," I said, my heart broken for my mother and the house.

"Has he seen the inside?"

Only the day we sat on the deck when my mother wore two different slippers. I shook my head. "He saw my room, and that was clean."

"Okay. Shelly. You're the only one who has been inside the house. You have to be prepared to explain the condition of the house in detail."

My heart sank into my shoes. *I can't go back there. I can't live there.*

"You'll do it?" he asked me.

Inhaling, I said, "I will."

Doyle glanced at his phone. "Then I think it's time we end this."

DAD, Joshua, and I walked behind our attorney into the courtroom, which was nothing like I expected. Instead of a dark-paneled room filled with chairs and a jury box, the room held about twenty padded chairs divided by an aisle. The judge sat on a raised platform behind a monstrous desk, an imposing piece of furniture that looked as if the building had been built around it. Near the front, two tables sat on either side of the aisle, and substantial texts filled a bookcase behind the judge. The walls were painted an uninteresting beige.

My breath caught in my throat when I found my mother seated beside her lawyer.

Joshua held my hand, his eyes offering silent encouragement.

Doyle and Dad took seats at the table. We sat behind them. When my mother realized we were there, she started from her chair, her wild eyes on me. Her attorney grabbed her arm and held her back. After a few heated moments, my mother sat down, her spine rigid and gaze fixed straight ahead. She wore a simple blue summer dress I never saw before and hoop earrings my father gave her years ago. Her hair was pulled back into a twisted knot at the back of her head.

Who was this woman? I hadn't seen my mother outside, dressed up, in so long. My determination wavered. Could I do it? Could I take her world away from her? If I didn't tell the truth, what then?

Joshua squeezed my hand, bringing me back to the moment.

Living with my mother nearly killed me. Going back would finish the job.

Doyle and my mother's lawyer rose as the female judge entered the room. We hurried to stand as well.

"You may be seated," the judge said as she took her seat. She fixed her gaze on the case file in front of her. "William and Madeline Frank?"

"Yes, Your Honor," Doyle announced.

"Yes, Your Honor," Mom's attorney replied.

"Good. And Shelly Frank? She's here?"

I rose slightly out of my seat as my mother hit me with an icy stare. "Yes. I'm Shelly."

"Good," she said again. "All right. We're here today because of a complaint filed by the former Mrs. Frank indicating William Frank has interfered with her sole custody of Shelly Frank. Is that correct?" She glanced toward Mom's attorney.

"Yes, that's correct," the attorney said.

"Care to explain?"

Mom's lawyer stood and straightened the back of her jacket. "Yes. Shelly Frank is a minor and has lived with Madeline Frank since the dissolution of her marriage to William Frank, nearly eight years ago. Prior to the divorce, the Franks were separated for almost another full two years."

The judge wrote at her desk. "Okay. So how did Mr. Frank interfere with your client's custody? Mr. Frank resides in Florida. Is that correct?" She directed her last question to Doyle.

"Yes, Your Honor. Mr. Frank has lived in Florida for nine years," our attorney replied.

"So, how did Shelly Frank get from her mother's home in New Jersey to her father's house in Florida?" Her gaze drifted to me. I tensed.

"He took her!" my mother snapped. "He took her from me!"

"That's not true," my father responded.

The judge held up her hand, silencing my parents. Her gaze fell on me. "Shelly. Can you explain how you ended up at your father's house?"

Doyle motioned for me to stand.

I avoided looking at my mother as I took a deep breath, filling my lungs and buying myself an extra instant to get my head together. "My home situation wasn't good. My father sent me a plane ticket to Florida for my birthday, but he didn't know if I would actually use it."

"But you did?" the judge asked.

"Yes," I told her.

"How old are you, Shelly?" she asked.

"I'm seventeen."

The judge tapped her pen on the desk. "And you left on your own?"

Distraught, I glanced at my mother's frantic pallor.

"No," I replied, my heart shriveling in my chest. "I told my mother about the ticket and explained I wanted to go visit for a while. She screamed at me and told me to get out, that I was just like my father. She threw me out."

"No! Not true!" my mother insisted. Her lawyer leaned over to calm her.

"Mrs. Frank, you need to keep your comments to yourself for the time being. You'll get your turn to talk," the judge said with firm patience.

"But she's lying," my mother complained under her breath to her lawyer. The woman guided her back into a seat. Mom's cheeks flushed red.

The judge turned back to me. "You left your mother's house? Where did you go?"

I cleared my throat. "I left at night after we argued. I slept in my car until the morning. Joshua drove me to the airport."

The judge glanced at her notes, then at Joshua. "You're Joshua Evans?"

"Yes, ma'am," he said, standing beside me. He smoothed his tie with nervous fingers.

"And you are Shelly's boyfriend?"

"Yes."

"Were you aware of the situation Miss Frank has explained to us here?"

He nodded. "Yes. I knew her life at home was bad, but I only met her mother once."

"And how was the meeting?" The judge leaned forward.

"Her mom was nice to me but very confused. She was

wearing two different shoes and couldn't seem to remember my name."

Ah. Joshua noticed more than he let on.

"I was glad she decided to leave and go to her father's," he continued. "It wasn't a healthy situation for her to live in." And there it was. The lead-in to the question I never wanted to answer.

"What do you mean by unhealthy?" the judge asked.

My chin jutted up. I had to say the words. I had to. This was the only way she would get help. Telling the truth was the only thing I could do for her. "My mother is a hoarder, Your Honor. Our house is a total disaster."

Across the courtroom, my mother gasped.

"A hoarder?" the judge glanced from my mother to my father. "You knew about this?" she asked him.

Dad nodded. "Some. I didn't know how bad it had gotten until Shelly came to live with me. My wife's illness, and her refusal to get treatment, caused the demise of our marriage."

"My God, how can you lie?" My mother gaped at him. "You left to live with that woman in Florida. You didn't care about Shelly! How can you say you do now?"

"Mrs. Frank. You will have your turn to speak." The judge stared at my father. "Mr. Frank, I tend to agree with your wife, to an extent. If you were aware your daughter's living conditions were so bad, why didn't you attempt to have her removed from your wife's care?"

He hesitated as he rose to his feet. "Because I was afraid, Your Honor." My father stood behind the table, and I fixed my gaze on the back of his suit coat. "When we were negotiating the divorce, Maddy and I discussed custody of Shelly. At that time, Maddy told me she would kill herself if I attempted to take custody away from her." His tear-filled eyes found me. "They were so close when Shelly was young. I couldn't let that happen. If she did kill herself, because of me, how could I ever look at my daughter again? Knowing what I'd done?"

"Is this true?" The judge observed my mother.

"He's lying," she said flatly, her tone enraged.

"So then, Shelly has been living with you. I understand she's had a medical emergency in Florida," the judge said, her appraising eyes on me.

"Yes, Your Honor," Doyle said as he lifted a file from the desk. "This is a copy of Miss Frank's medical record surrounding the emergency. She was released just a few weeks ago." He handed the paperwork to the judge, who read it silently. My mother slumped forward in her chair, studying her hands.

"Shelly? Would you please come forward?" The judge waved me toward the desk.

Joshua squeezed my hand as I passed him.

I swallowed and walked between the tables where my parents sat. "Yes?" I asked her.

Some of the sternness left her when I approached. "You don't have to be afraid to answer my questions. Considering the nature of your illness, it's best if you and I chat about what happened to you up here. Okay?"

I nodded and gripped the edge of the desk.

"You were diagnosed with a perforated stomach ulcer. Is this correct?"

"Yes," I replied. I kept my chin up, my back straight.

She paused to write something down. "That's a life-threatening illness. How are you doing now?"

"Better. The ulcer has healed. I'm gaining my weight back. I can eat again."

The judge studied me for a moment. "What will happen if I return you to your mother's home?"

Tears sprang into my eyes, propelled by an eviscerating guilt. "Please. Please don't. I'm trying to get better. I have to keep going to my counselor. Please."

Her face softened by a degree. "I understand. You can take your seat."

I dragged my feet back to Joshua's side, keeping my gaze from my mother.

"It seems we have an impasse," the judge advised us. "But I'm inclined to side with Mr. Frank and Shelly in this instance. I believe it is in her best interest to continue her treatment for her illness, but the custody agreement negotiated at the time of divorce is still valid. As a result, I will order the following: an inspection of the Frank home within the next fifteen days. This can be accomplished as early as tomorrow. If the inspection finds a home in perfect repair, this case is dismissed, and Shelly will return to her mother's home until her eighteenth birthday in accordance with the custody agreement. If the home is found as Shelly and William Frank have described, we will reconvene no later than the twenty-fifth of this month to discuss what is in the best interest of the minor." She shifted her gaze to me. "Shelly, until the inspection is complete, you are to remain with your father."

"Thank you," I said. The breath I held deflated.

"Mrs. Frank," the judge addressed my mother.

"Coradoni, Your Honor." Her attorney lifted out of her chair, a silencing hand on my mother's shoulder. "My client has just informed me of her intent to retake her maiden name."

The judge frowned. "Ms. Coradoni. Do you have any questions for the court? Are you prepared to allow an inspection of your home?"

My mother leaned toward her attorney, and her eyes were wide. The judge waited while they conferred. "Your Honor, Ms. Coradoni asks for more time before the inspection."

"Denied," the judge told her.

Mom must be in a panic. She had to understand what they'd find in the house.

"Your Honor?" I spoke up.

"Yes?"

Doyle motioned for me to sit down and shut up. I ignored him.

"There are some things in my room at my mother's house. I'd like to get them."

My mother glowered at me. I wanted to squirm in my seat. "Things?" the judge asked.

I nodded. "My grandmother's recipes. An afghan and quilts she made. That's all." I held my breath as the judge considered my request.

"I don't think a box of personal belongings is a lot to ask." She turned her attention to Mom's lawyer. "Will you ensure Miss Frank has access to her things?"

The lawyer spoke to my mother. "That's not a problem."

"Good. You can go get your things from the house, and we'll have a quick inspection within fifteen days. This should be settled within the month." She rapped her gavel on the desk.

My mother gripped the edge of the table with her nails. Her face . . . God, her face. She looked as if I staked her through her heart. In a way, I guessed that was true. Some stranger was going to knock on the door and ask to be let inside the house. No way were they going to say the house was a place I should be forced to live in. The smell alone would seal the deal.

Dad reached back and clasped my hand as Joshua squeezed me in a one-armed hug. Doyle looked like he wanted to smack me for opening my mouth. I didn't care. He could go jump in the lake. I wanted my grandmother's things—I needed to save something of my past if I was going to make a future. As my mother walked out of the courtroom with her attorney, her back straight and her head high, I realized I would make Grandma's recipes in my father's kitchen with Mindy.

Within a few days, my mother's secrets would be exposed. Because of me. I won the right to live in a good place. The reality? I lost so much more.

TWENTY-SEVEN

"I'LL GO with you to the house," my dad announced at lunch after we drove back to the hotel, changed out of our court clothes, and ordered food at the hotel restaurant. None of us wanted to celebrate our hollow victory, no matter how relieved I felt I would be going back to Florida. Thanks to the ruling, it was nearly assured. Once the inspector took a look at my mother's house? She'd be lucky if they let *her* back inside.

"Mr. Frank?" Joshua said. "It's probably not a good idea."

My father scowled at him, but I agreed. "Dad, she hates your guts. I want to get in, get my stuff, and get out without a fight. It's going to be bad enough with just me dealing with her."

His phone vibrated on the table. "You need a witness. Maybe we can have a police officer go with you. She's not thinking clearly, Shelly. She could accuse you of stealing something, though God knows how she would prove what was in the house." Dad picked up his phone and read a text. "I've got to call the office. I'll be back. Order some coffee, okay?" He stood and headed for the hotel lobby.

"You okay?" Joshua asked me. It was the first time we spent alone since the hearing.

I shook my head, momentarily unable to speak. I would not cry in front of my father. He didn't need to know my stress tangled up in knots. "I'm just a wreck. I don't want to go over there. But she's my mother. I have to love her, no matter what, right?" I cleared away the tears in my throat. "What if this is the last time I see or speak to her? Once I go back to Florida, I'm not coming back here."

"Remember when I told you not to let your parents' problems screw with you?"

"Yeah, I know." My voice quavered.

He reached for my hand. "I don't mind going with you. It'll be quick. In and out, okay? Maybe if I'm there, she'll keep it together."

"It's terrible in there," I warned him.

"I can handle it."

Considering her outbursts in court, I doubted my visit home would be painless. Still, I smiled despite the turmoil brewing inside of me. "How come you're so wonderful?"

He bent down and kissed the tip of my nose.

When Dad returned to the table, we told him our plans.

"Well, it's better than going alone. Still, make sure you have your phone. Leave if there's trouble. Call the police. We'll work through the courts to get what you need."

"It'll be fine, Dad," I assured him, not feeling the least bit certain.

"AT LEAST THE front yard looks good," I noted as Joshua parked his truck in the driveway. The magnolias had finished their early summer bloom, but the roses on either side of the steps had taken up the slack. Brilliant red and yellow blossoms filled the front of the house. If I were home, I'd be trimming back the azaleas for next year's blooming cycle. Without care, the plants would grow huge, eventually snuffing the life out of the roses.

"This is amazing."

"Yeah. I wonder if my plants miss me."

Joshua squeezed my hand. "Let's get this over with. Remember what you have going for you. Your new garden in Florida. Your job at the nursery."

"I know." Happy visions didn't make facing my mother any easier.

The front porch rockers swayed in the breeze. How many times had I hidden from my life on the front porch, waiting for pizza and watching the neighborhood kids? Pretending I was normal? Too many to count.

We climbed out of the truck and headed around the side of the house for the back door. My stomach twisted and turned, almost as bad as it used to. At least going in the back would avoid the horrible conditions of the front room where Mom spent most of her time.

Some tragic part of myself hoped and wished maybe Mom would do something inside to make the courts happy. Maybe she spent time packing up and throwing out her collections since I left. Maybe the pizza boxes were history. Because if she cleaned the house, her actions would mean she wanted me more than her nest.

"You have a key?" Joshua asked.

"Yeah." I pulled the key from my purse. My hand hovered over the lock for a moment. What would I find on the other side of the door? I turned to Joshua. "You don't have to go in there. I'll only be a minute."

He grabbed my wrist. "Your dad asked me to stay close. I'm not going anywhere."

I gave him a shaky smile and opened the door. The smell was instant, rank, and offensive. Worse than anything I remembered from living here. Like sour milk, warm trash, and rotting food. I covered my mouth with my hand.

"Oh, my God," I murmured.

Joshua gagged beside me.

My mother waited on the other side of the door, dressed in her court clothes. If she weren't standing in the middle of the wreck, I could mistake her for any other middle-aged professional, just home from her office job. Her hair escaped the knot and curled above her shoulders. Dark streaks of mascara smudged under her eyes.

"I knew you'd come back," she said.

Joshua laid a steadying hand on my back.

"Mom, I'm here to get my things. You heard the judge."

"This is my house," she snapped.

"I know. I just want some stuff out of my room. Then I'll go."

Her voice broke. "You're my child. You have to stay, Shelly. You can't leave me."

I shook my head, a hand pressed to my nose. "I can't live here, Mom. I can't. It smells like death."

She backed into the kitchen, and I flicked on the lights. Worse—it was worse. The kitchen was destroyed. The little bit I threw out every week made a ton of difference. Without those bags of trash leaving on a regular basis, the house descended into chaos. I choked on the foul, thick air as tears coursed from my eyes.

"What are you crying for?" she asked me. "You don't live here anymore. He took you from me. And you!" She pointed at Joshua. "You're responsible for this. Before Shelly met you, we were fine. Happy!"

"Mom, I was never happy here."

Her expression crumbled.

I pushed past her into the book-lined hallway and gasped when I flicked on the lights. My door stood open, the lock smashed to pieces. Beside the door sat a sledgehammer. Where had she found it? In the garage? Did she order it on Amazon with the sole purpose of breaking into my sanctuary?

With hesitant steps, I approached the bedroom. My legs went weak. My mother had been living in my room —that much was obvious thanks to the empty water bottles, foam plates, and take-out containers littering the floor. She moved on from pizza to spaghetti, it seemed.

Blankets tangled with clothes, newspapers, and books. The top of my dresser held four old coffee cups and an empty shipping box. A spill stained the carpet.

Inside my closet, clothes ripped from the hangers lay in a heap on the floor.

I stood in the middle of the destruction, shaking.

"Shelly?"

I forgot Joshua was with me. I turned to stare at him, mute, unable to express the incredible sense of loss grinding me into the floor, turning my bones into dust, my will into water. My mother stood in the hallway, a mix of loathing and fear burning in her gaze.

"You broke into my room," I whispered. "Why?"

"He took you. This is my house. My bed now. This is where your father and I slept, all those years ago. What do you think about that?" The emotion she wore changed, turned sad. "I love you. You're my daughter. My only! How can you leave me and run to him? After all he's done to us?"

"Mom, he left because of this," I told her, waving my arms at the destruction. "How can we live like this? In this trash? This isn't a house, Mom. It's not. You're sick; you need help. Please, Mom. Let me help you." I never wanted Joshua to be part of this, to experience how I lived, to witness me fracture because of who I was. But it was too late. He was with me, and he was my witness.

"You never appreciated anything I did for you," she said, pacing the length of the room and kicking packages out of her path.

"You need help," I said.

She turned on me. "I need help? I need my family back." Her words shattered what was left of my soul. "*My* daughter. *My* husband!"

But the crack came too late. Too much damage had

been done to acknowledge the new, deeper furrows. "The only way that can happen is to get rid of all of this. Mom, I don't want to live this way. I want a clean house. Have you seen the outside? You must have on the way home from court. I want a clean house on the inside, too."

"Maybe we can do that," she said, suddenly hopeful. Her eyes brightened with a frightening, fevered light. "We can fix it up together. Stay. We'll do it tomorrow." She brushed her hair back.

I glanced around the room. "I can't sleep here. Not until it's cleaned out." I reached under my bed for one of my trash bags. Mom stood stock-still while I opened it and began to fill it. This was a big test. I was pushing her hard.

"Here. Let me hold the bag." Joshua took it and opened it wide. I stuffed the water bottles and containers, papers, and magazines. My mother stood to the side and wrung her hands, agitated. I picked up my blankets and shook them clean. When I reached for the old coffee cups, my mother came alive.

"Enough! Enough for now." She grabbed at the cups, spilling old coffee on the floor. "Leave these. I'll drink them in the morning."

"Mom! You can't drink this. Look! This one has mold spots on top of it."

"It's fine. What do you know?"

I took the bag from Joshua and held it out to her. Her eyes followed me. "Right now, Mom. Make the decision. It's me or the coffee cups. You dump them right now, and I'll believe you're serious about changing." I learned Marie's lessons well.

She stared at me for a long time, her gaze flicking between me and the trash bag. Her hands shook, sloshing old coffee. Without a word, she turned and left the room.

I broke.

"I'm sorry," he said. He took the bag from my hand and set it on the floor. "It's over. Grab your stuff and let's get the hell out of here."

"I tried, Joshua! All she had to do was choose me. Why couldn't she?" I choked back a sob, and my body wracked with tremors. "It's all I ever wanted from her."

He pulled me into his arms. "I know. I wish I could make it better. You have a way out of this. You gotta take it."

"I know. I know."

"What do you need me to carry?"

I handed him a box of Christmas ornaments that belonged to my father's sister before she passed. I filled a tote bag with my grandmother's recipe cards and a small jewel box. An afghan my mother had made early in her marriage layered on the top of the bag with one of my grandmother's quilts.

"This is all I need," I told him. Somewhere in the house were photo albums from when I was little. Videos of special events when Dad still lived at home. But those were gone forever, swallowed by the sickness my mother couldn't battle.

The deepest, darkest secrets. They were mine to hold.

With one last look at my room, I left. My mother stood in the middle of the ruined kitchen, smoking a cigarette. I hadn't seen her smoke in years. I wondered where she got them. Did her lawyer stop on the way home? Did she have them delivered from some grocery store?

She flicked ash on the floor. I lost it.

"Look at this! This is why Dad left you! Left me." My voice tore across the years of heartache, falling flat on the grimy tile. We faced each other, and I finally felt free, even though I was still breathing in the noxious combination of decaying food and damp, moldy trash.

"How dare you," she snarled, a clear warning in her words. She pointed at me with her cigarette. "Your father married that woman. That's why he left. Not because of me. My house is messy, but I was a good wife. You've taken his side. Get the hell out. Go away."

To my mother, the worst she could do was cast me out. Her only threat was a hollow one. All I'd ever wanted was to escape this life that wasn't worth living.

"Mom, this is garbage! All of it! There's nothing in here worth keeping. You can't live this way. You're going to die in here under some pile of trash that's more important to you than I am."

"Get out! Get the hell out!" Mom stormed from the kitchen between the piles of boxes, snagging papers and bits and casting them onto the floor. The boxes swayed ominously overhead, bumping into one of the three surviving blades on the ceiling fan. Her fingers dug into my hair, and she dragged me back toward the door. I struggled and pushed her, as hard as I could, screaming as a chunk of my hair yanked free in her hand.

"Knock it off!" Joshua roared, trying to get between us.

She barely stumbled before she attacked again, her

eyes glazed and unseeing. Fingernails found my skin, drawing blood to mix with my tears. I didn't want to hurt her, but it was too late.

My hand drew back and slapped her as hard as I could. The cigarette flew into a pile. She crumpled to her knees in a tangle of newspapers and bubble wrap.

Joshua quickly moved to stamp the smoldering cigarette out.

"Enough!" My hatred echoed through the cavern of her hoard. "Enough!" I ran out the back door so she couldn't get to me and did the only thing I could to save her.

Tell. I called the police.

"9-1-1. What's your emergency?"

"My mother is sick. She needs help. I need help."

THE COPS FOUND us sitting on the grass outside my impeccably landscaped house. The breeze was perfumed with roses and lavender. From here, in the midst of my flower garden, even I couldn't believe what happened inside. The years of shame were hidden behind strategically closed blinds and thick drapes.

Out here, there was peace. Serenity.

Inside, my mother awaited her sentence, one I alone deliberated on and delivered.

Joshua laid his hand on my knee. "You did the right thing," he said as he draped an arm over my shoulders and pulled me close. I rested my head on his shoulder.

Inside, I felt carved out, hollow. Part of me would never recover from the last hour of my life.

A police car pulled up to the front of the house. My heart skipped, and I pressed a hand to my chest. I wished I could talk to Marie.

"Are you Shelly Frank?" A female cop with a blond ponytail cautiously stepped toward me. "You called us?"

I nodded. "My mom's inside."

"Did she do that to your face?" Her name tag said Norris.

Tentatively, I reached up to the side of my head. My fingers come away sticky. Apparently, Mom damaged more than hair when she attacked me.

"Yes."

Our neighbors crept out onto their front porches.

"Did you see this happen?" she asked Joshua.

"Yeah. I was there."

Turning to me, she asked, "How old are you?"

A hundred? A thousand years old? "Seventeen," I managed. The shaking began in my toes, crawled up my legs, and sent my torso into spasms of tremors.

I shoved out of Joshua's arms and vomited on the grass until my stomach was empty.

Bright spots invaded my vision. There would be no hiding our secret any longer. Everyone on the street would find out how we lived. We would be in the paper. On the news.

"Shell. Take deep breaths." Joshua pulled my hair back from my sickness.

Norris knelt beside us. "Shelly, put your head down,

between your knees. Brennan, find out where the ambulance is," Officer Norris called to her partner.

"Got it," Officer Brennan said.

I breathed in and out of my mouth, holding the blackness at bay by inches. Slowly, my vision cleared, and I edged away from my pile of sickness.

"Can you get up?" Joshua asked me.

"Yes," I whispered.

Norris tucked a hand under my elbow, and I stood on wobbling legs as Joshua led us to the rockers on the front porch. The emotions I clung to burst through my defenses.

"Who are you in all this, son?" she asked him as he settled me into the rocker and wrapped his jacket around my shoulders.

"He's my boyfriend," I managed to tell Norris.

She glanced between us and seemed to decide he could handle me for the time being. "Stay with her while we check on her mother. You said she was sick?"

"Wait." Joshua stopped her. "You need to understand what you're walking into." His eyes found mine, and I reluctantly nodded. He was stronger than me. He could say the words I couldn't.

"Her mother is a hoarder. The place is full of stuff. Floor to ceiling. Be careful. Some of it is unstable. Her mom's out of it."

Norris waved her partner over and relayed the information. "We need PPE. Gloves." She turned to me. "Thanks. You two just hang here."

The police officers headed back to their cruiser, opened the trunk, and removed gloves and protective masks. Laughter bubbled up my throat from somewhere I couldn't define. Madness. My mother had finally broken me.

"You okay?" Joshua rubbed my arms until a tingle indicated the circulation returning. I could face this. Thank God my father stayed away.

I wiped my eyes on my shoulders. "Yeah. It's just I've lived there for my entire life. Look at them going in there with masks and gloves. I never had any protection from her illness."

His fingers stroked my arms. "Maybe they'll finally get her some help."

"That's what I want," I said, my voice hollowed out by grief and loss as more sirens sounded down the street.

"Let's take a look at your face." He sucked in a sharp breath when he saw the damage my mother inflicted. "Damn it!"

I turned my gaze to the twilight sky while he probed my wounds. Orange and purple blended with darkness in the west over the tops of the trees. His fingers grazed an oozing wound on the side of my head. "Ouch!"

"You might need a couple stitches, Shell." His eyes sparked with anger. "I should've stopped her."

Dabbing at the blood with my fingertips, I shook my head. "Then we'd never have gotten to this point. She'd never get help."

The ambulance stopped behind the police car. EMTs pulled on their protective suits and gathered their gear before heading into the house with barely a glance in our direction. Apparently, the cops had informed the emergency crew about the house.

"What will they do with her?" Did they put people in straitjackets anymore, or was that an old movie ploy? I couldn't imagine her going quietly.

"I don't know. Counseling maybe? A hospital?" Joshua drew me into his arms.

My fingers pressed to my lips as frenzied shouts carried across the lawn. Nope. I had my answer. Mom wouldn't go quietly. She hadn't been out of the house in six years except to go to court. The driver removed a stretcher from the back of the ambulance and wheeled it toward the porch.

"A hospital would be good," I said, my thoughts a jumble of steps I needed to take. I needed to call my father. I needed to do something about the house. I needed to leave New Jersey and never come back.

More yelling and pleading from inside. He stopped me when I moved to get up. "It won't help to have you in there." His hand on my arm held me back. He tugged me close, and I leaned against his chest. Joshua was safe. He never judged me. Not once. He didn't care about the house or what was inside it.

Several minutes later, the arguing faded, and an unnamed fear took hold of me. Somehow, the quiet was worse than the screaming.

"What do you think they're doing?"

The blinds blocked our view. "She's quiet. Maybe they were able to reason with her?"

We looked at each other, neither believing rational discussion was going to work.

Moments later, the stretcher appeared at the side of the house with my mother on it. She wasn't screaming anymore. Her gaze found the evening sky and stayed there.

Joshua's arm went around me as the driver and a paramedic loaded her into the ambulance. The other paramedic made his way toward us, his face grim.

"Are you her daughter? Son?"

I pointed to my chest. "I'm her daughter."

His lips pressed into a line as he nodded. "Okay. She's going to the hospital. We had to sedate her to get her out of there." He cocked his head to the side. "What about you? Looks like you've got a good-sized gash on your head. Did that happen in there?"

"Yes," I told him.

"Then you need to have it looked at. The house is loaded with bacteria," he said.

"I'll take her," Joshua told him. He helped me to my feet. "We'll follow the ambulance."

"Okay. There's lots of dirt inside the house. You need to be careful about infection."

Our neighbors stood gathered across the street. I wondered how much of this they could hear.

"Okay," I told him, weak with relief I didn't have to ride in the ambulance with my mother. Sedated or not, closeness was a recipe for disaster.

The female cop and her partner strode across the yard. "You'll need to explain what happened here. We couldn't get much out of your mother." She turned to the paramedic and pointed at me. "Is she going in to get checked out?"

"Yeah. Her friend offered to transport."

"Probably for the best," Norris said to me. "Your mother's still pretty upset."

I swallowed the lump of tears riding up my windpipe. "At least she's not screaming."

"She's going to be all right." The EMT turned back to the ambulance.

Officer Brennan motioned to the truck. "We'll meet you at the hospital."

Joshua led me to the truck and helped me sit inside. He dropped the tote bag of mementos behind the seat.

My fingers couldn't seem to make the seatbelt click with one hand. With the other, I clutched the old afghan to my chest. "Here," he said. "Let me." Gently, he tugged the buckle free of my grip and snapped it into place. His hand drifted over my hair like he was afraid to touch me, like I might shatter into a million fragments of myself.

Like that hadn't already happened.

The ambulance pulled away, lights only. My mother lay inside, staring out through the window at the sky.

"YOU'RE HOME NOW. Good. Things can get back to normal." My mother sat up in a hospital bed in a stark, powder-blue room, smiling at me like we were at the nail salon.

"Yeah," I told her for the thousandth time. It was what she wanted to hear. I'd yet to discuss with her the reality of her situation—the house had been condemned and deemed unfit to live in. Two visits to the police station later, I still didn't know what could be done. I carried a weighty list of conditions in my purse, including having the house professionally cleaned. Dad was looking into a service.

The problem was, we were running out of time.

"The doctor said I could go home, Shelly. Isn't that great? I'm so glad you're home." She beamed at me from the bed, completely oblivious. A steady stream of counselors and social workers failed to make her understand sense in the past week. She still believed she could go home to her nest and live her life.

"Mom, you can't go back to the house. They told you."

She waved a dismissive hand toward me. "Oh, nonsense. Of course, I can go home. It's where I live. You live there too."

I sighed wearily. There was no getting through. "I'm going to head out, Mom. I have to meet Joshua."

"When am *I* going to meet this Joshua? I swear, Shelly. I'm starting to believe he doesn't exist." It was as if she completely blocked out memories of the night we fought, of Joshua pulling me out of her clutches, of talking to him on the deck.

"He was at the house. The night you went to the hospital." I turned to stare at her. "You don't believe I have a Joshua, but you believe the town is going to let you move back into a condemned house?"

Her mouth set in a furious line, and her face turned scarlet. "What do you know?"

"Me?" I asked, throwing up my hands. "Apparently nothing." I stomped out before she could reply.

DAD MET me at the house that afternoon. I asked Joshua to stay away while we met with the cleaning crew for an estimate. This was something we had to do as a family. We stood in the driveway, gazing up at the sweet yellow house I loved and hated with every fiber of my soul. None of what happened here was the house's fault. Just like it wasn't mine. But that didn't mean the circumstances hadn't exacted a horrendous price from us both. I nearly lost my battle, and the war for my health wasn't over.

The house was poised to lose its fight for life. I knew that as soon as my father read the estimate. No cleaning meant the bulldozers were not far away. This would be my last visit, my last chance to take anything from the house.

"How do you want to do this, Shell?" he asked me. The weather turned steamy. Although it wasn't hot outside by Florida standards, maybe eighty degrees, the humidity stuck my clothes to my back and dampened my hair at my nape. I prayed the air conditioning was still on inside the house. Otherwise, we were doomed.

"I'll go in the back. It's closest to my room. She moved in there when I left. We need to see what we can salvage for Mom. The less time I spend in there, the happier I'll be." I removed a box of trash bags from the backseat of my car, along with two sets of heavy work gloves and two respirators. I handed a pair of gloves to my father.

He stared at them for several minutes. "Jesus," was all he said.

I led the way around the side of the house, checking on plantings and flower beds. Without my constant attention, weeds had begun incursions into various areas.

Before I left, I would make sure the insidious invaders were cleaned out. I cut the health department's seal on the back door and opened it with my key. Being away from the house for the past week left me totally unprepared for the odors that assaulted my nose. Had it always been this bad? Was this how I lived?

Dad pressed a hand over his mouth. "Oh, man," he murmured as he tugged the respirator over his face.

"Yeah," I agreed.

We stepped into the kitchen. It was worse in the daylight. The bags of trash I ferreted out of the house had truly been the only thing saving the place from total destruction. Now, decaying vegetables sat on the counter, and the kitchen trash can overflowed onto the floor. I made a point of cleaning out the new refrigerator when I could, but the practice was abandoned in my absence, and my mother unplugged the appliance. The whiff of rotting pizza had been pleasant compared to the overwhelming bouquet of utter despondency inside the shiny refrigerator.

"How did this happen?" Dad asked as tears streamed down his face, darkening the edge of his mask. "Shelly?"

"She doesn't see it. She doesn't." I kicked boxes and empty vegetable cans out of my path as I headed toward my room. How did she imagine she was coming back here? The only person coming into this house would be the man riding on the bulldozer.

I shimmied down the hall between the book stacks and stopped dead. My door was open again. In the time we waited for the ambulance, my mother exacted her rage on my room with the sledgehammer. Holes peppered the plasterboard. My dresser mirror shimmered up from the floor in a thousand shards.

Dad made a strangled sound in his throat, but I didn't turn. I was frozen to the gleaming floor, unable to process or understand what occurred.

"She did this," Dad said. It wasn't a question. I left. This was her way of getting back at me. He opened a trash bag and removed the pizza boxes. I opened the windows to air out the foul, throat-clogging odors and plugged my air fresheners in with new cartridges.

"I forgot this the other night," I told him. In the craziness that ensued, I'd rescued the ornaments but left without the bin I'd returned for. Deep in my closet, I located it. Somehow, my grandmother's things avoided my mother's wrath. I popped the lid and set the box on my bed.

"That's my mother's quilt," Dad said. "She used to have it on the bottom of her bed. You kept it."

"And I have the one she made for you. I took it that night. I wanted to have it when I got away from all this." Beneath the quilt was a picture of my grandparents on their wedding day.

He laid a hand on my shoulder. "Are you going to be okay? You get what's going to happen to this place, right?"

"Yes," I said as fresh tears flowed. "It has to be done." The town would tear down the house, load it in a dumpster, and plant it in a landfill somewhere. I wondered if my flowers would sprout over its grave.

Dad wiped his hands over his eyes. "Is there anything else you want in here? We should leave. I'd rather buy your Mom the things she needs than dig through this mess."

I shook my head. "No." I turned to him then and pulled off the respirator. Fresh air flowed into the room, enough so I could breathe. "Can you take this out to my car? I want a minute alone." My voice trembled on the verge of breaking.

He drew me into his arms and held me as sobs wracked my body. If I hadn't been sick in Florida, I wouldn't be strong enough to face this—the destruction of my childhood. Marie would tell me to get over it, put on the big girl panties, and she would be right. As bad as my past suffering was, it would live with me forever in whatever form I allowed it to take. I couldn't give it space inside my head or my heart. Maybe someday, but not now.

I backed out of his embrace. "I'll just be a couple of minutes."

"Okay," he said, heaving the plastic bin into his arms. "I'll be on the deck."

We maneuvered the box down the narrow hallway and out the back door. When he'd gone, I stood in the middle of the vandalized kitchen. It was as if a tornado suddenly appeared in the center of the room and tossed the contents of the sunny space up against the walls in a mirror of an invisible funnel. I stood in the center vortex, the sole survivor of a merciless storm.

"I'm so sorry," I told the house.

In the dining room, I followed the narrow path between the forest of china cabinet and buried table. At the cabinet, I brushed aside the junk blocking the door and opened it. My parents' toasting flutes from their wedding sat on a shelf beside a tiny teacup and saucer painted with pink roses. I emptied a box of many months' worth of mail and carefully set the flutes and teacup inside.

The china my mother never used bore a graying grime I didn't want to consider, so I passed over the dishes. From the wall in the dining room, I lifted a framed picture of our family. I had to have been five or six at the time. We wore shades of blue that exactly matched the color of my mother's eyes.

I gazed down at the photo, making dusty tracks on the glass with my finger. We'd been so happy once. A heavy sigh escaped my lips as I trudged through the house.

In the living room, I stopped and simply stared at my mother's abandoned chair, reduced to one cushion corner sagging toward the floor. The couch disappeared in the time I'd been gone—swallowed whole by a rogue wave in the hoard. And books. Books were everywhere. I set down my box and picked up a copy of *Gone with the Wind,* complete with a movie tie-in cover. It was brand new. Beside it sat four other pristine copies of the same book.

"Damn it! Damn it!" I ripped the cover off the book, shredding pages and bindings. When I finished with one, I attacked the others until there was nothing left but a pile of paperback and a picture of Scarlett and Rhett staring at each other across the ages. I stomped their faces as I snatched my box and stormed from the house.

My father met me around the side of the house. "Everything okay in there?" he asked.

"Fine," I told him as I loaded the box in my car and slammed the door.

"What's in the garage?"

"I don't want to know. I haven't been in there in years." A car pulled up to the end of the driveway and stopped. "Who's in the car?"

"Looks like an unmarked police car," Dad said. We waited while the officer got out and walked up the driveway.

"Are you residents?" he asked, eyeing the boxes in the back of my car.

"Yes. I'm Shelly Frank. This is my father."

The police officer's gaze shifted to my father. "Do you own this house, sir?'

Dad shook his head. "Not anymore. My wife got the house in the divorce. My daughter has lived here, up until last month. She came to collect the last of her things."

"Does your mother know you've been inside, miss?"

I bristled at the insinuation. "I lived here for seventeen years. My mother's hospitalized."

"I'm aware," he said levelly. "This property was condemned."

"Was?" my father asked him.

"Ms. Coradoni's attorney has won a stay through city council." He handed me an envelope. "She has thirty days to clean and make the necessary repairs to the interior of the house before the order is reinstated."

I took the envelope with a shaking hand. My father and I read the letter while the police officer waited. "So, she can come back here tomorrow when they discharge her?" I asked, incredulous.

"Yes. She has thirty days."

Dad stepped forward. "Have you been in there, son? It's not a place for a sick woman."

The officer nodded curtly. "That's your family's matter, sir."

I stood rooted to the driveway as the policeman got into his car and drove away. I wished the concrete would crack open and swallow me alive. "She can't come back here, Dad. She can't."

He laid his hand on my shoulder. "There's not much we can do, Shell. She has thirty days. I hope she'll do something with it."

The hoard loomed behind me like a malevolent specter waiting to drag me through the door when I wasn't looking, back into the life I set firmly in my past. Yet here I was, back at the threshold of hell. "I can't go back to Florida," I told him. "I can't leave her with this." Someone should stay and work on the house so my mother could come home.

"Shelly, come on." He gripped my arm. "You can't save her from this. You know by now. You've talked to her. She's ill, and she's not getting the help she needs." Dad gazed back at the house. "She's never going to get better when they let her back in there. They should have demolished the damn thing the day she left."

She's never going to get better. Never going to escape. Neither am I.

"You're right, Dad." I dragged my hands across my eyes. "I need to leave." I took my keys from my pocket and slid behind the wheel, knowing Dad would never understand the damage done to me—inside and outside. I didn't have the words to educate him. I clenched the letter from the town in my fist. There were no words and no time.

Dad stood in the driveway, as if unsure of what to do. Was this how he felt the day he decided to leave? Did he stand undecided in the driveway or had he simply thought of himself? What did he think now? Maybe someday he would tell me.

Maybe someday I'd care.

Finally, he opened the passenger door and slid inside. I started the car and cranked up the air conditioning, turning the vents so it hit me in the face. Clean. Cool.

He leaned his elbow on the door and cupped his chin as he stared at the house. "It's going to be all right, kiddo. I'll talk to the attorney and the town. Let me see what we can do."

I nodded in agreement because he expected it of me. Compliance. Agreement. Submission. I had my fill of them all. "Okay. Thanks."

"I'll stay in town until we figure it out." His eyes met mine across the car. They were wet. Mine were finally dry. "You go home tomorrow. Mindy will get you at the airport."

"Thanks, Dad." I paused. "I'm going to stay at Joshua's house tonight. It's our last night here."

His eyes darkened, and his expression told me he didn't want to agree to my plan. Still, he sighed and relented. "All right."

TWENTY-EIGHT

AFTER I DROPPED off my father at the hotel to make his useless phone calls, I drove to Joshua's house. I didn't call him on the way over, preferring to be alone with my thoughts and the familiar sound of Bennie's tires scratching on the road. Dad was absolutely correct about one thing: If Mom went back into the house, it would consume her. Slowly or quickly, the nest would crush her in its fist.

Mom refused treatment. In fact, she didn't believe the cancer living inside the yellow walls was real. I knew better. I'd seen and smelled it up close. But if the cancer were treated and cut away, survival odds rose dramatically.

He met me at my car and hugged me as soon as I got out. "Are you all right? I've been going nuts over here. Why didn't you call?"

My throat closed, and for a moment, I felt the horrid nasogastric tube bumping into my windpipe, the ghost of another cancer that had only gone into remission.

"Here," I said, holding out the crumpled letter from the city.

He skimmed the letter, his face registering shock then horror. "They can't do this, Shelly. They can't let her back in there." He handed the letter back to me, and I stuffed it in my pocket.

"It's done." I leaned wearily against Bennie's fender. "They're letting her out tomorrow or the next day—soon —right back into the nest."

He gripped me gently by the forearms to force my gaze up to his. "What are you going to do? What did your dad say?"

I breathed in once, heavily. "He's calling the lawyer, the town, the social workers. Whoever he can get to talk to him. But he's not her husband anymore. He doesn't own the house." Neither did I, for that matter.

Joshua kicked the ground with his toe. "It's her house. It has to be her problem."

No. It was my problem. I was still the adult in the house, the one who paid the bills and kept back the dam of the hoard. I had to be the one to make it go away.

"Shell. What aren't you telling me?" He shook me slightly.

"She can't go back there. I can't let her." I dragged my lip through my teeth. "Remember how it was last week? It's a hundred times worse now. There's food everywhere. She destroyed my room." My breath caught on a sob.

He brushed the hair out of my eyes as I struggled to center myself. "What are you going to do?"

It took several moments of deep breathing exercises before I could answer. I always wanted control of my life.

I wanted my mother to get better, for her to be my mother. This was the moment I'd been waiting for.

"I'm going back to Florida tomorrow," I told him. "As soon as I finish this."

I WAITED until everyone in Joshua's house fell asleep before I slipped out. His aunt and uncle were oblivious in their room upstairs, Joshua asleep in his basement suite. As a way of explanation, I left a note on the table.

J,

I needed to get an early start. I'll call you later.

Love you,

Shell

The streets were deserted, and I drove without haste through familiar neighborhoods until I parked three blocks away, checking to make sure no traffic cameras followed Bennie in the gloom. It would make sense if anyone looked later that I drove in this direction. One last time to visit my old house before I left town forever. It made perfect sense.

My shoulders hunched in my dark jacket as I raced through the humid darkness toward the house. I skirted the edge of our yard and headed directly for the shed where I kept the hedge clippers and push mower. And the gas cans.

Footsteps sounded behind me. I reached for a shovel and spun to challenge whoever was out there.

"Shell! What the hell are you doing?" Joshua held up

his hands as I brandished the shovel. His hair stuck up all over.

"Get out of here," I told him, my voice steady in the darkness. "You don't need to be part of this."

"Part of what?" He glanced around the interior of the shed using his phone screen for a light. "Did you forget something? What are you doing?" His worried gaze dropped to my face. "Shelly. Tell me."

I leaned the shovel back in the corner. "I can't. You need to get out of here. Now."

He grabbed me, turned me around, his eyes wild in the half-light. "You're not thinking."

"I'm thinking clearly for the first time in months." A steady calm came over me, washing away any of the doubts I clung to on my drive across town. There was no way out for my mother, or me. Not as long as the house survived.

"Do you know what they'll do to you?"

"They'll never find out. You need to leave." I ripped my sleeve from his grasp. "It'll never end, Joshua. Not as long as she can come back here. I'll be in Florida, and I'll know how she's living. She's slowly killing herself in a pile of filth. We're so alike, my mother and me. You need to get away from me. Save yourself. We're cancer. We'll eat you from the inside out."

He gripped my arms and shook me. "Do you hear yourself? Shelly. Come on. You're not making sense."

I laughed softly, sadly in my chest. "I'm making sense. I'm the only one making sense." I drew away, reached inside the shed, and found one of my gas cans. I swished it back and forth. It was half full. "My dad was right. They should have destroyed it the day they took her out. I should have."

He reached for my hand and slowly peeled the can out of my cold fingers.

"I'm sorry," I told him. "I never should've brought you into this. You should've run when you had the chance." Tears dripped off my chin.

He leaned in and kissed me, soft then fierce, until I clung to his shirt with both hands as he held the can an arm's length away. "I care about you. And none of the rest matters to me," he whispered against my lips.

I led the way to the back door and silently inserted my key. "It's going to be bad in here. The air conditioning isn't running." The tell-tale hum of the central air unit had fallen silent. The noxious odor slammed me in the face as soon as the door opened.

"Shit," Joshua gasped. "What's that smell?"

"Death," I replied. "Stay close to the door. You don't want to get stuck in here."

My stomach heaved. I crept into the kitchen, into the dining room, and then to the living room. I picked up the remnants of *Gone with the Wind*. My gaze drifted over her chair and the piles of books. The pizza boxes, the china cabinet, the boxes and bags that once held my mother's treasures. The blue bedroom. The hall bathroom.

Rubbish. All of it. The gas can shook in my grip. I set the can on the floor and breathed in the reek. My mother was safe, I told myself. Free of the nest and finally getting help. Once the house died, she would be able to move on. The only way I could help her and myself was to empty her nest.

But her nest held my memories too. The early days when my dad still lived at home. A few Christmases when there was room for a tree. A meal cooked in a semi-clean kitchen. The memories didn't simply exist in a place like a spirit haunting a box. They were part of me. If I wanted or hoped to make new ones with my mother, I had to sever our pasts forever.

Right now.

I pulled a box of matches from my pocket and lit one. The flame blazed like a tiny sun in the darkness. Drop the match and the pain would end. I wished I found my dog so I could have buried his body. I wished I'd been strong enough to look for him then. In the amber glow, I saw the inside of my hell for the last time before I flung the match into the nest.

The heat was instant, intense, burning up my nose, searing down my throat. Paper and plastic ignited in a blaze of cleansing fire. Joshua grabbed me by the arm and dragged me out the back door. We stumbled and fell in the dewy grass.

"C'mon Shelly. Get back." His fingers dug into my skin.

I crawled to my knees beside my rusted swing set. Tears coursed down my cheeks, but I didn't move, couldn't—not until the kitchen window exploded in a rain of fiery, bright glass, and sirens wailed in the distance.

"Shelly! We have to go!" He pulled me away, taking the matchbox from my hands and jamming it into his pocket. We ran toward the trees as a deep thud echoed across the yard; a miniature explosion I felt through the soles of my shoes. Oil tank? Propane? Lord knew what was stored in the garage.

In the safety of the trees, I stopped and turned to stare at the inferno, but the violent heat pushed me further into the stillness of the woods. The house blazed into the sky as if the fire could propel my mother's compulsions up to the stars where beings stronger than me might find a way to cope with them. Peace remained elusive for me, but maybe Mom would find some. I'd always remember what I'd done to help her, no matter how far I ran. The burning house was scorched into my brain, a brand forged by what I lost and what she gained.

Joshua moved away, heading through the vacant lots like a wraith in the darkness.

I breathed deep of smoky air and followed him through the woods to where I parked the car, feeling lighter than I had in months.

My mother was free.

So was I.

TWENTY-NINE

I STARTLED awake in Joshua's aunt's spare bedroom to the sound of raised but indistinct voices in the hallway. Groaning, I reached for my phone in the dimly lit room. It was not nearly morning, but I had already missed a dozen calls from my father.

My stomach flopped over as the vivid images from last night collided in my brain with the reason for his calls. Bile rushed up the back of my throat. He knew. My father knew about the fire.

Of course, he did. He called the township about the thirty-day stay, trying to get them to listen to why the house should be condemned. Because of his efforts, I bet they kept his number as a contact person and told him about the fire.

I squeezed my eyes shut. Today began the clean-up— the repairs to my mother's psyche now the nest was destroyed. A surge of warmth brushed away my spiking anxiety. Mom would finally heal. Without her house, she would be freed. It was worth it, no matter what happened to me. I truly believed this. Burning the nest meant everything.

My phone buzzed angrily. I had to call him back, and when I did, I should act surprised, shocked, and saddened by the loss of the house I loved on the outside but hated on the inside.

"I need to talk to her!" My father's voice sounded in the hallway.

Dad? He was here in Joshua's house. I froze in bed and grappled with my composure. *Oh, no.* He'd see through me. He'd see through the lies.

A door banged, and frantic voices ended right outside my door. I hastily shrugged into the bathrobe I borrowed from Joshua's aunt and opened the door just as my father reached it.

"What's going on?" I asked him. Joshua's aunt and uncle stood at the end of the hall. His aunt wiped her eyes with her fingers. Why was she crying? Where was Joshua? What did he tell them? Was something wrong with him? In my chest, my heart pounded an uneven rhythm that frightened me almost as much as the sorrow on my father's face.

"Dad? What's going on? Where's Joshua?" Seeing Dad there, standing in the hall outside my door, enhanced the shock I needed to show. Dirt streaked his face.

I smelled fire on his clothes. My body trembled.

He leaned an arm against the doorframe as if the wall were the only thing keeping him on his feet. His voice sounded hoarse, charred. "Shelly, I need to talk to you." I let him pass, my fragile heart thudding madly. Did he know? Could anyone suspect my crime?

"Did you hear the news?" he asked, his voice barely a whisper.

"What news?" I shook my head and clutched my bathrobe to my throat. "I just woke up when I heard you in the hall. Where is Joshua?"

"He's in the living room." Relief nearly took my legs from beneath me.

A grave, haggard darkness shadowed my father's eyes as if he aged since I saw him yesterday. In fact, he wore the same clothes I'd seen him in at the house. "There's been an accident."

My stomach flopped, and I pressed a hand to my mouth, stopping the reflux just in time. "What do you mean?"

"Are you going to be sick?" He suddenly picked up on my gesture.

I held up a steady hand, swallowed, and breathed, remembering the lessons Marie taught me about controlling my reflux. "I'm okay. What accident?"

He scrubbed his filthy face with a hand, smearing his tears with soot. "The house burned. Last night. This morning. Whatever the hell time it is."

"The house?" My eyes widened as I stared at him.

"Mom's house. It's gone," he told me.

Weakness flooded my system, and I quickly sat on the edge of the bed before I landed on the floor. *It's over. Done.*

"Gone?" My thoughts spun wildly, imagining a blacked-out hole surrounded by burnt rose bushes.

"I just came from there. The fire crew is still working. It's a total loss."

Tears of relief crested my lids. It was over. I did it. "What now?"

Dad paced to the window and stared out at the pinkening sky as dawn chased the night out of view. His shoulders lifted and fell, lifted and fell with his breath. "There's more. The police are investigating the fire."

I stared at his back, my body trembling with fear. *Oh, no. God, no.* Somehow, someone saw us at the house. Police lights flashed outside, as if a car turned into the driveway. I'd admit to it and make sure Joshua was cleared. This was my nightmare. Not his.

"Dad, why are the police here?" my voice trembled as fear clenched a bruising fist around my throat. *Oh, Joshua. What have I done to you now?* Steady, solid Joshua, always trying to save me from myself. This time, I yanked him under with me.

My father struggled for a moment, as if he were trying to understand the words he wanted to say. "Your mother turned on a heater. It caught fire."

"What? Wait. How?" Confusion swept over me in a tidal wave of conflicting emotions that made absolutely no sense. "Why would they think that? She's in the hospital."

Dad turned to look at me, a mask of regret and conflict where his smile should be, and sorrow sliced a deeper channel into my heart. And I finally understood what he was trying to tell me.

Mom ...

I felt myself falling, falling, crashing into the darkest parts of my soul, the places devoid of light, of joy. I fell for what seemed like hours into the pit of despair I tried to destroy with half a gallon of gas and a match.

He crossed the room and dropped to his knees in front of me. "Shelly, I'm sorry. I don't know how to tell you this. I can't grasp it myself." He gripped my hands, and his tears dripped onto our clasped fingers. "The hospital called me yesterday, late afternoon. They were looking for a ride for Mom. She was ready to go home." He shook his head. "If I'd known for an instant she could do this. That she could—"

"No," I cut him off. I covered my ears with my hands.

"I picked her up. Got her some food and dropped her off at the house. She seemed *fine*. She said she was tired. They gave her something to help her sleep. Why would they let her go if she was unstable?"

"No. Dad—"

"God, kiddo." He breathed, and I felt his shudder to the core of my bones. "They found her on the back deck outside your old room. She's still alive."

THIRTY

DAD and I held hands in the hospital waiting room, my secret a black presence occupying the space between us. I held the words on my tongue a dozen times in the past hour, trying to work up the courage to tell him the truth. So far, I'd been unsuccessful.

"She's going to be okay," he assured me for the thousandth time. "They said it was too much smoke."

Physically, she would be okay. But what would happen when she saw the blacked-out hole? Would she finally understand she couldn't return to the house? I took her nest away. I almost killed her in the process.

"Dad, I need to tell you something," I whispered.

"What?" He shifted in his seat to find my eyes.

"I—"

"Mr. Frank?" A nurse waved him over near the ER door.

"Come on," he said, pulling me up out of my seat.

We followed the nurse to a small conference room.

"The doctor will be right in. Don't worry. It's good news." She smiled before hurrying away.

Dad's shoulders sagged in relief. "What did you want to say?" he asked.

"It can wait until later," I said. The door opened, and a doctor in green scrubs entered. A mask dangled under his chin.

"Mr. Frank?"

"Yes. This is my daughter, Shelly."

The doctor shook both our hands. "I wanted to talk with you about your wife's condition. She's inhaled a lot of smoke. We've done a bronchoscopy to look for damage. She's on oxygen, and I don't think we're looking at intubating her. She has some nasty cuts on her hands, so those were stitched. We're going to keep her tonight for sure and reevaluate tomorrow. If she continues to improve, she'll go home in a day or so. She can follow up with her family physician."

"Can we see her?" Dad asked.

"Soon. A couple of hours. She's sedated at the moment because of the test. We're moving her out of the Emergency Department. She'll be monitored on another floor."

Dad shook his hand again. "Thank you."

"You bet. Good luck to you." The doctor stepped out of the room.

My father enveloped me in a hug, his chin on the top of my head. "Thank God," he whispered.

"We're going to have to find a place for her to live," I said.

"We will. Let's get her healthy first."

A wave of emotion crashed over me. My chin trembled. She would never go home again, not to the little yellow house. I couldn't imagine how she'd handle seeing the destruction I wrought on her nest. She might lose what little grasp on reality she still held.

"What's wrong?

"Can we go to the house? I want to see it."

He gripped my arms. "Are you sure?"

I nodded. "I'm sure."

"YOU CAN SMELL IT FROM HERE," Dad said as we turned into my old neighborhood. The stench intensified the closer he drove to the house. A firetruck sat in the driveway, and two firemen poured water into the steaming wreckage.

A few neighbors stood across the street talking.

He parked the car a few houses down. "We'll have to walk over," he said. "You sure about this, Shell?"

"Yeah." From where we sat, a partial wall on the left side of the house remained, but the siding melted in a dirty yellow blob of plastic. The magnolias waved at the end of the driveway, oblivious to the carnage behind them.

A fireman stopped us at the driveway. "I'm the homeowner," Dad told him.

"I'm sorry for your loss. Is your wife okay?" The man didn't appear to be much older than Joshua.

"She's recovering. Thank you for all that you've done. Can we walk around the yard?"

"Sure. Be careful of the hoses."

"Thanks," Dad said. He led the way around the side of the house. The deck survived although the roses had been trampled by the fire crew.

I pressed a hand over my mouth to stifle the screams.

Dad led the way to the rear of the house. Beyond the deck, the wreckage steamed and smoked, a blackened pile of indistinguishable items. How many books perished in the flames? Hundreds, probably. More than enough to feed the fire of my loathing and scorch the nest from existence. It was what I wanted: the nest destroyed, my mother free, but I almost lost her in the process.

"It's a total loss," my father said. "Did she have insurance?"

"Yes. I paid it every month."

"Well, at least there's that."

The shed still stood. I left him beside what remained of the house and headed for the small structure. In my haste last night, I forgot to lock it. I opened the door and stepped inside. My tools hung neatly on their hooks. A bag of potting soil sat beside a cluster of pots awaiting new blooms. At the bench I ran my fingers over the gouged wood, playing along the edges of my father's initials.

"Are you okay?" Dad stood in the doorway.

I shook my head. "No." My eyes met his. I swallowed around the wave of sadness. "I set the fire."

"What?" He strode across the floor in two steps. His fingers dug into the flesh of my arm. "What are you talking about?"

Breathing deep, I said, "I came here last night. I didn't

know they would release her. I wanted to destroy the house before she came back." My body began to shake. "I almost killed her." He pulled me into his arms. Sobs wracked my spine, heaving smoke-scented breath out of my lungs. Several minutes passed before I could collect myself enough to look at his stunned face. "Say something."

"I can't. I don't know what to say." He moved to stand in the doorway, his back to me.

"I had to do it, Dad. I couldn't let her go back in there." I swiped at my streaming eyes with a pair of clean garden gloves. "What should I do?"

"Stay put. I'm going to make a phone call."

I leaned against the workbench as he paced the far edges of the lawn with his phone to his ear. I broke the law. My mother lay in the hospital because of me. For so long, my life was about protecting my family's secrets at all costs. I didn't know if I had it in me to hold on to another one.

DAD'S ATTORNEY met us at the hotel. I hadn't seen Joshua since last night, and he wasn't returning my texts. I couldn't bear to think our relationship was another victim of the nest, this one by merit of its destruction. His silence spoke in ways my imagination struggled to fathom. My mother survived, but Joshua might be collateral damage.

"Thank you for coming out," Dad said at the door.

Doyle's grave countenance didn't give me much hope.

They sat at the tiny table while I took a seat on the bed. "I understand you're responsible for the fire," the attorney began.

"Yes," I said.

He opened his briefcase and took out his laptop. When he was ready, he said, "Perhaps you can walk me through what happened."

I told him about the officer coming with the letter stating Mom could move back in. I searched for the words to explain the terror I experienced, knowing she would live there alone and not comply with the order. When I mentioned my mother's previous threats of self-harm, Dad backed me up. The only reason I burned the house was to save her from it.

"You didn't know your mother was present in the house?" Doyle asked.

"No. Not until much later that night. When I visited her in the hospital, they said she'd be there for a while longer. I decided if I was going to do something, I had to do it immediately."

"Explain to me what you did up to the point the house caught fire."

I edited out Joshua's presence. "I took a gas can from the shed and let myself into the house. The air conditioning wasn't running. It was horrible." Bile-tainted memories rushed up my throat, gagging me.

"Take your time, Shell," Dad said.

"I took the can with me, but I couldn't do it. I stood there for a while. Finally, I lit a match and dropped it. The paper caught fast."

Doyle tapped on his laptop keys. "And you never entered your old room when you were in the house?"

"No. I was in the living room when I dropped the match."

The attorney typed for a bit before he glanced up at us both. "I think this was a terrible accident. One which should not have happened."

"But I did it. I set the fire." I gripped the edge of the bed with my fingernails.

"There will be an investigation, won't there?" Dad asked him.

He removed a thin file from his briefcase. "I have the preliminary here. Because the contents of the house were so tightly packed, the cause is being listed as accidental. They did discover the remains of the gas can, but no broad distribution of fuel, which matches Shelly's account. While most people don't keep a gas can in their living room, knowing your wife suffered from hoarding disorder, the fire marshal cannot rule out the can wasn't there all along. It will be difficult to prove the fire didn't originate from, say, a candle. Or a bad electrical connection. The house was packed with paper and other debris."

My lungs deflated in a rush. "So that's it?"

"As far as I am concerned, yes. If you decide to talk to the police, I can give you the name of a defense attorney." Doyle closed his laptop. "While you did something very foolish, I understand why you did it. As misguided as your actions were, you were trying to help your mother. Let's thank the Lord no one was seriously injured." He stood and picked up his bag. "I hope your family can heal after this. You know where to reach me if you need me."

When the door closed behind him, Dad sat on the bed next to me. "Are you okay?"

"I don't know. I feel like I should be punished for what I've done. I could have killed her."

He gathered my hand in his. "I think you've suffered enough for your parents' problems, don't you?"

"How can I live another lie? Where will she go now?"

"Let me worry about that." His fingers tightened on mine. "I'm going to call Mindy." We both started as my phone vibrated on the night table. "Sounds like someone wants to talk to you, too."

THIRTY-ONE

SIX MONTHS LATER

I LIT the citronella candle on the patio table and counted the napkins. Dad and Mindy were coming for dinner to help us christen our new house, and a flurry of nervous energy buzzed in my veins. The three-bedroom ranch smelled of new paint and fresh carpet, and the windows stood open to the humid breeze. Outside on the patio, the palm trees whispered overhead, dappling the backyard with shade. Although the calendar read March, the Florida evening was warm enough for outside dining, especially for us northern transplants.

Joshua appeared at the door, carrying a pitcher of iced tea. "Here. Your mom said to bring this outside."

"Thanks. Is she doing okay in there?"

He flopped in a chair and stretched his long legs out in front of him. His feet were bare and tanned. "Seems to be. She was frosting cupcakes, so I figured I better leave." He hooked his finger in my direction. "Come here."

His arms went around me as I sat on his lap. For several minutes we stayed there, listening to the breeze tinkle the windchimes we hung at the edge of the house. My heart ached from fullness. A year ago, I would never have believed this blissful peace was possible. But here we were, resettled in Florida away from the bad memories of New Jersey. We were close enough to my father's house to maintain our relationship, but far enough away that Mom didn't feel awkward.

Lifting my head, I smiled at him. "I better go see if she needs help."

Joshua kissed me lightly. "I'll fire up the grill."

"That's a very manly occupation," I teased.

"That's why I'm here." His lopsided smirk flipped my stomach for all the right reasons.

I found my mother in the kitchen wearing an apron and wielding a spatula. While it looked as if a miniature tornado had attacked the counters, I suppressed the moment of anxiety and dipped my finger into the icing bowl. Since the house burned, she began seeing a therapist regularly and taking the medications prescribed for her. In so many ways, she blossomed into a different person, one I remembered from those sacred images of my childhood.

"That's delicious," I said.

"Thanks. I'm glad you kept Grandma's recipe books in a safe place. She made the best icing."

"Just the right amount of vanilla. Want some help cleaning this up? Joshua's warming up the grill."

She smiled at me, her face sun-kissed and healthy. "Thanks. I'll get the chicken out of the fridge."

I washed the bowls while she shuttled chicken and vegetables out to the grill. From my place at the sink, I could see her and Joshua laughing about some confidence they shared. A car door closed in the driveway. Wiping my hands on a towel, I hurried to meet Dad and Mindy.

"Hey," I called from the door. Dad carried two potted plants, his gift for our new house. I recognized the dark, shiny leaves of hibiscus and the long, flat leaves of butterfly bush.

Mindy held a covered dish. "The house is adorable. I told your dad you needed your own Orange Sceptre."

I took the plants from him. "Thank you. I hope you'll help me plant these."

"Of course, I will," he promised.

"Joshua's out back. He might need help taming the grill."

Dad smiled. "I'm on it."

My heart was full. After enrolling in college, Joshua took over the spare bedroom, and I kept my job at Beth's. We settled into a quiet rhythm of normalcy—and I still couldn't believe it was real. But it was. Somehow, someway, we survived. Slowly, Mom was building a life for herself. She even volunteered with a support group for people recovering from hoarding disorder. Little by little, she was learning to forgive my father, Mindy, and herself for the years we lost.

She found her hope. So had I. Tonight's dinner would be a big step. We spent so many years burying our secrets under guilt and shame. Tonight, we'd step out from beneath the burdens of our past and into the sunshine breezes of our future.

AUTHOR'S NOTE

As a mystery and thriller writer, *Buried Beneath* is a departure from my typical book. The story idea came to me in a literary agent's Twitter post when she asked for a book for children of hoarders. Over the next few months, the story developed slowly, and I found myself reading heart-rending accounts of children who survived by hiding their homelives behind stoicism and a genuine fear of losing their parents. While Shelly's story is based on an imagined house in a fictional town, I worked to understand the way in which a teenager might be affected by growing up with a terrible family secret and a dependent mother. *Buried* was at times difficult for me to write, but I wanted to tell Shelly's story in a way that offered hope for what could be.

Thank you to the wonderful staff at Zenith Publishing for the dedication they've shown to this story. A heartfelt thanks to my friend, the wonderful Cindy Dorminy, for reading and critiquing from first draft to final. Thanks also to Annika Ball for the beautiful cover artwork that perfectly portrays Shelly's internal and external struggles.

And finally, I could not pursue my love of writing without the unending support of my husband and family. Hugs to all.

THANK YOU

Thank you for reading *Buried Beneath*.

Please consider leaving a review so that other readers can find this title. It may just end up being their favorite.

OTHER ZENITH TITLES YOU MAY ENJOY

The Facts and Legends of Callie Catwell by Sophia Derise

A Love Across Time by Genevieve Jane

More Than Us by Ryan Jones

Not Always Blu Skies by Gabrielle McMaster

Twist in the Wind by Gabrielle McMaster

www.ingramcontent.com/pod-product-compliance
Lightning Source LLC
Chambersburg PA
CBHW030920050726
47498CB00003BA/827